Christy® Juvenile Fiction Series

VOLUME THREE

Christy® Juvenile Fiction Series

Christy® Juvenile Fiction Series
VOLUME THREE

The Princess Club
Family Secrets
Mountain Madness

Catherine Marshall
adapted by C. Archer

Tommy nelson™
A Division of Thomas Nelson Publishers
Since 1798
www.thomasnelson.com

VOLUME THREE
The Princess Club
Family Secrets
Mountain Madness
in the *Christy*® Juvenile Fiction Series

Published in Nashville, Tennessee, by Tommy Nelson®,
a Division of Thomas Nelson, Inc.

ISBN 1-4003-0774-0

Printed in the United States of America

05 06 07 08 09 BANTA 9 8 7 6 5 4 3 2 1

The
Princess
Club

The Characters

CHRISTY RUDD HUDDLESTON, a nineteen-year-old girl.

CHRISTY'S STUDENTS:
    CREED ALLEN, age nine.
    LITTLE BURL ALLEN, age six.
    BESSIE COBURN, age twelve.
    WRAIGHT HOLT, age seventeen.
    LIZETTE HOLCOMBE, age nine.
    GEORGE O'TEALE, age nine.
    MOUNTIE O'TEALE, age ten.
    RUBY MAE MORRISON, age thirteen.
    CLARA SPENCER, age twelve.
    LUNDY TAYLOR, age seventeen.

GRANNY O'TEALE, a superstitious mountain woman. *(Great-grandmother of Christy's students Mountie and George.)*

DR. NEIL MACNEILL, the physician of the Cove.

ALICE HENDERSON, a Quaker missionary who started the mission at Cutter Gap.

DAVID GRANTLAND, the young minister.

IDA GRANTLAND, David's sister and the mission housekeeper.

GRADY HALLIDAY, a traveling photographer.

BEN PENTLAND, the mailman.

FAIRLIGHT SPENCER, a mountain woman.
JEB SPENCER, her husband.
    (*Parents of Christy's student Clara.*)

OZIAS HOLT, a mountain man.

NATHAN O'TEALE, father of Christy's students
    Mountie and George.

DUGGIN MORRISON, stepfather of Christy's
    student Ruby Mae.
MRS. MORRISON, Ruby Mae's mother.

LETY COBURN, a mountain woman.
KYLE COBURN, her husband.
    (*Parents of Christy's student Bessie.*)

BIRD'S-EYE TAYLOR, father of Christy's
    student Lundy.

PRINCE, black stallion donated to the mission.
PRINCE EGBERT, unwilling frog captive.
OLD THEO, crippled mule owned by the mission.
GOLDIE, mare belonging to Miss Alice Henderson.
CLANCY, mule owned by Grady Halliday.

⊰ One ⊱

"Touch that frog, Clara Spencer, and you'll be covered with warts from head to toe!" Ruby Mae Morrison warned.

The two girls stood at the edge of Dead Man's Creek with their friend Bessie Coburn. It was a sparkling, warm afternoon, and the icy water burbled over their bare feet.

Clara rolled her eyes. "That ain't true about frogs, Ruby Mae. Miz Christy says frogs is am-phi-bians. We're goin' to study 'em for science class. And I'm gonna catch me this here one for her to teach us with." She pointed to the fat green frog sitting on a boulder in the shallow creek, sunning itself happily.

Ruby Mae sighed. Sometimes Clara acted like the biggest know-it-all in Cutter Gap.

"Warts," Ruby Mae repeated firmly. "Hundreds of 'em. Granny O'Teale says they start

5

on your nose first-off." She nudged Bessie. "Ain't that right, Bessie?"

Bessie watched as Clara took another careful step toward the frog. "'Member that fairy tale Miz Christy told us where the girl kisses a frog and he turns into a prince?"

"'Course I do. Anyways, you oughta be careful how far out you wade, Clara," Ruby Mae advised. "We ain't never been this far up the creek before."

Clara took a deep breath and lunged for the frog. She grabbed him with both hands. Then she slipped him into the deep pocket of her worn dress and returned to the bank.

"I'm a-callin' him Prince Egbert," she announced, peeking into her pocket.

"Can't call him Prince," Ruby Mae said. She picked up a smooth stone and flung it far down the rushing creek. "We already got ourselves a Prince, in case you forgot. And the mission's stallion is a whole lot purtier than any warty ol' frog."

"Prince *Egbert*," Clara repeated. "And he don't have warts, I'm tellin' you."

"Kiss him then," Ruby Mae challenged with a sly grin. "Prove it."

Clara lay back on the grass, her hands behind her head. "Don't need to kiss a frog, 'cause I don't want to be a princess. I'm a-goin' to be a doctor when I grow up. Just like Doc MacNeill."

Bessie groaned. "Gals can't be doctors, Clara. That's just plumb foolish."

"How about Miz Alice?" Clara sat up on her elbows. "She's got a bag full of herbs and medicines. And she births babies and fixes up broken bones and such, just like the doc."

Bessie joined Clara on the bank. "Well, I'm a-goin' to be a teacher, just like Miz Christy. Only in a much fancier school than ours. One with lots of books and pencils, and no hogs under the floor. And no bullies like Lundy Taylor, neither. All *my* students will behave nice and proper-like, with citified manners."

Ruby Mae turned to stare at her two friends. They were lying side by side on the grass, staring up at the sky. They looked alike, the two of them. They were both smaller than she was, with long blond hair. Of course, there were differences, too. Bessie had plump, rosy cheeks and a silly grin. Clara had a thinner face, with sensible brown eyes, like she was always fretting over something or other.

She usually was, too. Clara was a thinker. She was always asking how or why or when— questions that would make a normal person's head spin like a top.

Bessie, on the other hand, was more of a dreamer. She was the kind of girl who would forget her head if it wasn't attached.

Ruby Mae knew both girls leaned on her. After all, she was a year older, and that made her a whole year wiser. She was taller than they were, with long, curly red hair. If only she could get rid of her freckles, she figured she'd be just about perfect.

"Doctor Clara Spencer," Bessie said in a wishing kind of voice, "and Pro-fess-or Bessie Coburn."

Ruby Mae sighed. Of course, they were only twelve. They weren't so smart about the way the world worked.

"Hate to tell you, but you ain't a-goin' to be doctors or teachers or frog princesses," Ruby Mae said as she stooped to get another stone.

"Since when can you see the future, Ruby Mae?" Clara demanded.

"Only Granny O'Teale can see the future," Bessie said. "And that's if she's reading the innards of a squirrel on a full moon night."

"What I'm sayin' is, you need cash-money to get those highfalutin' jobs. 'Cause first you need your schoolin'." Ruby Mae tossed another rock upstream. "And in case you ain't noticed, we're just kinda short of cash-money."

"Still and all, Ruby Mae," Bessie said, "what do you want to be when you're all growed up? If'n you could be anything you wanted, I mean."

8

Ruby Mae didn't have to think for a second. "I'd be a mama in a big house in a big city, like Asheville. Maybe even Knoxville. And I'd have me a beautiful golden horse, the fastest in the world. And about twenty-seven kids. All of 'em little angels, mind you . . ."

"Not like their mama!" Clara teased.

"And a husband as handsome as . . ." Ruby Mae paused. "As handsome as the preacher and Doc MacNeill, all rolled up into one. Only he'd comb his hair more often than Doc does. And wear fancy clothes with no patches. He'd have the preacher's eyes. And the doctor's smile. And he'd have a voice like—"

"R-R-R-R-IBBIT!" cried the frog in Clara's pocket.

"Like Prince Egbert!" Clara exclaimed. She started to giggle. Before long, she and Bessie were rolling on the grass, laughing so hard tears came to their eyes.

Furious, Ruby Mae rushed up the bank. "Ain't funny!" she cried, grabbing for Clara's pocket. Prince Egbert popped out and made a flying leap. He landed on the edge of the bank, eyeing the girls suspiciously.

"You made me lose Prince Egbert!" Clara cried. "Now help me get him back, Ruby Mae Morrison, or I'll tell Miz Christy what you done!"

9

Ruby Mae sighed. "You stop laughin' at me, and I'll help you get your frog. Deal?"

"Deal."

Carefully the girls made their way toward the frog. But as soon as Clara reached for him, he hopped into the air. He landed on a big rock farther down the creek.

"Pretend you're huntin' squirrels," Bessie whispered as they made their way toward the rock. "Nice and slow and quiet-like."

"If we was huntin', my papa's hound would be doin' the hard work," Clara said.

"We need us a froghound," Ruby Mae joked. Bessie giggled, but Clara was still too mad to laugh.

"This time, we'll surround him," Clara advised as they waded closer. "When I say three, we grab him. I'll do the countin'. One, two, THREE!"

All three girls lunged for poor Prince Egbert. He took another leap and landed at the water's edge underneath a thick, overhanging bush. Ruby Mae reached down in a flash and scooped him up, along with some rocks and sand from the bottom of the creek.

She held him up, nose crinkled. "Hope you're satisfied," she said, depositing the frog into Clara's pocket. "I'll be covered with warts by morning."

Ruby Mae dropped the stones she'd scooped

up back into the water. As she started toward the bank, something sparkling on the bottom of the creek caught her eye.

Was it just the sun, bouncing off the water? Pieces of shiny metal? Maybe a belt buckle or some nails?

"Come on, Ruby Mae," Clara urged. "It's gettin' late. And I need to take Prince Egbert home and find a place to keep him till school tomorrow."

Ruby Mae bent down. The bottom of her dress was soaking wet. The icy water swirled around her legs.

She scooped up the shiny things into her hand. For a long time, she just stared at the handful of rocks.

"Confound it, Ruby Mae," Bessie whined in her high-pitched voice, "what *are* you a-starin' at?"

"Rocks," Ruby Mae whispered.

"Well, toss 'em, already. My papa'll whop me good if'n I'm late again for supper."

Slowly Ruby Mae smiled at her friends. "You don't understand. These here ain't just rocks. These is the most beautiful, purtiest, shiniest, amazin' rocks in the history of rocks!"

She held out her hand. The rocks glistened like tiny pieces of sun.

"Fiddlesticks, Ruby Mae," Bessie said. "Them's just creek rocks."

"That's where you're wrong," Ruby Mae

whispered. She could feel her heart leaping inside her like a kitten in a burlap sack. "These is creek rocks made of *gold!*"

For a moment, nobody spoke. The only sound was the musical babble of the creek.

Clara finally broke the silence. "Come here, Ruby Mae," she said. "Let me see those."

Ruby Mae waded over and held out her hand. Bessie and Clara bent close. Bessie held one of the golden stones between her fingers. Her mouth was hanging open.

"Sakes alive," she whispered, "I do believe this here is real gold!"

"But where did it come from?" Clara whispered. "I ain't never heard of no gold in these mountains. Coal and such, sure. But *gold?*"

"Who cares where it came from?" Ruby Mae felt like her smile might just be too big for her face. "Do you know what this means?"

Bessie nodded, eyes wide. "Means we found us some cash-money."

"Wrong, Bessie," Ruby Mae said. "It means we're rich! It means we don't have to kiss us a frog to become princesses!"

✌ TWO ✌

Miz Christy! Miz Christy! The most amazin' and fantastic thing has happened!"

Christy Huddleston watched from the porch of the mission house as Ruby Mae, Bessie, and Clara sprinted across the field at high speed.

"What's gotten into them, I wonder?" Christy asked Doctor Neil MacNeill, who was staying for supper.

Doctor MacNeill ran his fingers through his unruly auburn hair. He was a big man, with a big grin to match. "With Ruby Mae and her gang, sometimes I'm afraid to ask."

The girls rushed up the wooden steps, panting for air. They were grinning from ear to ear.

"What on earth happened to you three?" Christy demanded. "You're all wet! And your hands are covered with mud! Do you realize

13

you were supposed to be here half an hour ago to help set the table, Ruby Mae?"

"Yes'm, and I'm right sorry, but wait'll you hear what happened! It all started with—"

"R-R-R-I-B-B-I-T!"

Doctor MacNeill laughed. "Sounds to me like you have a classic case of indigestion, Clara."

"Ain't my stomach a-growlin', Doc," she said, reaching into her pocket. She pulled out a fat, green frog. "It's Prince Egbert. I got him for you to learn us science with, Miz Christy!"

Gingerly, Christy gave the frog a pat. She'd been living here in the Great Smoky Mountains for several months now, but she was still getting used to the wild creatures her students befriended. "That was very thoughtful, Clara. And a prince, no less!"

"And we," Ruby Mae added proudly, "are real, live princesses!"

"Well, you need to head inside, Your Royal Highness, and set the royal table," Christy said. "And Clara and Bessie, you two had better head for home before your parents start to worry. It's getting late."

Ruby Mae winked at her friends. "Don't need to set no table," she said. "From now on, I aim to just hire me a maid for doin' my chores."

"A maid?" Christy repeated, shaking her head.

Ruby Mae glanced over her shoulder. With a sly smile, she held out her fist and slowly opened her fingers. "And here's how I aim to pay her!"

Christy and Doctor MacNeill exchanged a glance. Several small, damp yellow stones glistened in Ruby Mae's palm.

"That isn't . . ." Christy began. "I mean, it couldn't be . . ."

Doctor MacNeill picked up one of the stones. He held it between his thumb and index finger, squinting at it carefully.

"My, my," he murmured. "Where exactly did you find this, if you don't mind my asking?"

Clara cleared her throat. "Nothin' personal, Doctor," she answered, "but we all sort of agreed we'd keep that a secret between the three of us. You understand."

Just then, Miss Alice appeared in the doorway. "Ruby Mae!" she said sternly. "It's about time, young lady!"

Ruby Mae jumped at the sound of her name. Christy tried not to smile. Alice Henderson, a Quaker mission worker who had helped start the school, definitely had a way of commanding attention.

"Miz Alice," Ruby Mae said quickly, "you got to understand, somethin' mighty important's happened."

"I'm listening," said Miss Alice, tapping her foot.

"Me and Bessie and Clara is goin' to be richer than the king of England hisself!"

Miss Alice barely hid her smile. "You don't say?" Her eyes fell to the gold stone in the doctor's hand. She joined them on the porch.

"Neil? What's this all about?"

"Well, it seems our three little prospectors may just have found themselves some actual gold."

"So it *is* gold?" Clara asked. "Real, live, for-sure gold?"

The doctor shrugged. "I can't say absolutely, Clara. I've never actually held a gold nugget in my hand. But judging from the weight and color, I'd say—"

"We're rich!" Ruby screamed.

"We're a-goin' to be princesses!" Bessie cried.

"Who's a princess?" called David Grantland, the young minister at the mission, as he rode up to the house on Prince.

Ruby Mae ran over to greet the preacher and Prince. "We are," she announced.

Clara groaned. "Now, that does it for sure. Nobody else can know about the gold, 'ceptin' the people right here. Understand?" She glared at Ruby Mae.

"How come you're lookin' at me?" Ruby Mae demanded.

"Could be 'cause you got the biggest mouth this side o' Coldsprings Mountain," Bessie suggested.

"'Tain't true!" Ruby Mae cried.

Bessie rolled her eyes. "'Tis so."

"Ladies," David interrupted as he dismounted. "For the moment, let's set aside the question of Ruby Mae's communication skills. What's all this about?"

"The girls have discovered some very interesting rocks," Christy answered. "Neil thinks they might actually be gold nuggets."

The doctor passed the gold rock he'd been examining to David. "What do you think, Reverend?"

"Hmm. I had an uncle who was a collector of minerals and such. This definitely isn't 'fool's gold.' Pyrite's lighter and more brittle."

"I thought gold deposits were mostly out west," Christy said, "in California or Colorado—but Tennessee?"

"Gold has never been found in these parts before," said Miss Alice. "That's definitely a story I would have heard by now," she smiled, "a hundred times."

"Just 'cause it ain't been found here before don't mean this ain't gold," Ruby Mae said, sounding a bit worried.

David shook his head in disbelief. "I don't know how it got here, but this is gold, all right, Ruby Mae. As hard as it is for me to believe."

"Now that we know for certain, nobody more's got to know about this," Clara told her friends. "The preacher and the doc and Miz Christy and Miz Alice, well, they're the kind of folks can keep their mouths shut. But that's all can know."

"And Prince," Bessie added. "And Prince Egbert."

Clara nodded. "And our mas and pas. But that's it. Final. Right, Ruby Mae? That's what we promised each other on the way here."

Ruby Mae shrugged. "Don't see why we can't tell a *few* folks. Lordamercy, what's the point in bein' rich if'n you can't let folks know it?"

"I think Clara's right," Miss Alice said. "When the word gets out about this, this mountain cove is going to change overnight."

"Just like us," Bessie said dreamily. "Like plain ol' frogs turned into beautiful princesses."

"I fear it won't be anything quite that magical," Miss Alice said.

Christy could hear the concern in her voice. "What are you worried about, Miss Alice?"

"The same thing these mountains have seen way too much of. Feuds. Pain. Greed. Even death."

Ruby Mae held out her hand. The gold nuggets glistened like a wonderful promise. "Ain't no bad goin' to come from these," she said confidently. "We're havin' ourselves our very own fairy tale."

"I hope you're right, Ruby Mae," Christy said softly.

❧ Three ❧

That evening, Christy ran a brush through her sun-streaked hair and slipped into bed. She retrieved her diary and her fountain pen from her nightstand. Slowly she thumbed through the pages of the little leather-bound book.

She smiled wistfully when she looked at the very first entry:

> *. . . I have begun my great adventure this day, and although things have not gone exactly as I had hoped, I am still committed to my dream of teaching at the mission. . . .*

Farther down the page she read:

> *The truth is, I have not been this afraid before, or felt this alone and homesick. Leaving everyone I*

love was harder than I thought it would be. But I must be strong. I am at the start of a great adventure. And great adventures are sometimes scary.

She'd been right about one thing, that frosty day in January when she'd started her diary. Coming here had certainly turned out to be an adventure. Teaching at this desperately poor mission had been a challenge and a joy beyond anything she'd imagined. It had helped her discover strengths in herself she hadn't known were there.

She'd discovered love, too. Love for the beauty of these rugged, ageless mountains. Love for her friends and her students. And even the love of two very special men—Neil MacNeill and David Grantland.

But tonight, as she glanced over the pages filled with her careful writing, she felt strangely troubled. Christy looked across the room to her big trunk. Tucked inside of it was a little wooden jewelry box her mother had given her. And inside the box was a handful of stones. Golden, glittering, precious stones.

After some discussion, Ruby Mae, Bessie, and Clara had decided that their gold should stay at the mission house for safekeeping. Christy had offered to lock the stones up in her trunk until the gold could be deposited at the bank in El Pano.

Since the mountain road leading there had

been blocked by a recent rockslide, it could be awhile before anyone could get to the bank.

In the meantime, her wooden trunk was the closest thing the mission had to a safe. After all, everyone here was poor, and that included the staff at the mission. And this wasn't like Asheville, Christy's former home. In Cutter Gap, nobody locked their doors. Some people didn't even *have* a door.

Christy opened her diary to a fresh page.

I can't help but feel uneasy tonight. In a place as needy as Cutter Gap, the discovery of gold should be a wonderful blessing. But as Miss Alice pointed out, greed and envy can make people do strange things. I keep wondering how this will affect the children. I still remember how they looked at me that first day of school. Me, in my fancy patent leather shoes, when almost all the children were barefoot! "Silly, silly shoes," David called them. He was right, of course.

A soft knock at the door startled Christy from her writing.

"Come in," she called.

Ruby Mae, who lived at the mission, poked her head in the door. She was wearing her blue cotton nightgown. Her wild red hair was tied back with a ribbon Christy had given her. "Can I come in, Miz Christy?"

"It's late. You should be asleep, Ruby Mae. Tomorrow's a school day."

Ruby Mae leapt onto Christy's bed. "Can't sleep. I'm too excited about gettin' rich. I tried countin' sheep, but they kept turning into gold nuggets." She gazed at Christy's trunk longingly. "Can I see 'em one more time?"

"Ruby Mae . . ."

"Just a peek, I promise. I know it's crazy, but I keep fearin' they'll up and disappear. I mean, don't get me wrong, Miz Christy, I trust *you* and all. But it's like the only way I can believe in 'em is to look right at 'em with my own two eyes, you know?"

Christy set aside her diary. "All right. Just this once. But I'm not going to have a daily show for you and your friends. Understood?"

"Oh, no'm. Bessie and Clara won't let me tell anyone no how. My lips is glued tighter than a bear paw to a honey hive."

Christy retrieved the key to the trunk from her nightstand drawer. She opened the trunk, pulled out the small cedar jewelry box, and sat down on the bed next to Ruby Mae.

When Christy opened the box, Ruby Mae gasped. "Oh, my! They're even more beautiful than I remembered!"

"You just saw these gold nuggets a couple hours ago, Ruby Mae."

Ruby Mae picked up one of the stones.

22

"It's like these tiny little rocks have magic power. More than one of Granny O'Teale's herb potions, even. More than all the doc's medicines. This rock can make me into anything I want to be."

Christy started to argue that money couldn't buy happiness. That what mattered was that Ruby Mae be happy on the inside. That material things didn't matter.

But when she looked into Ruby Mae's shining brown eyes, she couldn't say a thing. Christy had grown up in a lovely home, with pretty dresses and fine food and loving parents and all the shoes she'd ever needed.

Not long ago, Ruby Mae had actually visited Christy's old home. Bessie had needed an operation at a hospital in Asheville, and Ruby Mae, Christy, David, and Doctor MacNeill had traveled there together. Christy could still remember the look on Ruby Mae's face when she'd first stepped into Christy's old bedroom. Seeing it through Ruby Mae's eyes, Christy had felt ashamed at the way she'd always taken her own good fortune for granted.

"Magic rocks," Ruby Mae repeated in a whisper. "That's what they is."

Christy touched the red ribbon in Ruby Mae's hair. "You know, that ribbon looks pretty in your hair," she said softly.

"Finest present I ever got," Ruby Mae

declared, still staring at the gold. "Practically the onliest one," she added with a smile.

Gently Christy put the gold nugget back in the box with the others.

"Miz Christy?" Ruby Mae asked thoughtfully. "You figure a gal from these here parts could ever make somethin' of herself? Maybe be a doctor or a teacher or have a passel of kids in a big city mansion?"

"I think a girl from these parts can do just about anything she sets her mind to, if she works hard at her schooling," Christy said, "and gets enough sleep." She placed the box back inside the trunk. "You head on to bed now."

"One more thing," Ruby Mae said when she got to the door.

"Yes, Ruby Mae?"

"I was wonderin' if you'd mind hidin' that key o' yours someplace more secret-like. I know I can trust everyone, but just in case . . ."

Christy stared at the brass key. She'd never bothered to lock her trunk before today. She eased the key into the lock and turned it until it clicked. Then she slipped the key under her mattress.

"How's that?" Christy asked.

"Much better. Now I can get me some sleep."

Christy sighed. "I hope I can say the same for myself."

✺ Four ✺

"Now, there are several differences between frogs and toads," Christy said the next afternoon in the schoolhouse.

Prince Egbert sat on her battered desk in a small wooden box Clara had borrowed from her father. It was nice, Christy realized, to have any kind of educational aid—even if it *was* just a disgruntled frog.

When Christy had first come to the mission school, she'd been shocked at the lack of supplies. There'd been no paper, no books, no pencils, no chalk. In the winter, there wasn't even enough heat.

It still amazed her that she had sixty-seven students of all ages and abilities. Some could read and do math. Some couldn't even hold a pencil. And no matter what their grade level, they were all crowded into one tiny schoolhouse—a school that doubled as the church on Sundays.

On a hot, sunny day like today, it was especially hard to control so many children. It didn't help one bit that Ruby May, Bessie, and Clara had been disrupting class all morning with giggles and whispers.

Creed Allen, a mischievous nine-year-old, waved his hand frantically. "Teacher!" he called. "I got me a question about that there frog!"

"Yes, Creed?"

"How come Clara Spencer gets to bring her pet to school, but I can't bring Scalawag?"

Christy sighed tolerantly. Scalawag was Creed's pet raccoon. She'd made his acquaintance on the first day of school, when Creed had hidden the animal in his desk.

"This frog—" Christy began.

"Prince Egbert," Clara interjected.

"Excuse me. Prince Egbert," Christy continued, "is here as part of our science class, Creed. We're learning about amphibians, and—"

"But Scalawag's got manners to spare compared to that slimy ol' frog," Creed persisted.

"I'm sure he does, Creed. But he's such an entertaining fellow that we'd never get any learning done with Scalawag around, don't you think?"

"I s'pose," Creed said crankily. "But he's a

heap more good for learnin' than some warty fibian."

"Amphibian," Christy corrected. "And that brings me to an interesting point. Who can tell me the difference between a frog's skin and a toad's?"

"Tell you this," came a loud voice from the back of the room. "Ruby Mae's got more warts than either of 'em!"

"That will be enough, Lundy," Christy said firmly. At seventeen, Lundy Taylor was the oldest boy in school. He was also the source of most trouble. He was a vicious bully, and although he'd been better behaved lately, Christy never let her guard down around Lundy.

"Shut up, Lundy Taylor!" Ruby Mae shot back. She jutted her chin. "I'm better 'n you every which way there is. 'Specially 'cause now I'm a-goin' to be stinkin' r—"

"Hush, Ruby Mae!" Clara elbowed her hard.

"Stinkin' is right," Lundy crowed. "You stink like them hogs under the schoolhouse. Only they smell better!"

Christy clapped her hands. "That will be quite enough," she said. She was beginning to wonder if she should have let the children have a longer lunch break. The way things were turning out, it was going to be a long afternoon.

"Lizette?" Christy said. "Can you answer my

question about the difference between frogs and toads?"

Lizette Holcombe shrugged. "Nope," she grumbled.

Christy was surprised at her tone of voice. Lizette was one of her best students. "Is something wrong, Lizette?"

Lizette glared at Ruby Mae and her friends. "Nothin's wrong."

"Are you sure?" Christy asked gently.

"Why don't you just ask the *princesses* to answer? They think they're so smart. But you could take all the brains they've got, put them in a goose quill and blow 'em in a bedbug's eye!"

Christy knelt by Lizette's side. She was a tall, pretty girl, with long brown hair. But her face was splotched and red, as if she'd been crying.

"What's wrong, Lizette? What do you mean, 'princesses'?"

Christy feared she knew all too well what the answer was going to be.

"Ruby Mae and Clara and Bessie," Lizette said. "They started them up a club for princesses and such."

"Ruby Mae?" Christy asked sternly. "What's this about a club?"

Ruby Mae grinned. "We started us a club during the break. We're callin' it 'The Princess Club.' Nobody but me and Bessie and Clara can get in. It's glue-sive."

"I believe you mean *exclusive*," Christy said. "Did it ever occur to you girls that you might be hurting other people's feelings?"

"It's for their own good, Miz Christy," Clara explained in a reasonable voice. "We have our secret, after all." She gave Christy a knowing smile.

"You can have your dumb old secret," Lizette muttered. "You three have been carrying on all day like you've gone plumb crazy."

"Ain't crazy," Clara said. "We do have a secret. A gigantic secret."

"Big deal."

"A real big deal," Bessie said.

"Just ignore her," Clara advised. "She's just jealous."

"'Course, she'd be lots more jealous if'n she knew we found us some gold!" Ruby Mae cried.

Suddenly the room went still. Ruby Mae slapped her hand to her mouth. Bessie's jaw dropped open. Clara groaned.

"It's just as I said, Ruby Mae. You've got the biggest mouth this side of Coldsprings Mountain," Bessie hissed.

Ruby Mae's cheeks flared. The rest of the class stared at her in stunned disbelief.

"Well, it don't rightly matter if'n I told, anyhow," she said. "As long as I don't say where we found it or where it's hid, what harm is there in tellin'?"

"What do you mean, you found gold?" Lizette demanded. "There ain't no gold in these mountains."

Lundy jumped to his feet. "You oughta whop her good for tellin' lies, Teacher!"

"If'n you found real live gold," Creed cried, "show it to us, Ruby Mae! That's a heap more edu-cational than that ol' frog!"

Instantly, the class erupted into shouts and jeers. Christy clapped her hands to get their attention, but it was no use.

In desperation, she climbed onto her chair. She tried yelling. She tried waving. When nothing else worked, she decided to try a trick David, who taught math and Bible study, had shown her. She put two fingers in her mouth and let out an ear-splitting whistle.

At last, the room quieted. "Wow, Teacher," Creed said in an awed voice, "you whistle better than a feller!"

"Sit down, everybody," Christy instructed as she climbed off her chair. "Now, I want one thing made clear. This is a place where we are all equal, and we are all here to learn."

"But Teacher," asked Mountie O'Teale, a shy ten-year-old, "is it really true they're rich?"

Christy put her hands on her hips. Now that Ruby Mae had let the cat out of the bag, she couldn't lie.

"It's true that Ruby Mae and her friends found some interesting stones that are probably gold." Her words caused a fresh gasp from the class. "But that is their business, and I do not want it to be part of the discussion in this classroom. As a matter of fact, I do not want to hear anyone uttering the words 'gold' or 'rich' or 'club' in this class."

"I thought only cows had udders, Teacher," Creed said.

"I meant 'don't talk about these things,' Creed," Christy said. "And while we're at it, the only princesses I want to hear about are in fairy tales. Understood?"

She looked directly at Ruby Mae and her two friends. They nodded obediently.

"Now I believe, when we were interrupted, we were about to discuss the difference between frogs and toads," Christy said. She held up Prince Egbert. "To begin with, a frog has smooth skin and long limbs. Can anyone tell me any other differences? Creed? How about you?"

Creed didn't answer. He was staring at Ruby Mae and her friends, eyes wide.

Christy scanned the room. Not a single student was looking at her. All eyes were glued to the three smug "princesses," as if they really were royalty.

In a way, Christy realized suddenly, here in Cutter Gap, that's just what they were. From now on, nothing in her classroom would be the same.

✺ Five ✺

I now declare the first official meeting of The Princess Club is a-startin'," Ruby Mae announced after school.

The three girls were outside the small shed that David had built to house Prince; Goldie, Miss Alice's palomino mare; and Old Theo, the mule. Ruby Mae was carefully brushing Prince's glossy flanks. Clara was scratching his ears. And Bessie was feeding him a carrot from Miss Ida's vegetable garden.

"Before we start," Clara said in a whisper, "check all around to make sure we wasn't followed."

"Don't be a fool, Clara." Ruby Mae rolled her eyes. "Ain't nobody followin' us. You're actin' jittery as a squirrel with a hungry hound on his tail."

"Wouldn't need to," Clara shot back, "if'n

you coulda kept your mouth shut. I heard Lundy talkin' after school, sayin' how he was going to figure out where we found the gold and get some of his own."

Bessie gulped. "And you know Lundy. He'd as soon steal it as find it his own self."

"Listen here, you two lily-livers." Ruby Mae could tell she was going to have to be stern with her friends if she wanted any peace. "People was goin' to find out about the gold, one way or the other. You told your parents, right?"

Both girls nodded.

"Well, how long do you think a secret like that's goin' to keep here in the Cove?" She moved to Prince's other side and began brushing his silky mane. "Remember that time Violet McKnapp run off with Elroy Smith to get hitched? Remember how she only told Mary Allen and made her promise not to tell a soul?"

"Yep," Bessie said.

"Well, how long do you figure *that* secret lasted? A day, maybe two? *Our* secret is a whole lot bigger than Violet's."

"I s'pose you're right," Bessie admitted. "It's plumb unnatural for a secret like ours to stay a secret. People bein' how they is."

"And people's mouths bein' as big as they is," Clara added, glaring at Ruby Mae.

"There ain't no use snifflin' about spilled milk." Ruby Mae set down her brush and gave Prince a hug. "Besides, we got things to talk about. Princess Club things."

Ruby Mae hopped onto the slat fence and motioned for the others to join her. "Let's do our meetin' here. Nice and proper-like."

"I ain't never been a member in an actual club before," Bessie said excitedly.

"You ain't never had a reason to be special before," Ruby Mae pointed out.

Clara cleared her throat. "I think the first thing we should do is figure out what we're a-goin' to do with the gold. Pa says we got to take it to the bank and split it up three ways, nice and fair, Morrisons and Spencers and Coburns. But part of the road to El Pano's blocked by a rockslide. That's why Mr. Pentland hasn't brought mail in so long. So it'll likely be awhile before we can go to the bank."

"It'll be fine with Miz Christy," Ruby Mae said. "'Course, I'd feel better if'n it was in a nice, safe bank."

"I think Pa wants to build us a better house with the cash-money," Clara said. "Maybe one with real floors instead of dirt."

Ruby Mae nodded. "It's true the grown-ups will have their own ideas about what to do with all the cash-money. But I figure we found it, so we oughta get to spend some of it. Besides, there'll be plenty to go around."

"I want to buy me a dress all frilly and

puffy, with silk ribbons," Bessie said in a far-away voice.

"And I want to get me a horse of my own," Ruby Mae said. "I love Prince, but I got to share him with the preacher. My horse'll be the color of gold, with a white star on his head. And faster than the wind!"

"And I want—" Suddenly Clara stopped. The sound of someone whistling floated on the air. "Everyone hush!" she instructed.

"It might be Lundy, or one of the other big boys, come to find out about the gold," Bessie whispered.

"I told you we should have made sure we weren't followed!" Clara said. "People get mighty greedy when they hear the word 'gold.'"

Just then, a lone figure emerged from the woods. He had a large belly and a red beard. On his back, the man carried a strange-looking black contraption with long wooden legs. Behind him trudged a gray mule laden with packs. The mule seemed to be limping.

When the man noticed the girls, he waved and turned in their direction.

"Wonder what a stranger's doin' in these parts," Bessie murmured.

"Flatlander, I'll bet," Clara said. "He looks lost. Whatever you do," she added under her breath, "not a word about the gold, Ruby Mae Morrison!"

"I ain't entirely feeble-minded, thank you kindly," Ruby Mae snapped.

"Ho, young ladies!" the man called as he neared. "What luck to find you. Where exactly am I, if you don't mind my asking?" He wiped his brow with a white handkerchief. "I'm ashamed to admit it, but I haven't the foggiest idea."

"Lordamercy, you must be lost!" Ruby Mae exclaimed.

"Most folks who end up in Cutter Gap aim to come here on purpose," Clara added. "Or they was born here and don't know no way to get out."

"Cutter Gap," the man repeated, chuckling. "Well, I'll be." He patted his mule on the head. "Seems we're a bit lost, Clancy, old fellow."

"It's easy to get lost in the mountains if you're a city fellow," Bessie said kindly.

The man pointed to the mission house. "And whose house might that be?"

"That's the mission house," Bessie said. "So I s'pose it belongs to the Lord, in a manner of speakin'. But He's lettin' Miz Christy and Miz Ida borrow it."

"You suppose I might find a bite to eat there? Clancy and I have been wandering these lovely mountains for weeks, and I haven't seen a home-cooked meal in all that time. He's pulled up lame, poor guy.

Slipped on a rock near a creek awhile back. Thought he was better, but he's been favoring that hind foot today."

"Creek?" Ruby Mae asked.

"Up on the west face of that mountain," he said, pointing past Ruby Mae's shoulder. "By the way, name's Grady Halliday."

"I'm Ruby Mae, and this here's Bessie and Clara."

"What's that strange thingamajig you're carryin'?" Clara asked.

"This, my dear, is a camera. The finest made. I'm a photographer by trade."

Bessie frowned. "You mean a picture-taker?"

"Indeed. Although I don't take pictures of people. Not anymore."

"What else is there?" Clara asked.

Mr. Halliday swept his hand through the air. "Why, all this, my dear. Nature itself. These grand mountains. These majestic trees. Flowers. Streams. Rocks."

"You take pictures of rocks?" Ruby Mae cried. "I never heard of such a plumb fool thing!"

"Yes, it is a foolish occupation," Mr. Halliday agreed. "Which is probably why I'm such a happy man."

"You say you've been up in the mountains for weeks?" Clara asked.

"Took a little longer than I'd planned," Mr. Halliday said. He pursed his lips. "Got a little sidetracked, looking for something . . . important. But as they say, fortune is fickle . . ."

"Can't say as I understand your meanin'," Ruby Mae said, scratching her head.

Mr. Halliday shrugged. "No matter. Now, if you'll provide the introductions, I'd be most appreciative if you could escort me to the mission house."

"I'll feed Prince," Ruby Mae said. "You all go on ahead. It's almost time for supper."

Mr. Halliday nodded. "So nice to make your acquaintance, Ruby Mae."

Ruby Mae watched as Bessie and Clara, who were staying for supper, led Mr. Halliday to the mission house. She wondered what it was he'd been looking for, up there in the woods. She wondered where Clancy had gone lame. Could it have been near Dead Man's Creek?

"Nice to make your acquaintance," he'd said. Fancy talk, when a simple good-bye would have done just fine.

He seemed nice enough, but Ruby Mae couldn't shake the uneasy feeling that she was going to be very sorry to have made Mr. Halliday's acquaintance.

❧ Six ❧

My, my, I never dreamed when I happened upon your mission house that I'd be met with such a welcoming committee!" Mr. Halliday exclaimed as he settled into a chair in the parlor two hours later. "And I must say again, that was the finest piece of apple pie I've ever had the pleasure of devouring!"

Miss Ida, David's sister, handed him a cup of tea. "It's an honor to have you as a visitor, Mr. Halliday."

"Miss Ida's right," Christy said. "Imagine us hosting a man who's photographed the Wright brothers and Ty Cobb and even President Taft himself!"

"No longer, Christy. My professional days are past. I met many interesting folks along the way. A few scoundrels, too, come to think of it. I worked hard and made plenty of money. Now I take the photographs *I* want to take. Mountains are much more interesting subjects than people. Sit still longer, too."

"How long can you stay, Mr. Halliday?" Miss Alice asked.

"Oh, I can't impose. Just until Clancy heals up."

"You should know that the road to El Pano is blocked," David said. "Rockslide. Happens all the time in these parts."

"I'm headed in that general direction," Mr. Halliday said. "But I don't mind a detour or two. I enjoy stopping here and there to say hello. People around these parts strike me as the salt of the earth. Decent, kind. If a little shy."

"They are fine people," Miss Alice agreed, "despite their hard lives."

Mr. Halliday nodded sympathetically. There was a kindness about him that had made Christy instantly like him. Everyone seemed to like him, in fact—except, perhaps, Ruby Mae and her friends, who hardly said a word during supper. And now they seemed to have vanished from the house.

"I've encountered such poverty in these hills," Mr. Halliday said. "You have your work cut out for you."

"Poverty, but dignity, too," Christy said. "When I first came here, the hunger and ignorance and pain really frightened me. But then I started to see the goodness in these people."

40

"I'm sure life here can be very trying," Mr. Halliday said. "Living without hope is a hard thing indeed."

"Of course, hope can turn up in unlikely places," Christy said. "For example, the bottom of a creek."

"A creek, you say?"

"It seems Ruby Mae and the other girls you met came upon some gold nuggets the other day."

Mr. Halliday went very still. He cast a sharp glance at Christy. "Some . . . gold?" he repeated softly.

"We'd hoped to keep it quiet, but of course the whole Cove's abuzz with the news," Christy said.

"The prospect of that kind of wealth," Miss Alice added, "in a place like Cutter Gap—well, you can imagine the excitement it's kindled."

"Indeed," Mr. Halliday said.

David grinned. "Ruby Mae told me she hopes to buy a companion for our horse Prince."

"A friend for Prince?" Mr. Halliday echoed.

"She's quite the horse buff, you see."

"And Clara's even talking about going to medical school," Christy said. "Of course, their parents will have their own plans for the money."

Mr. Halliday set down his teacup. The china rattled slightly. "Yes," he said, "I imagine they would."

"Naturally, we're all curious as to where the gold came from," Miss Alice said. "After all, Tennessee isn't exactly known for its gold mining. And the nuggets had to come from somewhere."

Mr. Halliday nodded slowly. "Well," he said, "you know what the Bible says—'With God all things are possible.'" His voice trailed off.

"It's quite possible someone will still show up to claim the gold," David said. Then he shook his head. "But I'd certainly hate to be the one to deliver that news to Ruby Mae and her friends."

Mr. Halliday stared out the window, stroking his beard. For the first time since his arrival, he'd fallen silent.

"Mr. Halliday?" Christy asked.

"Hmm?"

"Are you feeling all right?"

Mr. Halliday waved his hand. "Of course. Just a little tired, after all my wandering."

For a moment, Christy wondered if she should have mentioned anything to Mr. Halliday about the gold. Something about the sharp way he'd looked at her made her uneasy . . . especially since the nuggets were hidden right here in the mission house.

On the other hand, he was bound to hear about them, anyway. If he was going to be staying here at the mission, Ruby Mae would tell him soon enough.

One thing was certain. Christy was going

to feel much better when the gold was safely locked in that bank safe in El Pano.

She was a teacher, after all, not a banker.

* * *

From her perch on the stairs, Ruby Mae listened to the grownups talking in the parlor. Bessie and Clara sat on the stair below her. They'd been eavesdropping for what seemed like hours. And the more they listened, the more Ruby Mae wished they hadn't.

She had a bad feeling growing in her stomach faster than a spring weed. She didn't like bad feelings. And she didn't like feeling confused.

Mr. Halliday had been looking for something, he'd said.

Mr. Halliday had been near a rocky creek when Clancy had gone lame.

Mr. Halliday was the kind of man who might have lots of cash-money. Maybe even gold.

Clara sighed loudly. "It just don't make any sense, Ruby Mae. If'n the gold belongs to Mr. Halliday, why didn't he just up and say something when Miz Christy told him about it just now?"

"Come to think of it, he did sound a little funny when she brought it up," Bessie said. Her eyes went wide. "I have an idea. . . ."

"Uh-oh," Ruby Mae said.

"Maybe he stole the gold, and that's why he can't own up to it!"

"Or maybe we're just imagining things," Ruby Mae said. "Maybe it ain't his gold at all."

"Still," Clara continued, "he could have been up near Dead Man's Creek. And he was lookin' for somethin'. It *is* kind of a . . . what's the word Miz Christy taught us? A coincidence."

"He had his chance to claim the gold just now," Ruby Mae argued. She hated it when Clara got to thinking too much.

"Maybe you're right," Clara said, chewing on a fingernail thoughtfully.

"'Course I'm right."

"So then where *did* the gold come from?" Clara asked.

"You heard Mr. Halliday. Maybe God put it there for us to find. Like a miracle. You don't go askin' questions about miracles, Clara. You just say 'Thank you kindly' and feel mighty grateful."

"How come you happen to know so much about miracles?" Bessie asked.

"Because I been prayin' for one my whole life, that's how come." Ruby Mae stood, brushing off her dress. "Besides, it don't matter who the gold used to belong to. It's ours now. Finders, keepers. That's the rule."

"Finders, keepers," Clara repeated, as if she were trying to convince herself.

"Trust me," Ruby Mae said. "That gold was meant for us to have."

❧ Seven ❧

When Ruby Mae went down to breakfast the next morning, she was surprised to find Mr. Halliday sitting in the parlor, staring down at the floor. Photographs lay at his feet like a strange, patchwork carpet.

"Good morning, Ruby Mae!" Mr. Halliday said cheerfully.

"Did you take *all* these pictures?" Ruby Mae asked in amazement.

"Oh, this is just the tip of the iceberg." Mr. Halliday hooked his thumbs in his suspenders, contemplating the floor. "I was just trying to sort the wheat from the chaff, if you know what I mean."

"Can't say as I do."

"It means I'm trying to pick out the good photographs from the not-so-good ones. There are things to consider, like composition.

That's the way the parts of a picture all fit together."

Ruby Mae knelt down. She examined a picture of an evergreen tree. "I like this one," she said. "It's not like you're just lookin' at any ol' tree. It's like you're lookin' at the tree and up at the sky, too. Like the tree and the sky are hitched up together."

"You've got a good eye," Mr. Halliday said.

"Factually speaking, *both* my eyes work just fine."

Mr. Halliday gave a hearty laugh. "No, no. That's a way of saying you look at the world like an artist."

"I don't mind drawin'," Ruby Mae said, moving to another picture of a waterfall, "when Miz Christy's got pencils and paper for us, which ain't often. But truth to tell, I'd rather be ridin'."

"Ah, yes. The reverend mentioned you're quite an avid horsewoman." Mr. Halliday paused, as if he were about to say something, then seemed to reconsider.

"Ruby Mae!" Miss Ida called from the kitchen.

Ruby Mae stood. "Well, I got to go set the table for breakfast or Miss Ida'll have my head." As she turned to leave, she noticed a fat book near Mr. Halliday's chair. "What's that? I ain't never seen such a big book before!"

"That," Mr. Halliday replied, "is the Sears

Roebuck catalog. I was thumbing through it for supplies. You've never seen it before?"

Ruby Mae shook her head.

"Here. Take a look. It's chock-full of interesting things. Some useful. Some not." Mr. Halliday passed the book to Ruby Mae. "It's a catalog. That means you find things in it you want, and then you order them. A few weeks later, the item is mailed back to you."

"If'n you have cash-money," Ruby Mae said softly.

Mr. Halliday nodded. "Yes. That's how it works, all right."

Ruby Mae turned the crisp pages one by one. Hats and plows and hammers and shoes! Drawing after drawing of the most amazing things! It was like going to the general store in El Pano, only with a hundred times more shelves.

"It's like the world's biggest store," she marveled.

"Yes, I suppose in a way it is."

"Ruby Mae!" Miss Ida called again. "You stop bothering Mr. Halliday and march on in here. Breakfast is almost ready."

Slowly, carefully, Ruby Mae closed the amazing book. "I have to go," she said, gazing longingly at the catalog as she handed it back to Mr. Halliday.

"Tell you what," he said, "why don't you borrow it for the day? I'm in no need of it."

"You mean keep the book? For a whole entire day?" Ruby Mae cried in disbelief. "Why, I'd be tickled to death! Thank you ever so kindly!"

Clutching the book tightly, Ruby Mae started for the kitchen. But she hadn't gone far before she paused.

"Mr. Halliday," she asked, "can it be that you would have money enough to just out and buy things from a book like this?"

Mr. Halliday looked up from the picture he was examining. "Some," he said. "Enough."

"What kind of things do you buy?"

"Oh, supplies, mostly. I have them sent on to the post office in the town where I'm heading next. Last order, I bought a canteen and a horse blanket for Clancy. Some handkerchiefs for me. Odds and ends."

"I guess you made all kind of cash-money," Ruby Mae said, trying to sound casual, "takin' pictures of powerful folks like the President."

"I suppose you could say I made a good living," Mr. Halliday said gently. "But more importantly, I got to experience wonderful things. Traveling the world. Meeting many different kinds of people."

"Princesses, even?"

"Princesses, presidents, working men, thieves."

Ruby Mae gulped. "Thieves?"

"A few." Mr. Halliday smiled. "They're not

as frightening as you might imagine. Just people like you and me, trying to get by. People who took the wrong fork in the road."

"Well, I'd best be getting on to the kitchen," Ruby Mae said quickly. "Thank you again for the catalog. I promise I'll take real good care of it."

"I trust you completely," Mr. Halliday said.

❧ Eight ❧

So, what do you think of our guest Mr. Halliday?" David asked that afternoon.

He sat beside Christy under a sprawling oak tree in front of the schoolhouse. It was the noon break—what the children called "the dinner spell." As usual, the students had broken off into small groups to eat. Some sat on the schoolhouse steps, but most lay on the wide blanket of green grass, soaking up the hot sun. A knot of children surrounded Ruby Mae, Bessie, and Clara. They'd become quite the celebrities, it seemed.

Christy unwrapped the sandwich Miss Ida had prepared for her that morning. "I like Mr. Halliday. What a fascinating life he must have had."

David gave a wistful nod. "Sometimes, when I hear talk of travels like his, I wonder if I'll stay in Cutter Gap forever."

"You're needed here, David," Christy said. "And being needed is a wonderful gift, don't you think?"

"Yes, I suppose it is." He reached for Christy's hand, then looked away shyly. "I guess we always want what we can't have, hmm?"

Christy wondered if David was referring to his recent proposal. She'd told him she wasn't ready to get married yet, and since then, things between them had been a little awkward. Perhaps it was because David thought Christy was really in love with Doctor MacNeill.

"Sometimes we don't really know what it is we want," she said softly.

David let go of her hand. He sighed, his dark eyes shining. "Maybe you're right."

"Are we talking about us?" Christy asked. "Or about Mr. Halliday?"

"Both. But let's stick with Mr. Halliday. He's a much safer topic." David managed a grin. "It's not his talk about knowing famous people that made me . . . well, a little envious. It was his freedom, I suppose. And the money he'd made. The things I could do for the mission, Christy, if only we had a little more money!"

"I know it sounds like Mr. Halliday's well off, but did you see the way he looked at me when I mentioned the gold the girls had found?"

"It's perfectly natural. Who wouldn't be intrigued?" he said, accepting the half sandwich

Christy offered him. "You know, it actually occurred to me that the gold might have belonged to him. I mean, *somebody* had to lose it. But I guess we may never know its true owner."

Suddenly, the tranquil air was filled with the sound of sobbing. Christy scanned the area. Near the schoolhouse, she noticed George and Mountie O'Teale together. Mountie was crying uncontrollably. George, her nine-year-old brother, was patting Mountie on the back, trying to comfort her.

Christy dropped her sandwich. "I just hope this isn't Lundy, up to his old tricks." Mountie was one of Lundy's favorite bullying targets.

Christy rushed to Mountie's side. "What's wrong, sweetheart?"

Mountie rubbed her eyes. "The p-p-p-princesses say I c-c-can't—" She stopped to take a gulp of air.

"Can't what?" Christy asked. She glanced over her shoulder at Ruby Mae and her friends. They were huddled over the Sears Roebuck catalog that Ruby Mae had borrowed from Mr. Halliday.

"The princesses say Mountie can't get herself a doll she set her sights on in that there book," George explained. He stroked Mountie's tangled hair. "Say she ain't got no gold. Say she's poor as a church mouse and they's rich folks now and that's that."

Christy wrapped her arms around the children. "Don't you listen to those girls. They aren't princesses. They're just Ruby Mae and Bessie and Clara, like they've always been."

Mountie sniffled, her sobs subsiding. "I-I knew I couldn't buy me the doll," she whispered. "I just wanted to *look* at her, Teacher. So later I could pretend in my head she was mine."

"You know what, Mountie?" Christy said, wiping the girl's dirty, tear-stained cheeks. "You can pretend right now. You don't need that picture. You can use your imagination to come up with the prettiest doll in the world. And when you're done, she'll be yours forever."

Mountie considered. "Just make her up, right here on the spot?"

"George will help you. What color eyes should she have?"

Mountie pursed her lips. "Blue, like George's. And sparkly."

"Good. And what color hair?"

"Just like Mountie's," George pronounced. "She's got right purty hair, even if'n it do have some tangles in it."

"There you go. Now you get the idea. I want you two to come up with the perfect doll for Mountie," Christy instructed. "Meantime, I'm going to have a little chat with Ruby Mae and her friends."

❧ Nine ❧

Christy marched across the lawn, hands on her hips. She shooed away the other children and led Ruby Mae, Bessie, and Clara into the empty schoolroom.

"Give me the catalog, Ruby Mae," Christy said as she sat at her desk.

"But, Miz Christy, Mr. Halliday said . . ."

"Now."

Reluctantly, Ruby Mae set the catalog on Christy's desk. "We was just plannin' on what we might could buy ourselves," she said in a pouty voice.

"I found me a dress with a puff-out skirt and a straw hat to match!" Bessie exclaimed.

"And I . . ." Clara began, but Christy held up her hand.

"Did it ever occur to you that your good fortune doesn't mean you can forget about your

54

friends' feelings?" Christy asked. "Mountie was in tears just now because you told her she could never buy the doll she wanted. Why would you say something so cruel?"

"We weren't tryin' to be hurtful, Miz Christy," Clara said. "But she was gettin' so all-fired excited, lookin' at the doll picture . . ."

"We just didn't want her to get her hopes up," Bessie added. "I mean, just 'cause we found gold don't mean everybody in Cutter Gap's goin' to be rich."

Christy took a deep breath. She knew the girls weren't being deliberately thoughtless. But she had to put a stop to this before it got out of hand.

"Here's what you three need to understand," she said slowly. "Your good luck isn't a blessing at all if you end up making other people feel badly. You need to understand that there's going to be a certain amount of jealousy about the gold you found."

"Can't help it if'n folks got the envy in 'em," Ruby Mae declared.

"You can make it easier for them, though. These people are your friends, girls. That hasn't changed. Calling yourselves princesses, setting yourselves apart with a private club . . . well, that's just bound to make other people unhappy and angry. It's as if you're saying that because you may have more money, you're somehow better than they are. And that hurts."

Clara frowned. "We ain't sayin' we're better, Miz Christy. But the whole truth is, we are different now. Can't help it."

"But you can," Christy insisted. "You can be the same kind, generous, thoughtful friends you've always been. Have you forgotten the Golden Rule? How would you feel if Lizette and Mountie and George had found the gold instead of you?"

"'Tain't likely," Ruby Mae said, jutting her chin. "They ain't exactly bosom buddies."

"The *point* is, what if they had? What if Lizette had brought a catalog to school, full of things you might never be able to afford?"

Ruby Mae cocked her head. "I s'pose I'd be a mite jealous."

"Exactly," Christy said. "I realize you're excited about what's happened. But from now on, I want you to try as hard as you can to think about the feelings of your friends. Understood?"

"Yes'm," Clara said.

Bessie nodded.

"Can we still have The Princess Club," Ruby Mae asked hopefully, "if'n we do it private-like?"

"That's up to you," Christy said. "But I want you to think about how you'd feel if some of the other children wouldn't let you join their club."

"Speakin' factually, Miz Christy," Ruby Mae said with a sly grin, "you got us doin' so much thinkin' about other people, I don't see as how there'll be any room left for thinkin' about our 'rithmetic test."

Christy laughed. "Nice try, Ruby Mae."

That afternoon, after the children left school for the day, Christy sat at her desk, grading papers. The sun cast long yellow rays through the windows, spreading onto the floor like melted butter. The sweet smell of honeysuckle carried on the warm breeze. A scarlet tanager warbled joyously from the branch of a hickory tree.

Christy loved this time of day, when the echoes of the children's voices still lingered and the chalk dust still hung in the air. It was a time to reflect on her day. How could she help the children learn better? What could she do tomorrow and the next day to make their hard lives a little easier?

She scanned Ruby Mae's math test. Four wrong answers out of seven. No, Ruby Mae definitely did not have her mind on "'rithmetic" today.

Christy piled up the math tests and straightened her desk. She'd grade the rest at home this evening.

Before leaving, she opened her desk drawer and removed the Sears Roebuck catalog she'd put there for safekeeping. Locking up temptation, she thought with a rueful smile. Just like the gold in her trunk, back at the mission house.

She thumbed through the pages. Page after page of *things*. Things people needed, things people didn't need.

When she'd first come to Cutter Gap, she'd wondered how these people could get by on so little. She still remembered the first mountain home she'd seen—the cabin belonging to Clara Spencer and her family. It was gloomy and cramped, just two rooms, side by side. The family owned a few sticks of furniture and a big iron pot in the kitchen—a pot that was empty, more often than not. And yet the love and happiness Christy had discovered in the midst of those tiny rooms had filled her with awe.

Christy flipped to the back of the catalog, where she happened upon a page of school supplies. Chalkboards, pencils, paper by the pound, even beautiful desks! How wonderful it would be to be able to order everything she needed and have it all magically appear. But that was not the way the world worked— a lesson Mountie had learned only too well this afternoon.

"Knock, knock!"

Christy looked up in surprise to see Doctor MacNeill standing in the doorway. He was holding a slightly wilted handful of wild violets.

"Neil! What brings you here?"

"I had to stop by to talk to Miss Alice about a scarlet fever case she's been helping me with. Thought you might want to take a walk." He gave an embarrassed grin. "Sorry about the violets. It's the thought that counts."

Christy grinned. "I'm sure they were lovely."

"What's that?" Neil pointed to the catalog.

"Trouble, that's what it is."

As she started to close the catalog, Christy's gaze fell on a beautiful dress. Back home in Asheville, she'd seen one of her old friends in a dress just like it. Blue satin, sleeves trimmed in lace, tiny pearl buttons down the bodice. It had been beautiful.

Christy traced her finger over the drawing of the dress.

Be the belle of the ball! . . . the description began.

Quickly, she slapped the catalog shut. There was no point in imagining such a thing. It wouldn't be the same as having it.

Like an imaginary doll, she thought with sudden sadness.

☙ Ten ☙

For sure and certain nobody followed us?" Bessie asked for what had to be the hundredth time that afternoon.

"For sure and certain, Bessie," Ruby Mae said. She peered through the thick woods behind her though, just to be on the safe side. "Would you stop actin' like a scared rabbit?"

At the edge of Dead Man's Creek, the girls stopped to catch their breath. The dense greenery around them rustled with every breeze. The sun dappled the creek with sunlight.

"I could have swore I heard somebody a-whisperin'," Bessie said nervously.

"We doubled back just to be sure," Clara reminded her. She sat on the bank and let her dusty feet cool in the creek. "Even Lundy Taylor would have had himself a hard time followin' us."

"I still don't see why we had to come all the way back here with Prince Egbert," Bessie complained.

"Now that Miz Christy's done teachin' with him, we owe it to him to set him back in his rightful home," Clara said. "Could be he has a wife and kids, you know."

"Let's just get this over with," Ruby Mae said curtly. She didn't like coming back here any more than Bessie did. For some reason, returning to the spot where they'd found the gold made her feel guilty.

"You know, that talk about the gold with Miz Christy got me to feelin' kind of bad," Clara murmured as they walked along the bank.

"You've been usin' your head too much again," said Ruby Mae. "I can tell by the way your forehead gets all crinkled up."

"Ain't crinkled." Clara felt her forehead, just to be sure. "But all that talk about the Golden Rule and all . . ." She sighed. "This bein' princesses is awful complicated, ain't it?"

Bessie nodded. "Lizette wouldn't even talk to me this afternoon. You'd a thought I had the typhoid or somethin', the way she run off."

"And last night," Clara confided, "I heard my ma and pa arguin' out by the woodpile. Somethin' about how to spend the cash-money. My pa wants a new roof and a floor. And my ma wants to save some of the money

61

for later. My pa started to yellin', sayin' how are we even goin' to have a later if'n we don't have a roof over our heads? It was somethin' awful to hear."

"For a blessin'," Bessie said, "this gold sure is a passel of trouble." She paused. "What's that? Did you hear anything? Kind of a rustlin' noise?"

"You're imaginin' things," Ruby Mae said.

"All I'm sayin' is," Clara continued, "this gold sure does seem to bring out the argufyin' in people."

Suddenly, Ruby Mae stopped. A flash of white under some reeds by the edge of the creek caught her eye.

She bent down and fished her hand in the icy water.

It was a white handkerchief.

"What'd you find, Ruby Mae?" Clara asked.

Ruby Mae stared at the white clump of fabric in her palm. "Nothin' much. A man's handkerchief. Or maybe it's just a piece of fabric off'n a shirt. Can't rightly say."

The other girls joined her. "Can so say," Clara said. "That's a man's handkerchief for certain."

"It looks like the one Mr. Halliday was carryin' with him," Bessie said.

Ruby Mae wrung out the little piece of fabric. "Prob'ly lots of people carry handkerchiefs."

"Not in these here parts, they don't," Clara said. "Are you thinkin' what I'm thinkin'?"

"Not likely," Ruby Mae said. "You think more than a whole roomful of teachers and preachers put together, Clara Spencer."

Clara put her hands on her hips. "I'm thinkin' we were right about what we were sayin' before. I'm thinkin' that gold might just have belonged to Mr. Halliday. And I know you're thinkin' it too, Ruby Mae. Even if'n you don't *think* you're thinkin' it."

"Start over," Bessie said, scratching her head. "That's one 'thinkin' too many."

"What Clara means, Bessie," Ruby Mae said, dropping onto the mossy bank, "is that our gold may really be Mr. Halliday's gold."

"It's like one of them mystery stories Miz Christy reads us," Clara explained. "We've got us some clues, see. We know Mr. Halliday said he was lookin' for somethin' out here. We know he and Clancy were by a creek when Clancy slipped. We know Mr. Halliday's handkerchief was here. That's a lot o' clues, no matter how you look at it."

"'Ceptin' for one," Ruby Mae shot back. "Like I said already—how come he doesn't just claim the gold then?"

Clara shook her head. "I don't know why. I admit it don't make a whit of sense. But flatlanders ain't always as sensible as regular people. Them that comes from the city don't always know which way's up and which way's down."

"Maybe we should say somethin' to somebody," Bessie said.

"Why?" Ruby Mae demanded. "Mr. Halliday had his chance to claim the gold."

Bessie shrugged. "I don't know. It just sort of feels a little like stealin', Ruby Mae. And the preacher always says, 'Thou shalt not steal.'"

"He also says, 'finders, keepers.'"

"I ain't never heard him say that," Clara said.

"Well, if'n we asked him, he *would* say it, I'm pretty sure." Ruby Mae fingered the handkerchief. She didn't like this ugly feeling inside her, not one little bit. "Look," she pleaded, "even if'n it *is* Mr. Halliday's gold—and I ain't sayin' it is—I got to talkin' to him this mornin'. He's got plenty of cash-money. He told me he's met real, live princesses his own self. And presidents and rich folks. A few nuggets of gold won't matter to him one way or the other." She sighed. "Not the way they can matter to us. With that gold, we can make somethin' of ourselves."

"Maybe you're right," Bessie said.

"It's true he ain't said the gold's his," Clara conceded.

Ruby Mae slapped her thigh and stood up. "Exactly! Now, no more disagreein'. The Princess Club has got to stick together."

Clara held up her hand. "Here's the spot where we found Prince Egbert." She opened the box she'd been carrying and gently set it on its side. Prince Egbert hopped out, blinked, and looked up at the girls.

"Without you, we might never have found the gold," Clara said. "Thanks, Prince Egbert."

Just then, the trees behind them rustled.

"That ain't no breeze," Clara whispered darkly.

A branch cracked. A bush shook.

"There's somebody comin'!" Ruby Mae cried.

Out of the trees leapt Lundy Taylor. In his hand was a heavy rock.

"Well," he sneered, "if'n it ain't The Princess Club. Fancy the luck. Just so happens I'm lookin' to join up."

❧ Eleven ❧

Lundy took a step closer.

Standing higher up on the bank, he seemed to tower over the girls. He lifted the rock over his head. His black eyes gleamed.

"Tell me where you found the gold," he growled. "Right now."

Ruby Mae glanced at her friends. Both stood frozen in place. Bessie looked as if she were about to cry. Clara's eyes were darting here and there, searching for a way to escape. But Ruby Mae knew there was nowhere to run.

"I said, tell me where you found the gold, Ruby Mae!" Lundy shouted.

Ruby Mae could feel her heart thudding in her chest. She'd known Lundy Taylor her whole life. She'd listened to him sass Miz Christy. She'd watched him beat up boys half his size. She'd even seen him throw a rock at little Mountie O'Teale.

Lundy had done those things out of pure spite. There was no telling what he'd do for a chance to get rich.

"Ain't no more gold to be found, Lundy," Ruby Mae said. She barely recognized her own squeaking voice. "We done found it all."

"Liar!"

Lundy lurched down the bank toward Ruby Mae. She stumbled and fell in the shallow water at the edge of the creek.

"You tell me or I'll knock your head clean in two!" Lundy cried. He waved the big rock in front of Ruby Mae's face. "I'll do it, too! You know I will!"

"Stop it, Lundy!" Clara said. "Ruby Mae's tellin' the truth. We found the gold in this here creek, only there ain't no more to be had. We looked and looked ourselves already."

Lundy lowered the rock, taking in this new information. "Right here, in Dead Man's Creek?"

"Up there, just a few feet," Ruby Mae said, slowly getting to her feet.

"How do you know there ain't no more gold?"

"W—we don't," Ruby Mae stammered. "Not for sure and certain."

Lundy dipped in a bare foot at the creek's

edge and stirred up the rocks on the bottom. Then he bent down and scooped some into his palm, still clutching the big rock in his other hand.

"Don't believe you," he pronounced at last. "These is just creek rocks. Nothin' special about 'em." He scowled at Ruby Mae. "You're a-tryin' to put one over on me."

"No we ain't," Bessie said in a quavery voice. "It was just one of them things, Lundy. We was just plumb lucky, is all."

Lundy stood. Angrily, he slapped the rock in his palm. "How come you all get to be plumb lucky, and I get nothin'? That seem fair to you?"

"That's how luck is," Ruby Mae said with a helpless shrug. "It don't make a whit of sense."

She looked over her shoulder, trying to plot an escape. They could try running for it, but Lundy would be faster. He was bound to catch one of them. Ruby Mae was one of the fastest runners in school—faster even than a lot of the boys. She'd probably be able to get away. But she couldn't risk leaving her friends behind. If she had to stay and fight, she would. Three to one, they might just have a chance. If only they were closer to the mission, they could try calling for help. But out here, no one would hear them.

Lundy moved close to Ruby Mae, so close she could smell the tobacco on his breath.

"Tell me this, Princess Ruby Mae. What makes you so all-fired special you should get all that gold?" Again he raised the rock high. Its sharp edges glinted in the sun.

"I . . . I have an idea," Clara said suddenly. "S'posin' we give you some of the gold, sort of like a reward. For not hittin' us and all."

"Clara!" Ruby Mae moaned, but secretly she was relieved. After all, she wasn't going to enjoy the gold much if her head was split in two.

"A reward?" Lundy repeated. He stroked his stubbled chin.

Clara nodded. "Like for instance, s'posin' we give you a nugget of gold if'n you let us go?"

"Or even two?" Bessie added hopefully.

"Let's not get carried away," Ruby Mae muttered.

"That's an idea, all right," Lundy said, sounding reasonable at last.

"For starters," Ruby Mae said, "how about you just toss that silly ol' rock aside?"

Lundy thought for a minute. His face darkened. "I got me a better idea. How about you three princesses just tell me where the gold's hid and give it all to me? Or else I'll bash your royal heads in!"

Lundy grabbed a lock of Ruby Mae's hair and yanked her closer. She let out a scream of protest. Bessie began to sob.

With the rock inches from Ruby Mae's temple, Lundy smiled a dangerous smile.

"Well?" he said. "I'm gettin' tired of your games. Just tell me where the gold is. I'd hate to have to get blood all over that pretty hair of yours."

"Run, Bessie! Run, Clara!" Ruby Mae screamed. "Get help!"

"Ain't nowhere they can run in time to save your sorry head," Lundy said. "Now, tell me how I can get me that gold . . ."

"Let her go, Lundy!" A booming voice filled the air. "Now!"

Lundy released Ruby Mae's hair and spun around.

To her amazement, there on the bank stood Doctor MacNeill and Miz Christy.

In two strides, the doctor reached Lundy. Lundy tried to resist, but he was no match. The doctor pinned Lundy's arm behind his back. The rock fell to the ground.

"Lemme go!" Lundy moaned. "My arm! You're a-hurtin' my arm!"

"Hurts, you say?" the doctor inquired.

"Burns like fire!"

"I want you to remember this feeling, Lundy," the doctor said. "Because if I ever catch you near these girls again, it's going to hurt a whole lot worse. You get my meaning?"

Lundy nodded.

"I'm sorry. I didn't quite catch your answer."

"Yes!" Lundy squawked. "Yes!"

Slowly the doctor released him. Lundy rubbed his arm. "Docs ain't s'posed to go around hurtin' people," he muttered.

Doctor MacNeill shrugged. "I went to a very unorthodox medical school."

"What's that supposed to mean?" Lundy demanded. "You know I don't know no fancy words."

"It means," Christy said sharply, "that you'd better watch yourself from now on, Lundy."

Ruby Mae blinked in disbelief. She'd never heard Miz Christy sound so riled, not even that time Lundy had hit Mountie O'Teale.

"But they said I could have a re-ward," Lundy murmured, pointing at the girls.

"Well, they were mistaken," said Christy. "They don't have the gold in their possession."

"Who does?"

"It's safely locked away."

Lundy's eyes narrowed. "I bet you got it, Teacher-gal."

Doctor MacNeill took a step toward Lundy, who backed up instantly. "Apparently, I didn't make myself clear," the doctor said with quiet rage.

Lundy spit on the ground, glaring at Ruby Mae. "You won't be princesses much longer," he said. Then he turned and vanished into the trees.

Christy rushed to Ruby Mae's side and pulled her close. "Are you all right?"

"Fine and dandy," Ruby Mae reported. "Sure am glad you two happened along, though."

"We were looking for violets," Christy said. Her blue eyes were shimmering with tears. "We almost headed in the other direction, toward Stony Peak. When I think what might have happened if we hadn't been here . . ."

"We'd have figured somethin' out, Miz Christy," Ruby Mae said reassuringly.

Bessie sniffled loudly. "I ain't so sure about that, Ruby Mae."

"What's that?" Christy asked, pointing to the white handkerchief Ruby Mae was still clutching.

"This?" Ruby Mae stuffed the handkerchief in her pocket. "Nothin'. Just some ol' scrap of fabric we found by the bank."

Christy sighed. "I still can't get over how lucky it is we were in the right place at the right time."

"Well, it's over now," Ruby Mae said lightly. "The doc sure scared the daylights outa Lundy. He won't be botherin' us again. His bark's worse than his bite, anyhow."

Doctor MacNeill was gazing off in the direction Lundy had run. "Don't be too sure about Lundy Taylor, Ruby Mae. Gold can do strange things to people."

Ruby Mae started to argue, but the look on the doctor's face made her fall silent. She'd never seen that look before, not on the doc. Doc MacNeill wasn't afraid of anything.

And yet, right now, if she didn't know better, she'd have sworn he looked awfully worried. Maybe even scared.

❧ Twelve ❧

"**G**rady Halliday," Christy said, "I'd like you to meet my dear friend, Fairlight Spencer, and her husband, Jeb."

"Pleased to make your acquaintance." Mr. Halliday shook hands with the Spencers. "Lovely morning for a church service. If a little on the hot side."

"I think you'll enjoy David's sermon," Christy said. "Church here in Cutter Gap isn't quite like anything you've ever seen before."

Mr. Halliday smiled. "I'm looking forward to it."

Christy surveyed the area outside the church. Knots of people stood here and there, chatting. Children and dogs chased each other in crazy circles. A group of men hovered near the entrance, chewing tobacco. Still, she couldn't help but notice there were a lot of faces missing.

"This is an unusually small turnout," Christy commented. "I wonder why?"

"Perhaps the fine weather is proving too tempting," Mr. Halliday suggested. He pulled a handkerchief from his pocket and wiped his brow.

"Something's temptin' them, all right," Fairlight said. Her lovely eyes sparkled. "But I'm guessin' it's not the weather."

"We passed Ozias Holt and Nathan O'Teale on the way here," Jeb said. "Both of 'em with shovels and picks. Said they didn't have time to look for the Lord." He shook his head. "Lookin' for gold instead."

"This gold discovery certainly seems to have had an effect on the community," Mr. Halliday said.

Fairlight sighed. "It's startin' to seem like a blessin' *and* a curse. Poor Clara ain't slept the last two nights, since Lundy Taylor went after the girls up by the creek. At first, I had such hopes about the gold . . . fixin' up the cabin, maybe. Or savin' for the children's schoolin'. But if it means my little Clara has to live in fear . . ."

"If I get my hands on Lundy, I'll show him a thing or two about fear," Jeb said gruffly, his hands clenched in anger.

Christy gazed at him sadly. It was only

natural for Jeb to want to protect his children. Still, he was usually such a gentle man. It hurt to see him so angry.

"I think Neil did a pretty good job of scaring Lundy Taylor, Jeb," she said, trying to sound reassuring. But she could see from his worried expression that he wasn't convinced.

They headed into the church. Even though the simple building served as Christy's schoolroom all week, it always felt fresh to her on Sunday. Maybe it was the hushed anticipation in the room. Maybe it was seeing David, dressed in his Sunday best—a dark suit, white shirt, and black tie. Maybe it was seeing the scrubbed faces and combed hair of her students, who were generally on their best behavior.

But Christy knew it was more than just those obvious things. The real reason the room felt changed was the feeling of joy and hope that filled the dusty, rough room like summer sunshine.

Today, though, as she settled into a pew with her friends, something was missing. The usual happy mood had been replaced by something much darker. People were grumbling, whispering, and pointing. Much of the attention seemed to focus on Ruby Mae, Bessie, and Clara, who were sitting together in a front pew.

A few rows behind them sat Kyle and Lety

76

Coburn, Bessie's parents. Next to the Coburns sat Duggin Morrison, Ruby Mae's stepfather, and his wife. Christy was surprised to see Duggin. He didn't come to church much. She imagined Ruby Mae was surprised to see him, too. She and her stepfather didn't get along well. That was one reason why Ruby Mae lived at the mission.

As soon as David cleared his throat, the room quieted. "It's nice to see all of you today," he began, "particularly since some seem to have gotten sidetracked en route by, shall we say, more earthly concerns—"

He was interrupted by some loud talk coming from the direction of Duggin's pew. Christy turned to see what the commotion was about. Bessie's father and Ruby Mae's stepfather seemed to be arguing about something.

"Gentlemen?" David said calmly.

"Er, sorry, Preacher," Kyle mumbled.

Christy smiled. By now, David had grown used to such interruptions. Two weeks ago, he'd had to suspend his sermon when a skunk had decided to join the congregation.

"Today," David continued, "I thought we'd reflect a bit on what it means to be wealthy in our society. Does it mean having a lot of material things? A nice home, perhaps even an automobile? Beautiful clothes? Money in the bank?"

"Ask them princesses, Preacher!" called a young voice. "They know all about bein' rich!"

That had to be Creed Allen, Christy thought, as the room exploded into laughter.

David laughed, too. "Thank you, Creed. You bring me to an interesting point. By now I suppose there's not a soul in Cutter Gap who hasn't heard about the intriguing discovery of some gold in these mountains. But is gold the way we measure true wealth? What about happiness? Love? What about the pride that comes from hard work? Which means more—a penny, earned by the honest sweat of your brow . . . or a dollar in ill-gotten gains?"

"Give me the dollar any ol' day!" someone cried.

Again, everyone laughed. But this time, Christy sensed tension in the air, too.

David waited until the room was perfectly still. Long moments passed. At last he spoke again.

"'What is a man profited,'" he said softly, "'if he shall gain the whole world, and lose his own soul?'"

His words hung in the air. Suddenly, Ruby Mae's stepfather leapt to his feet. "Is *so* more Ruby Mae's!" he screamed. "She's the one what found it!"

Bessie's father jumped up, fists raised.

"Wouldn't have found it a-tall, without my Bessie's frog!"

"Bessie's frog!" Clara cried in outrage. "Weren't Bessie's frog! Prince Egbert was *mine!* I'm the one oughta get more of the gold, if anyone does!"

"Clara!" Fairlight said in embarrassment. "You sit down this instant and apologize to the preacher!"

"But Ma—"

David held up a warning hand. "I think we all need—"

Wham! Duggin let loose with a powerful punch to Kyle's belly.

"Fight!" Creed yelped in glee, jumping onto a pew.

Kyle swung back wildly. After several tries, he connected with Duggin's nose. Blood trickled onto his dirty shirt.

Suddenly the whole room went crazy. Kyle and Duggin bumped into the benches, grunting as they threw punches at each other, most of which missed. Soon a few other men were drawn into the fight. Somebody threw a chair. Somebody else knocked over the blackboard. Two babies began to squall. In the corner, somebody was taking bets on who would win.

Into the fray ran Christy, David, Mr. Halliday, Jeb, and Fairlight. But before they could separate the combatants, Granny O'Teale appeared.

The tiny, frail woman stood in front of Kyle and Duggin, her cane poised over her head.

"Stop it, you pig-headed, greedy geezers," she commanded, "or I'll whop you both to kingdom come!"

Kyle and Duggin stopped in mid-swing. They looked at Granny and gulped. The rest of the room fell silent, too.

"Granny," David said, giving her a hug, "I couldn't have said it better myself!"

"My, my," Mr. Halliday whispered to Christy. "I see you weren't exaggerating before. This certainly is very different from any service I've ever attended!"

"It's usually a little calmer," Christy said with a weak smile. "I'm sorry you had to see this."

Mr. Halliday didn't answer. He seemed to be lost in thought. "You know, Christy," he said at last, "I'm sorry, too."

✥ Thirteen ✥

That afternoon, Christy was sitting in the yard writing a letter to her parents when Ruby Mae emerged from the mission house. She was carrying a napkin full of oatmeal cookies.

"For you," Ruby Mae said. "Miss Ida just made 'em."

"Thank you, Ruby Mae. I could use a little pick-me-up. After that fight at the church, I didn't have much appetite at noon."

"I brung some for Mr. Halliday, too."

"He's in the storage shed," Christy said. "We told him he could use it to develop his photographs." She put down her pen and paper, then reached for a cookie. "Come on. I'll walk over with you."

"That was quite a commotion at church today," Ruby Mae said as they started across the lawn. She paused. "You think the preacher was mad?"

"Mad? No. But I do think David's worried about the effect this gold seems to be having on everyone."

Ruby Mae took a bite of cookie. Christy could tell from the faraway expression on her face that something was bothering her.

"I noticed you had a long talk with your stepfather after church today," Christy said gently.

"My step-pa asked if maybe I wanted to come back home to live."

"Oh? What did you tell him?"

"I told him I was right happy livin' here at the mission house. And if'n I moved back home, it'd be such a long ways to school I might hardly never go."

"And what did he say?"

"Said that was all right with him. As long as I didn't get uppity and forget to honor my pa and ma and give them what's rightfully theirs."

"The gold?"

Ruby Mae nodded. "I told him how I maybe wanted to save the gold. You know, for the future. Told him all kinds of crazy dreams I have." She stopped walking. Her lower lip trembled. "Then he . . . he slapped me. Said I didn't have no right to be dreamin' dreams. He wanted to know where the gold was, so I told him you was holdin' it till it could go in

82

the bank and that was that. Then he got even madder and stormed off."

Christy put her arm around Ruby Mae. "This has all gotten awfully complicated, hasn't it?"

"Worser than those 'rithmetic problems you gave us to figure."

Mr. Halliday was emerging from the shed as they approached. He was wearing a black apron. In his hand was a large photograph.

"We brung you some fresh cookies," Ruby Mae said.

"Wonderful! I'll trade you." Mr. Halliday handed the photograph to Ruby Mae. She passed him the cookies.

"You're just in time to see my latest effort," he said. He bit into a cookie. "Wonderful cookie. My compliments to the chef."

Ruby Mae squinted at the photo. "It's a creek," she said. "Looks like Dead Man's."

"So? What do you think?"

Ruby Mae shrugged. "I don't mean to be hurtful, but it just kinda looks like a bunch of water to me."

"I think it's lovely, Mr. Halliday," Christy said quickly.

Mr. Halliday stroked his beard. "Thank you, Christy. But I've already appointed Ruby Mae as my primary critic. She has a wonderful eye."

"*Two* good eyes," Ruby Mae said.

"I stand corrected." Mr. Halliday took the photo and held it out at arm's length, gazing at it critically. "What's wrong with it, Ruby Mae?"

She leaned against the shed, lips pursed. "I don't rightly know. I guess it's just water. Your tree picture, that had the mountain and the sky, all wrapped up together."

"So it's the composition you have trouble with. Not the subject."

"What do I know?" Ruby Mae said irritably. "I ain't no expert."

"Of course you are. You know the beauty of these mountains as well as anyone. And if I'm not getting it on film, well then, I'm not really doing my job, am I?" Mr. Halliday took the photo into the shed, then returned. "Ah well, I shall have to try again. It's a hard task, capturing the riches of this place for posterity. Perhaps it can't be done."

"Ain't no more riches," Ruby Mae said. Christy was surprised at her angry tone. "I keep tellin' everybody, we done found all the riches there was. It was just plumb lucky, is all."

Mr. Halliday looked at her thoughtfully. "I wasn't referring to those riches, actually."

"What, then?"

"I was talking about the incredible beauty of the evergreen trees. The way the sun paints the garden with gold in the morning. The way the warblers argue in the woods."

"Shucks," Ruby Mae said. "That ain't riches. That's just the way the mountains is."

"Exactly." Mr. Halliday reached for another cookie. "There's something else, too. The way the people here love the mountains. And each other. You can't put a price on that."

"You didn't see too much of that at church today," Christy said with a rueful smile.

"Sure I did. By the time everything settled down and the congregation got to singing hymns and clapping and carrying on. I saw it, all right. There was so much love in that room I thought the roof might just pop right off." Mr. Halliday looked at Ruby Mae. "That's all part of the composition, don't you suppose?"

Ruby Mae rolled her eyes. "Beggin' your pardon, Mr. Halliday. But you talk in pure riddles sometimes."

He laughed. "I like you, Ruby Mae Morrison. You speak your mind."

"Well, my mind says I need to go help Miss Ida clean up. But before I go, I was wonderin' . . ." Ruby Mae glanced at Christy nervously.

"Wondering?" Mr. Halliday repeated.

"Well, I know Miz Christy gave that catalog back to you and all . . . but I was wonderin' if I could tear out one tiny little picture in it."

"I wouldn't mind at all. Let me go get the catalog. It's in the shed."

Ruby Mae gave Christy a sheepish smile. "I promise it ain't for makin' anybody feel bad, Miz Christy."

"Just remember what we talked about, all right?"

Mr. Halliday returned with the catalog. "There you go."

"Miss Ida has some sewing scissors," Ruby Mae said. "I promise I'll be right careful."

"Bring it back when you're done," Christy called as Ruby Mae dashed off. She smiled at Mr. Halliday. "I think she's a little preoccupied by all the commotion lately."

"Indeed. Who wouldn't be?"

"Well, I'll let you get back to your work. But I wanted to ask you something first. David and I were wondering if you ever take photographs of people anymore."

"Not really." Mr. Halliday gave a wistful smile. "I suppose I've seen all I need to see of people. Through the lens of my camera, at least."

"We were just thinking . . . well, that a photograph of the congregation—everybody, all together—might help the people here see themselves differently. As a whole, a group. Although I doubt we could even begin to afford such a thing."

"That's one photo I'd be happy to take."

"How much . . ."

"I've been paid in shillings and pennies and

moonshine and gold nuggets," Mr. Halliday said. He stared past Christy at the green mountains surrounding the mission. "But you've already paid me more than I deserve with your hospitality. If anything, I owe you. I fear I've rather complicated lives here."

"You? But how?"

"Oh, the catalog . . . and other things," Mr. Halliday said vaguely. "You tell the reverend I'd be delighted to take a picture of the people of Cutter Gap. I only hope I can do them justice." He gave a sad smile. "After all, I can't even seem to photograph a simple creek."

❧ Fourteen ❧

That evening, Christy went to her bedroom and closed the door. It was a beautiful night, warm and perfumed with flowers. A full moon lit her room like a golden lamp. She looked out the window and sighed. Mr. Halliday was right. Such beauty!

She walked to her bed and slipped her hand under her mattress. The key was there, just where she'd left it.

Slowly, Christy unlocked her trunk. She opened the jewelry box. The gold inside looked dull in the moonlight. How could a handful of rocks hold such power? The power to make grown men fight and young girls cry. The power to split families and change lives forever.

Where had it come from, and why was it here? Was it just "plumb lucky," as Ruby Mae had said? Or did this gold belong to someone . . . perhaps someone right here in Cutter Gap?

Again she went over her conversation with Mr. Halliday that afternoon by the shed. "I fear I've rather complicated lives here," he'd said. What had he meant by that?

He'd talked today of having been paid in gold. And he'd taken photographs near the very creek where Ruby Mae and her friends had found the nuggets.

Suddenly, she remembered the white piece of cloth Ruby Mae had been holding when Christy and Doctor MacNeill had confronted Lundy. It had looked like a handkerchief.

Like one of Mr. Halliday's handkerchiefs.

But why, if the gold belonged to him and he'd lost it, hadn't he told them the truth?

And could it be that Ruby Mae had the same suspicions?

Christy put away the gold. She locked her trunk and hid the key. Then she pulled out her diary and began to write.

What if my instincts are right? What if the gold that filled the girls with such hope—and this community with such anger—really belongs to Mr. Halliday? He's such a kind man. I doubt he'll ever be able to bring himself to say anything. But if Ruby Mae and the other girls know this gold isn't just the result of luck . . . If they know that their gold really belongs to someone else, and that they're taking advantage of his kindness, they'll never be able to live with themselves. The question is, am I right? And if I am, how can I find a way to reach the girls before Mr. Halliday leaves forever?

━ ━ ━

"Lots of children missin' today," Clara commented on Monday morning as she took her seat next to Ruby Mae and Bessie.

"Out gold-huntin'," Bessie said. "Pa said everybody from here to Asheville's heard about it by now. Said he wished he had some pickaxes and shovels to sell."

"At least Lundy ain't here," Ruby Mae muttered. "Probably scared to show his face." She turned to check the door. "Mountie O'Teale come yet?"

"Why are you so all-fired interested in Mountie all of a sudden?" Bessie asked.

"No reason."

The girls watched as more children took their seats.

"Am I crazy," Clara whispered, "or are we sittin' all by ourselves? How come everybody else is off in other rows?"

Bessie scanned the room. "You'd think we had the pox!"

"They're just treatin' us like royalty, is all," Ruby Mae said.

A few minutes later, Mountie entered the schoolroom. Ruby Mae leapt from her seat and pulled the little girl aside.

"I got something to show you," Ruby Mae said excitedly.

"Don't care," Mountie said softly. "I know I ain't no princess, but that's all right. 'Cause I got my 'magination. Teacher said."

Ruby Mae pulled a slip of paper from the pocket of her dress. "Here. This is to help your imagination. For when it gets tuckered out and needs some help rememberin'."

Mountie stared at the little piece of paper. Her mouth worked, but no sound came out. "I-it's my dolly!" she whispered.

"Mr. Halliday let me cut her out of the catalog."

"Can I keep hold of this for a little while?"

"You can keep it, Mountie. It's for you to have." Ruby Mae looked away. "I know she ain't a real dolly, but she's easier to carry."

"Th-thank you, Ruby Mae!" Mountie whispered.

Ruby Mae had never seen Mountie grin so wide. "Shucks, Mountie. Ain't nothin' much," she muttered. Quickly she ran back to her seat.

"What was that about?" Bessie asked.

"Nothin'. Just 'cause we're princesses don't mean I can't talk to the common folk, do it?"

"Don't get all riled," Bessie said. "You ain't

mad at me 'cause our pas was beatin' up on each other in church, are you?"

"Naw," Ruby Mae gave a short laugh. "You mad at me?"

Bessie giggled. "Naw. Can't help it if'n the grownups act like kids. It's a good thing we can act proper-like."

Ruby Mae glanced back over her shoulder. Mountie was hugging the little piece of paper to her chest as if it were a real doll. "Yep," Ruby Mae said softly. "It's a good thing we can act proper-like."

❧ Fifteen ❧

Instead of reading from a book today," Christy said later that morning, "I thought maybe I'd tell you a story."

Her announcement was met with enthusiastic applause. Even the older children loved it when she told stories. Fairy tales, myths, mysteries—it didn't matter what. She wasn't sure if it was her storytelling ability, or the fact that they preferred just about anything to the prospect of another arithmetic or spelling lesson.

Christy sat on the edge of her desk. The children pulled their desks and chairs closer. She couldn't help noticing that Ruby Mae, Bessie, and Clara were sitting apart from the others. She wondered if it was their doing, or if the other children were keeping their distance.

"This is the story of three fair maidens," Christy began.

"Teacher?"

"Yes, Little Burl?"

"What's a maiden?"

"A maiden is a young girl." Christy cleared her throat. "One day, these three maidens were walking through the woods when they—"

"Teacher?"

"Yes, Creed."

"Don't these maidens go by names?"

"That's a very good question, Creed. Let's see. Their names were Lucinda, Drusilda, and—"

"Pearl!" Creed exclaimed.

"Excuse me?"

"I'm right partial to Pearl, Teacher. If'n it don't get in the way of your storytellin'."

"Pearl it is." Christy smiled to herself. She'd long since learned that with the aid of her students, a ten-minute story could take an hour.

"As I was saying, Lucinda, Drusilda, and Pearl were walking through the woods on a bright summer day when suddenly the air was filled with the most beautiful sound their ears had ever heard. 'It sounds like the first call of birds in the morning,' said Lucinda. 'It sounds like a church bell on Christmas morning,' said Drusilda. 'It sounds like angels singing,' said Pearl."

"What was the sound, Teacher?" Mountie asked shyly.

"Well, the maidens didn't know for sure, Mountie," Christy said. Then she lowered her voice to a whisper. "Very carefully the maidens crept to the clearing that seemed to be the source of the wonderful sound. But Pearl tripped on a root—she had very large feet—and suddenly the sound vanished. All was still."

Christy glanced over at Ruby Mae and her friends. They were listening as attentively as the other children—maybe even more so.

"Well, the maidens went to the clearing. They saw footprints leading away into the woods. They saw a campfire, too, the embers still glowing from the night before. And next to the campfire, what do you think they saw?"

"A family of three bears?" Creed ventured.

"Well, no, Creed, that's another story. What they saw was a tiny silver flute. That's a long, thin tube with holes in it. It's a kind of musical instrument, just like the dulcimer Clara's father likes to play."

"Or like the piano over to the mission house that Wraight plays on?" Lizette asked.

"Exactly," Christy said, grinning. It was no secret that Lizette and Wraight Holt were "sweethearts," as the children put it.

Christy paused for a moment, considering

where to take her story. She was making it up as she went along, and she wanted to be sure she got her point across to three members of the audience in particular.

"Well, the maidens gave some serious thought to this flute," she continued. "'Maybe we should leave it,' Drusilda said. 'After all, it doesn't really belong to us. Maybe the music-maker was so frightened he left this behind. Or maybe he left it for us out of the kindness of his heart.' But Pearl was the leader of the group, and she said, 'No, if we found it, it's ours, fair and square.' So she picked up that silver flute and she put it in her pocket and off the maidens set for home."

"So then they played songs on it, Teacher?" George O'Teale asked.

"Well, that's the thing, George. Drusilda tried, and Lucinda tried, and Pearl tried. They blew on that flute till their faces were purple, but the only thing that came out was the most dreadful noise. A noise like a hungry hog and a balking mule and a howling hound all mixed up together. The maidens had to wear earplugs day and night while they tried to make that sweet music they'd discovered in the woods. But you know what?"

Christy looked over at Ruby Mae. She was staring at the ceiling with a strange, unhappy gaze, her mouth set in a frown.

"The maidens couldn't make the silver flute

play because it wasn't theirs. They'd taken something that didn't belong to them, and because of that, there was no joy in it." Christy paused. "Finally, in frustration, the maidens took the silver flute back to the clearing in the woods. Day after day they waited patiently, hidden in the trees, far enough away so the music maker wouldn't be afraid. On the last day, when they were just about ready to give up, what do you think happened?"

"Music!" George cried, and the other children laughed.

"Exactly, George. Music happened. The owner of the flute returned, and made the sweetest, most joyous, most angelic music the maidens had ever heard, even more beautiful than before."

"And is that the end, Teacher?" Creed asked.

"That's the end, Creed."

"Ain't no point to this story," Ruby Mae said darkly, speaking up for the first time. "They found the flute. They coulda kept it."

"But it weren't rightfully theirs," Clara said softly. "So they couldn't make music. You see, Ruby Mae?"

"Tell us another one, Teacher!" Creed urged.

"And make this one have a better ending," Ruby Mae muttered.

"I'm tellin' you, Ruby Mae," Clara insisted during the dinner spell that noon, "Miz Christy was tryin' to learn us a lesson. We're the three maidens, don't you see? And she's sayin' if the gold don't rightly belong to us, maybe we should give it back to the person it does belong to."

Ruby Mae lay back on the springy lawn, chewing on a blade of grass. "First off, we don't know who it belongs to. And second, who's to say we won't do more good with it than he would?"

"He," Bessie repeated. "You mean Mr. Halliday."

"I don't mean anyone!" Ruby Mae shot back.

"That was his handkerchief by the bank," Bessie reminded her.

Clara set her bread aside and brushed the crumbs off her dress. "I think we need to have an official-like meetin' of The Princess Club. Right here and now. We need to take a vote."

Ruby Mae sat up. "Vote on what?"

"On givin' back the gold," Clara whispered harshly. "What do you think? All for it, raise your hands."

Bessie's hand shot into the air. So did Clara's.

Ruby Mae couldn't believe her eyes. "Are you crazy? What about your education? What about your frilly dresses? Have you forgotten all our plans?"

"Don't matter havin' plans," Clara said, "if you got no friends to share them with."

"Besides," Bessie added, "I'm tired of all the fussin' and feudin'. Like with my pa and your pa. Craziness, all of it." She gave an embarrassed smile. "And to tell you the truth, it just don't feel right, spendin' money that ain't rightfully ours. Even if we haven't *really* spent any of it yet."

"But . . ." Ruby Mae threw up her hands in exasperation. "What's got into you two? Some silly story about a flute, and all of a sudden you want to give up your future? We all agreed that if'n the money was Mr. Halliday's, he shoulda owned up to it."

Bessie and Clara just stared at her blankly. "We took a vote, Ruby Mae," Clara said. "Fair and square."

"All right, then," Ruby Mae said. "How about this? How about we give it a day to sink in? You know, think about it longer. You love to think about things, Clara. You can fret over this for another day for sure. Then, we'll vote again tomorrow. And whatever the club decides, that's what we'll do."

Clara chewed on a thumbnail. "Well, I s'pose one more day wouldn't hurt. But that's all."

"Deal?" Ruby Mae turned to Bessie.

"I don't have to think any more on it, do I?" Bessie asked. "My head already hurts from all this frettin'."

"No, Bessie. You don't have to." Ruby Mae stood, arms crossed over her chest. "Then we're decided. Tomorrow we vote. Till then, no matter what, the gold's still ours."

✎ Sixteen ✎

May I be excused?" Ruby Mae asked at dinner that evening.

"I suppose," Christy said. "But you barely touched your chicken."

"Just ain't hungry, I reckon. It was fine chicken, though, Miss Ida."

"I'll second that," Mr. Halliday said heartily.

"As a matter of fact," the preacher said, "I'll eat that last piece on your plate, Ruby Mae. Unless you'd like it, Mr. Halliday."

"All yours, Reverend. Eat any more, and I'll burst."

Ruby Mae pushed back her chair and carried her dishes to the sink in the kitchen. She slipped upstairs without a sound.

At the top of the stairs, she paused in front of Miz Christy's room. Her heart was hammering inside her chest.

All afternoon, she'd known she was going to end up in this spot. But now that she was really here, she wasn't sure if she should go through with her plan.

Downstairs, the grownups were laughing and talking. Mr. Halliday had spent the whole dinner talking about his trips to faraway places. He'd even told them how he'd had dinner at the White House after he took the President's photograph. A fine meal, he'd said, but not as fine as Miss Ida's fried chicken.

The more he had talked, the more Ruby Mae had realized he didn't need the gold, even if it *was* really his. He was a man with a camera and a fancy catalog and lots of white handkerchiefs and a gold pocket watch. What did a little gold matter to him? If he needed more money, he could always take more pictures of fancy people.

With trembling fingers, Ruby Mae eased open Miz Christy's door and slipped into her bedroom. The setting sun had turned everything golden. The room smelled of lilac talcum powder, the way Miz Christy always did. Unlike Ruby Mae's room, everything was in its place, neat as a pin.

On the dresser was a picture of Miz Christy's family, smiling at the camera. Ruby Mae looked at it. Even though she'd seen it a hundred times before, tears suddenly spilled down her cheeks.

Miz Christy had a happy family. So did Bessie and Clara.

They could talk all they wanted about silver flutes and such, but the gold meant far more to Ruby Mae. She didn't have anyone she could really depend on. She didn't have the kind of family they did.

Sure, she'd talked about horses and mansions and dozens of kids. But what she truly wanted was a way to feel safe. What if Miss Alice and the preacher decided they couldn't let her stay at the mission any longer? What if her pa and ma wouldn't take her back in? Her pa had kicked her out once already. Where would she go then?

Ruby Mae wanted this gold. She wanted it just the way Mountie wanted that silly doll. Only worse.

She wiped away her tears with the back of her hand. She hated all this thinking. How did Clara stand it?

Taking a deep breath, Ruby Mae ran over to Miz Christy's bed, slipped her hand under the mattress, and found the trunk key. It took two tries to get it open, but finally the lock clicked.

Carefully, Ruby Mae opened the wooden jewelry box. There it was. Hope.

She scooped up all the nuggets and put them in her pocket. Her hands were shaking like leaves in the wind. Just as she started to lock the trunk, she heard voices on the stairway.

Her heart leapt into her throat. Leaving the key in the lock, Ruby Mae slid under Miz Christy's bed just as the door opened.

Miz Christy took another step, and another. Ruby Mae could see her teacher's shoes. They were close enough to touch. She feared she would scream from the awful waiting.

"That's funny," Miz Christy murmured. "I could have sworn I heard something."

"Coming?" the preacher called from downstairs.

"Just a minute, David. I'm getting my shawl. It's cool tonight."

Step. Step. Ruby Mae heard a drawer slide open. Step. Step. Step.

The door closed.

For the first time in what seemed like hours, Ruby Mae took a calming breath. She waited under the bed a long time, until, through the window, she heard the sound of Miz Christy and the preacher talking outside in the yard.

Ruby Mae eased her way out from under the bed. Her pocket bulged. There was something she needed to do, but what? Her head was still buzzing with fear.

Find a place to hide her gold, maybe that was it. Somewhere in her room where no one, not even nosy Miss Ida, would ever find it. Stuffed deep in her feather pillow, maybe.

Ruby Mae went to the door and peeked outside. It was safe.

She headed for her room, whistling softly.

A tune as pretty, she thought, as anything you might hear on a silver flute.

~ ~ ~

That night, Christy couldn't sleep. Maybe it was the full moon, lighting up the room. Or maybe it was the fact that David had thought he'd heard noises that evening around the mission house. He and Mr. Halliday had done a thorough search and hadn't found a thing, but still, it was hard to relax with the gold right here in her room.

It was a relief to know that Mr. Halliday was staying here. And David was in his bunkhouse, close enough to come if help were needed.

She went to the window and listened. Crickets thrummed noisily. A branch cracked. An owl hooted, soft and low: *HOO-HOO-HOO-HOOOOO*.

Nothing. She was just jumpy. She closed her window and returned to bed. But as she pulled the sheets over her, something glimmering in the moonlight caught her eye.

Her key. The key to her trunk.

For a brief moment, she thought maybe

she'd left it in the trunk latch by accident. But no, she distinctly remembered putting it under the mattress.

Christy rushed over to the trunk and opened it. The jewelry box was in its usual place. But when she opened it, just as she'd feared, the gold was gone. Not a nugget was left.

With a sigh, Christy sat on her bed, clutching the key. Who knew about the key? Miss Alice, David, Neil, Miss Ida.

And Ruby Mae.

No. She couldn't let herself think that way. Ruby Mae wouldn't, she couldn't . . .

Perhaps someone else had found out about the trunk. Rummaged through her room. Found the key.

But Miss Ida was almost always here. It didn't seem very likely.

Still, the alternative was more than Christy could bear to think about.

With a cold feeling in the pit of her stomach, Christy tiptoed to Ruby Mae's room. Gently she knocked on the door. When there was no answer, Christy eased it open a few inches.

Ruby Mae lay there asleep, snoring lightly. Asleep like this, she had the face of an angel.

Christy closed the door. She was going to try to remember that angelic face. And she was going to try very hard to think of some other way the gold might have disappeared.

❧ Seventeen ❧

Penny for your thoughts."

Christy looked up in surprise. Neil was standing in the doorway of the classroom, holding another bouquet of violets.

He handed them to her. "Not wilted this time. I'm improving."

"Thank you, Neil. They're lovely."

He leaned on the edge of her desk. "You looked about a million miles away just now."

"I was. I let school out half an hour ago, and I've been sitting here ever since."

"No problems with Lundy, I hope," he said, clearly worried.

"No. He hasn't shown up for school since the incident at the creek. From what I understand, he's probably out prospecting. A lot of the children are."

"What is it, then?" Neil touched her hand tenderly.

"It's the gold. It's been stolen. Right out of my trunk."

"That's all we need. Any suspects?"

"I'm afraid the most likely one has very red, very curly hair." Christy rubbed her eyes. "I told Ruby Mae and Bessie and Clara today about the missing gold. Clara and Bessie almost seemed relieved, believe it or not. I think the pressure was getting to them. But Ruby Mae . . . well, she didn't even blink. She was just a little *too* calm."

"Maybe she didn't take it."

"Maybe. But I can't see who else could have."

"Give her some time. Maybe she'll ''fess up' all on her own."

Christy went to the blackboard and started to erase the day's work. "Who'd have ever dreamed a handful of rocks could be so much trouble?"

"That's what they said in 1849 in California."

"Well, we're having our own Gold Rush of 1912." She sighed. "What am I going to do, Neil?"

He gave her a hug. "Pass me an eraser," he said.

～～～

"This here," Clara said that same afternoon, "is the last official meeting of The Princess Club. What with us not being princesses no more."

Ruby Mae sat on a bale of hay near the stable. The three girls had already fed Prince, Old Theo, Goldie, and Clancy. Now they were watching the animals munch contently on fresh grain and hay.

"Clancy looks to be gettin' much better," Ruby Mae said. "I wonder if'n Mr. Halliday will be movin' on soon. You think?"

"Ruby Mae!" Bessie cried. "You sure are takin' the news about the gold awful well. We ain't princesses anymore. Don't that bother you?"

"Sure it bothers me," Ruby Mae said quickly. "But ain't nothin' we can do about it."

"Still," Clara pressed, "don't you wonder who took it? Right out from under Miz Christy's nose like that? Who coulda done such a thing?"

Ruby Mae stroked Prince's warm, silky coat. She could feel her face heating up. Was Clara looking at her funny? Or was Ruby Mae's guilt getting the better of her?

"Anybody could have sneaked into the mission house," she said. "Ain't like it's locked up or nothin'."

"Still, they would have had to know where to look," Clara persisted.

"Easy enough to figure out where it was hidden," Ruby Mae pointed out. "There's only one thing with a lock on it in that whole house."

"But then they had to find the key," Bessie added.

"What does it matter?" Ruby Mae blurted. "Me, I'm plumb tuckered out, talking about that gold. If'n we ain't goin' to be princesses no more, let's just start actin' like plain ol' regular people!"

"Ruby Mae!" Bessie grabbed her by the arm. "Hush! Look, over yonder!"

Bessie pointed a trembling finger at a stand of nearby trees. There stood Lundy Taylor. In the crook of his arm was a long hunting rifle.

Bessie gulped. "H-he's got himself a gun!"

"Don't pay him no never mind," Ruby Mae said. "He's probably just out huntin' squirrels."

Suddenly, as quickly as he'd appeared, Lundy vanished into the woods.

"See?" Ruby Mae said. "Don't mean nothin'."

"Still and all," Bessie said, breathing a sigh of relief, "I'm just as glad to be rid of that gold. I didn't need the likes of Lundy after me the rest of my days!"

"Yep," Ruby Mae said, frowning. "I s'pose maybe you're right about that."

I thought I'd reached Ruby Mae.

━ ━ ━

Christy wrote in her diary that night. She paused, pen in hand, when she heard a howl coming from far off on the mountain. The woods were full of noises tonight. Even more than usual.

She turned to a fresh page.

Neil says to give it time, but how much time can I give it? Mr. Halliday will be leaving soon, and I'm more convinced than ever that the gold is his. But if I push Ruby Mae, I'm afraid she'll deny what I'm all too certain is the truth: she took the gold. I suppose all I can do is pray. Perhaps the answer will come to me if I am patient.

When she finally set her diary aside and tried to sleep, Christy tossed and turned, just as she had the previous night. Every now and then she awoke to a sound from the outside. But eventually, she somehow managed to fall asleep again.

Her dreams were full of flutes made of silver and red-haired angels . . . There was something cold in her dreams, too, something cold, pressed against her temple. There were people with her, but these weren't red-haired angels anymore. These people were dangerous. These people meant her harm . . .

Something clicked, like the sound of a rifle being cocked.

Christy's eyes flew open. In the milky moonlight, she could see them plainly— Lundy Taylor and his father, Bird's-Eye. Each one had a gun.

And they were both pointed straight at her.

❧ Eighteen ❧

Tell us where the gold be," snapped Bird's-Eye, a grizzled man with a permanent scowl. "If'n you do, we won't have to shoot you, Teacher-gal."

Slowly Christy sat up, trying to get her bearings. Miss Ida and Mr. Halliday were in rooms at the far end of the house. Only Ruby Mae's room was nearby. Christy could scream, but who knew what Bird's-Eye would do? She could smell the moonshine on his breath.

This wasn't the first time she'd faced down this man's gun. She knew better than to take him lightly.

Lundy cocked his gun. He jerked it at her. "We knows it's hid in here. So you might as well come clean."

Both men, Christy noticed, were whispering. That meant they didn't want to face Mr. Halliday and David. They just wanted the gold.

Well, she only had one choice. Tell them the truth.

"I don't have it," Christy said, as calmly as she could.

"Don't go lyin' to us, Teacher-gal. 'Thou shalt not lie.' Ain't that one o' your rules? We knows it's here."

"Gotta be," Lundy said. "That day by the creek, you said it was all locked up. That means you know where it is. And I figger it's gotta be here at the mission house."

"I'm telling you, I don't have it."

"Prove it."

"Fine." Christy went to the trunk and unlocked it. She pulled out her jewelry box. Her hands were trembling as she opened it.

"This is where the gold was hidden. But somebody stole it yesterday. I—I don't know who."

Lundy shoved the gun against her back. "You got it hid somewheres else."

"I'm telling you the truth, Lundy."

"Liar!" Bird's-Eye raised his hand to strike her.

"If I call out, I'll wake everyone in the house," Christy said calmly. "And . . . and Mr. Halliday has a gun." She wasn't sure if that was true or not. But she certainly hoped it was.

"I hit you hard enough, Teacher-gal, and you won't be able to scream," Bird's Eye growled. "I oughta—"

"No!" a small voice cried.

Christy spun around.

Ruby Mae stood in the doorway in her cotton nightgown. She was clutching her feather pillow to her chest. She rushed over and grabbed at Bird's-Eye's arm with her free hand.

"Let her be, Mr. Taylor," she whispered. "I know where the gold is."

Bird's-Eye and Lundy exchanged a wary glance. "I'm waitin'," Lundy said, jerking his gun at Christy.

Tears flowed down Ruby Mae's face. Frantically, she began digging into her pillow. Feathers floated everywhere as she searched.

"This better not be no trick," Lundy muttered as he brushed a feather from his face.

"A-choo!" Bird's-Eye sneezed. "If'n this . . . achoo! . . . ain't true, I'll . . . achoo!"

"There!" Ruby Mae cried. She dropped a sock onto the bed.

"Looks like a plain ol' sock to me," Lundy said.

Ruby Mae emptied the sock. Gold nuggets rained onto Christy's quilt.

Lundy's eyes went wide. "So they weren't lyin' about the gold! There it is, plain as day, Pa!"

"Weren't my gold." Ruby Mae looked at Christy. "It's Mr. Halliday's, I'm pretty sure. I shoulda told him I thought it was his a long time ago. But I was just so darn hopeful . . ." She frowned at Lundy. "And it ain't yours, neither."

Lundy dropped his gun and scooped up the gold into his hands. Bird's-Eye ran to join him.

"Looky here, Pa! We is kings now. Just like they was princesses!"

"I beg to differ with that assessment," came a voice from the hallway.

Mr. Halliday appeared in the doorway. He winked at Christy.

Bird's-Eye went for his gun, but before he could, there was a loud click. Mr. Halliday trained a silver pistol directly on Bird's-Eye's hand.

"Hand the guns to Miss Christy," Mr. Halliday said calmly. "And hand my gold to me."

❧ Nineteen ❧

I t's a good thing I'm a light sleeper," Mr. Halliday said.

Everyone was gathered around the kitchen table, drinking the warm milk a sleepy Miss Ida had prepared. David and Miss Alice had been roused in their cabins by all the commotion following Lundy and Bird's-Eye's rapid departure.

"I still can't believe the way Lundy and his pa high-tailed it out of here," Ruby Mae marveled. "They took one look at that pistol and left their rifles behind!"

"I still can't figure out why they didn't try to break in during the day," Christy said, shaking her head. "There are fewer people around."

"But I'm here," Miss Ida said, hands on her hips. She held up a frying pan. "And they know I'm well-armed!"

"One other thing I don't understand, Mr. Halliday," said Miss Alice. "Why didn't you just tell us that the gold was yours?"

Mr. Halliday looked at Ruby Mae. "I suppose I didn't want to dash anyone's dreams. The girls had such high hopes." He shrugged. "I've seen my share of good fortune. But things didn't turn out exactly as I'd hoped."

"Me neither." Ruby Mae sighed. "I'm right sorry I didn't 'fess up sooner, about figuring out who the gold belonged to. I pretty much put two and two together—that makes four, by the way!" she added, smiling at Christy. "But I wanted that gold more 'n I wanted to get it to its rightful owner. And look at what it got me. When I think how Lundy and Bird's-Eye might have hurt you, Miz Christy, I just want to up and die. I'm truly sorry."

"I accept your apology, Ruby Mae," Christy said. She reached across the table and squeezed Ruby Mae's hand.

"As do I," said Mr. Halliday. "And I happen to know a way you can make it up to me. I want you to be sure that everybody in Cutter Gap shows up for church this Sunday."

"I wouldn't mind that myself," David said with a chuckle.

"How come?" Ruby Mae asked.

"We've got a photograph to take, young lady. And we want to be sure we get the composition just right."

117

The following Monday, Mr. Halliday emerged from the shed. He handed a photograph to Ruby Mae.

"Before you give me your opinion," he said, "I want you to remember that it's been awhile since I took a photo of real, live people. Mountains sit still. Babies don't."

Ruby Mae studied the black and white photograph. There, in front of the church, were the residents of Cutter Gap. They stood stiffly, most barefoot. Some people smiled. Most did not.

Granny O'Teale was in the front row, leaning on her cane. Little Mountie stood beside her, clutching her hand. The preacher, Miz Alice, Miz Ida, and Miz Christy were there. Doc MacNeil was scowling at the camera in that way he had, looking gruffer than he really was.

Ruby Mae's eyes fell on three girls, clumped together at the end of a row. They were sharing a smile between them, as if they knew a secret. They looked proud and silly and happy, all at once.

If you squinted just right and didn't think too hard, they even looked a tiny bit like princesses.

"Well," Mr. Halliday said hopefully, "what do you think?"

"I think," said Ruby Mae with a grateful smile, "that the composition is just about perfect."

~ ~ ~

Early the next morning, Ruby Mae and her friends watched as Mr. Halliday packed up Clancy and prepared to leave.

"Don't forget these sandwiches I packed," Miz Ida said, tucking them into Mr. Halliday's knapsack. "And there's fried chicken, too."

"Ida, you are too kind," Mr. Halliday said. He kissed her hand and Miz Ida blushed.

"Where are you headed now?" Christy asked.

"Well, I'm starting toward El Pano. David tells me the road is more or less clear. And I've got some business to attend to there. Banking business, actually."

For a brief moment, Ruby Mae felt a sense of loss of her gold—her gold that was really Mr. Halliday's gold. He was going to put it in the bank, of course. Well, that was only natural. It needed safe-keeping. And it wasn't hers to worry about, anyway. Not anymore.

"I'm opening up a fund there," Mr. Halliday continued as he adjusted the pack on Clancy's back.

"Oh?" Miz Christy asked.

"An education fund, actually. You might be interested in it. It's for the children of Cutter Gap. I'm calling it the Princess Fund."

"For all us children?" Ruby Mae cried. "For us to go to college and such?"

Mr. Halliday nodded. "I'll be adding to it from time to time, as I can."

"You're a wonderful man, Mr. Halliday." Christy gave him a hug.

"We're most grateful," David added.

"You know what the Bible says—'God loveth a cheerful giver.' It's easier to part with money than you might imagine. There are many things worth more than gold. Friends, for example. Which reminds me."

Out of his pocket, Mr. Halliday pulled three white handkerchiefs, each knotted at the top. He handed one to Ruby Mae, one to Bessie, and one to Clara.

"A handkerchief?" Bessie asked, brow knitted.

"There's some gold dust in each of these," Mr. Halliday explained. "Not a lot, but perhaps enough to keep those princess dreams alive."

"Real live gold dust?" Bessie breathed.

"Oh, thank you!" Clara cried. "This is the bestest present I ever got!"

But Ruby Mae was silent. She stared at her handkerchief a long time. "I think," she said quietly, "we need to have one last meetin' of The Princess Club before you leave, Mr. Halliday."

He looked puzzled. "All right, then. I can wait."

Ruby Mae pulled her friends aside. A few minutes later, she went back to Mr. Halliday, carrying all three handkerchiefs. "We done had a vote," she said. "We're givin' these back to you, if'n you don't mind."

"But . . . why?" he asked, looking a little disappointed.

"We got somethin' else in mind for that gold," Ruby Mae said with a sly smile. "But we need your help."

❧ Twenty ❧

Five weeks later, on a sweltering afternoon, Ben Pentland, the mailman, arrived at the school. Christy was writing addition problems on the blackboard when he peered in the doorway.

"United States mail, at your service!" he called.

"Thank you, Mr. Pentland," Christy said. "Why don't you just leave the letters on my desk?"

"Can't do that, Miz Christy," he said politely.

"Why is that?"

"Mail ain't for you." Mr. Pentland grinned. He held up a box, wrapped in brown paper and tied with twine.

The children murmured excitedly. "Who's it for, Mr. Pentland?" Ruby Mae asked.

Mr. Pentland pretended to study the box at great length. "Why, it says here it's for none other than a certain Miss Mountie O'Teale!"

Everyone turned to stare at little Mountie. Her face was white. Her mouth hung slightly open. She gulped.

"Can't be," said one of the older boys. "Who would send a package to Mountie?"

"Let's just see about that," said Mr. Pentland. Again he studied the package. "Return address is kind of queer. Says 'Care of P.C., Cutter Gap, Tennessee.' Mountie, you know anybody with the initials P.C.?"

Mountie shook her head, bewildered.

With great flair, Mr. Pentland placed the package on Mountie's desk. "I guess you'll be a-wantin' to open it," he said.

Mountie barely managed a nod. She was trembling with excitement.

"Here, Mountie," Christy said. "I'll cut the strings with my scissors. Then you can open the rest."

When the twine was off, Mountie set about opening the package. The children gathered around in rapt attention. Christie noticed Bessie, Ruby Mae, and Clara standing off to the side, whispering to themselves.

Slowly, carefully, Mountie tore off the brown paper. Inside was a wooden box. George had to help her yank it open.

Layers of white paper came next. Mountie

123

pulled off each piece as if the paper itself were a gift.

Suddenly, she gasped. Her hand flew to her mouth. For several moments, she didn't move.

"Go on, Mountie," George urged gently.

With the utmost tenderness, Mountie reached into the box and lifted a beautiful doll into her thin arms. She stroked the shiny curls. She touched the lace-trimmed gown. Then she held the doll to her heart and kissed her.

Tears rolled down her face. "It's her," she whispered. "My 'maginary dolly."

Christy wiped away a tear. She heard quiet sobs behind her and turned.

Bessie and Clara and Ruby Mae were grinning from ear to ear, their own faces damp with tears.

Today, Christy thought proudly, *they really are princesses.*

Family
Secrets

The Characters

CHRISTY RUDD HUDDLESTON, a nineteen-
   year-old girl.

CHRISTY'S STUDENTS:
   ROB ALLEN, age fourteen.
   FESTUS ALLEN, age twelve.
   CREED ALLEN, age nine.
   DELLA MAY ALLEN, age eight.
   LITTLE BURL ALLEN, age six.
   WANDA BECK, age eight.
   WRAIGHT HOLT, age seventeen.
   VELLA HOLT, age five.
   MOUNTIE O'TEALE, age ten.
   MARY O'TEALE, age eight.
   RUBY MAE MORRISON, age thirteen.
   CLARA SPENCER, age twelve.
   ZADY SPENCER, age ten.
   LUNDY TAYLOR, age seventeen.
   LOUISE WASHINGTON, age fifteen.
   JOHN WASHINGTON, age ten.
   HANNAH WASHINGTON, age eight.

DOCTOR NEIL MACNEILL, the physician of the Cove.
HELEN MACNEILL, the doctor's grandmother.

ALICE HENDERSON, a Quaker missionary who
   started the mission at Cutter Gap.

DAVID GRANTLAND, the young minister.
IDA GRANTLAND, David's sister and the mission
   housekeeper.

JAMES BRILEY, former classmate of Doctor MacNeill.

BOB ALLEN, keeper of the mill by Blackberry Creek.
MARY ALLEN, Bob's wife.
(Parents of Christy's students Rob, Festus,
Creed, Della May, and Little Burl.)
GRANNY ALLEN, Bob's grandmother.

CURTIS WASHINGTON, new arrival to Cutter Gap
from Virginia.
MARGARET WASHINGTON, Curtis's wife.
(Parents of Christy's students Louise, John,
and Hannah, and of Etta, a baby girl.)
WILLIAM WASHINGTON, Curtis's grandfather, an
escaped slave.

LANCE BARCLAY, an old beau of Christy's from
Asheville.

GRANNY O'TEALE, a mountain woman.
SWANNIE O'TEALE, Granny's daughter-in-law.
(Mother of Christy's students Mountie and Mary.)

AUNT POLLY TEAGUE, the oldest woman in the Cove.

FAIRLIGHT SPENCER, Christy's closest friend in the Cove.
(Mother of Christy's students Clara and Zady.)

LETTY COBURN, a mountain woman.

SCALAWAG, Creed Allen's pet raccoon.
VIOLET, a pet mouse belonging to Hannah
Washington.
PRINCE, a black stallion donated to the mission.

✒ One ✒

This is without a doubt the messiest cabin I have ever seen!" Christy Huddleston exclaimed.

Doctor Neil MacNeill gave a hearty laugh. "I'm a doctor, Christy, not a housekeeper."

"Look at this dust." Christy wrote her name in the thick dust layering a cupboard full of medical books. "It's a good thing you don't perform surgery in this room."

"Actually, I do, on occasion."

Christy pointed to a stuffed deer head mounted on the wall. "Those antlers are covered with spider webs, Neil!"

Doctor MacNeill crossed his arms over his chest, hazel eyes sparkling. "I was under the impression you were sent here by Miss Alice to pick up some medical supplies. If I'd known there was going to be a housekeeping inspection, I would have prepared." Playfully, he tossed a feather duster at Christy. "Since you're so concerned, please feel free to take a whack at the dust."

"I can't stay *that* long. Besides, anyone who can perform delicate surgery can surely figure out how to operate a feather duster," Christy replied, laughing. "Before heading back to the mission, I thought I'd say hello to your new neighbors. How are the Washingtons doing, anyway?"

"Just getting settled in." The doctor began filling a small glass bottle with the dark, bitter-smelling medicine he and Miss Alice used to treat whooping cough. "They're in that abandoned cabin, but it's going to need a lot of repairs. Nice family. Four kids, three school-age."

"That'll bring my grand total up to seventy students," Christy said. "Amazing. When I decided to come here to Cutter Gap to teach, I pictured perhaps twenty children in my schoolroom at the most. But seventy! That's quite a handful."

The doctor grinned. He was a big man, with rugged, handsome features that looked like they'd been chiseled out of rough stone. His curly, sandy-red hair, always in need of a comb, gave him a boyish look. "For most mere mortals, that many students would be impossible," he said. "But for you, my dear Miss Huddleston, nothing is impossible."

Christy reached for the next empty new bottle and held it steady while the doctor filled it with medicine. His hands were rough and stained, the mark of long years caring for the desperately poor residents of this Tennessee mountain cove. Although Christy had lived here several months, her own hands seemed fragile and soft by comparison. They were the hands of a "city-gal," as the mountain people would say.

In some ways she still was that fresh-faced girl from Asheville, North Carolina—frightened, but full of big dreams. Her wide blue eyes and delicate features made her look younger than her nineteen years. She wore her sun-streaked hair swept up to make herself look older, but Christy knew it didn't fool anyone.

The doctor put a stopper in each of the two bottles he'd just filled. He gazed around the cabin with a critical eye. "Maybe you're right," he said. "This place could use a good cleaning."

It was a simple cabin, but well-furnished by mountain standards. A bearskin rug lay on the hearth. An old cherry clock ticked on the mantel. A rack of antlers served as a coat rack. A hunting rifle was propped against the wall in the corner, and a pipe with an engraved silver band rested in the pipe rack by a chair. Framed, inscribed photos, most from the doctor's years at medical school, peered out from the dusty shelves.

"Christy," the doctor said, "there's something I've been meaning to tell you. Um, ask you. It's about—" he cleared his throat, "well, about a wedding, actually."

Christy blinked in surprise. "A wedding?"

"Yes, that's right. And a confession I have to make."

The doctor's fingers were trembling as he reached for another empty bottle. It wasn't like him to be so nervous, and it certainly wasn't like him to blush!

Christy gulped. She'd already been through one proposal since coming to Cutter Gap. David Grantland, the mission's young minister, had asked for her hand in marriage not long ago. In the end, despite her affection for David, Christy had told him no. She'd explained that she needed more time to be sure of her feelings. She cared for David. But she also cared deeply for Doctor MacNeill—perhaps more than she was willing to admit, even to herself.

"What do you mean, 'confession'?" Christy asked, not sure she was ready to hear the answer. "What are you trying to say, Neil?"

He took a deep breath. "Is it hot in here?"

"Not really."

The doctor fanned his face with his hand.

"It's definitely hot. Why don't we go out on the porch?"

They settled into the old oak rockers on the cabin porch. Tulip trees and giant beeches formed a graceful canopy, shading out most of the hot late afternoon sun. "It's so beautiful here," Christy said, thinking it might be a good idea to change the subject.

"Yes, it is," the doctor replied. "I was born in this cabin, did you know that? So was my grandfather, and his grandfather before him. Sometimes I think these mountains are in my blood." He looked over at Christy, a pained expression on his face. "A man could do much worse. Couldn't he?"

"Neil," Christy said gently, "what is it you're trying to tell me?"

He rubbed his eyes. "It's silly, really. Crazy, even."

"Tell me."

"Well, it's like this." He took a deep breath. "I have an old friend by the name of James Briley. We went to medical school together. We were roommates, best friends— and competitors, I suppose. James went on to establish a thriving practice in Knoxville. He invited me to join him, and I was sorely tempted. But I felt an obligation to come back to Cutter Gap and help the people here. There wasn't a doctor within a hundred miles of this place. This was where I was needed."

"You did the right thing, Neil."

"I suppose." The doctor shrugged. "The thing is, it seems James is getting married, and he's invited me to the wedding."

"Oh!" Christy exclaimed. "So *that's* what you meant!"

"What did you think I meant?"

"I thought . . ." It was Christy's turn to blush. "I mean, I know it's crazy, but I thought you—"

"You thought I was going to propose to you?" The doctor threw back his head and laughed.

"Well, it isn't *that* funny," Christy protested.

"Isn't one proposal a year enough for you?" Doctor MacNeill asked, still chuckling.

"You can stop laughing now."

"I'm sorry. You'll understand why it's so funny when I explain my predicament. It's really quite amusing, actually. You see, James's letters are always full of automobiles and exotic trips and his beautiful house and his famous patients. My letters—well, let's just say a successful possum hunt can't quite measure up. I know I shouldn't feel that way, but it's hard . . ."

"No, you shouldn't. You have a wonderful life here in Cutter Gap."

"Seems it's even better now. A few letters

ago, when I learned James was engaged, I sort of let it slip that I'd become engaged myself." The doctor forced a laugh. "You'll get a good laugh out of this when I tell you . . ."

Christy tapped her foot on the wooden porch. "Try me."

"Well," the doctor said uncomfortably, "I sort of casually mentioned to old James that you and I were sort of . . ."

"Yes?"

"Sort of engaged."

❧ TWO ❧

You *what?*" Christy cried.

"I know, I know." The doctor held up his hands. "I can't believe I did it, either. But if you knew James, Christy, you'd understand. We were rivals over everything. We always came in first and second on exams. One week it would be James, the next week, me. We were even rivals for the same girls."

"Oh?" Christy asked with a cool smile. "And who usually won that little competition?"

The doctor jumped from his chair and began pacing the length of the wooden porch. "I don't blame you for being annoyed. It was stupid. Not like me at all, actually." He paused. "I love Cutter Gap. I chose to be here. I didn't want the fancy practice and the other fancy things."

"Just the fancy wife," Christy said.

He rolled his eyes. "It's not like that, Christy. I was just . . . spinning a little fantasy on paper. I was going through a dark time awhile back. I was having some doubts about my choice to stay here. David had just proposed to you, and maybe that put the idea in my head. I don't know. Obviously, I never thought it would come to anything."

"And now it has?"

The doctor pulled an envelope from the pocket of his plaid hunting shirt. "Yes, in the form of that wedding invitation. James insists on meeting you. He can't wait to see you dance with the waltz champion of Tennessee."

"And that would be—"

"Uh, me." Doctor MacNeill gave a sheepish grin. "What can I say? I exaggerated a little."

"Is there anything else you exaggerated about?"

"Well, your father is a wealthy industrialist. Very well-off. And you speak four languages."

"Only four?"

"I didn't want to get carried away."

Christy stared at the doctor in disbelief. This was so unlike the down-to-earth, practical Neil MacNeill she knew! She was torn between teasing him, yelling at him, and feeling sorry for him.

"I also told James," he continued, "that you were the most beautiful girl I'd ever set eyes on. Not to mention the toughest and smartest."

"More lies . . ."

"No," the doctor said softly. "All that was the truth."

Christy felt her cheeks burn.

"Well, I appreciate your telling me this, Neil. As long as you tell James the truth, I suppose there's no harm done."

"That's the thing, Christy," the doctor said, then hesitated. "I was thinking maybe we could go."

"*Go?* And pretend to be engaged and all the rest?"

"What could it hurt?"

"Well, I can think of a few little problems with your plan. First, I speak one language, not four. Second, my father is not a wealthy industrialist. Third, I'm not much of a dancer—even if you *are*. And—oh yes. There's that little matter of our imaginary engagement." Christy folded her arms over her chest. "Besides, it would be lying, Neil. And that would be wrong."

"You wouldn't have to lie." The doctor winked. "I'll present you as Miss Christy Rudd Huddleston of Asheville, North Carolina."

"Neil, you know very well that James will presume the rest. What if he speaks to me in Italian while we're waltzing?"

"You just bat your eyes and smile. I'll say you're very shy. Besides, your dance card will be full." The doctor took her hand and

138

gave an awkward bow. "You'll be dancing with me all night. After all, whom do you think I won my imaginary waltz champion- ship with, anyway?"

"Let me guess—your imaginary fiancée?"

"How'd you guess? Actually, I did win a local dance contest a few years back. So I've only partially stretched the truth."

Before she could object, the doctor pulled Christy from her chair and swept her into his arms. "May I have this dance, Miss Huddleston?"

"Neil," Christy said, groaning, "I am not going to go along with your plan—"

"Just one dance."

She allowed herself a small smile. "Well, all right. I mean, *oui, monsieur.* Which, inciden- tally, is the sum total of the French I know."

Humming an old mountain tune, Doctor MacNeill swept Christy around the porch in dizzying circles. "That's not exactly a waltz, you know," she chided.

"I know. But I'm better at this."

"How is it you managed to win that imagi- nary championship, I wonder?" Christy teased.

"The judges were swept away by my partner's beauty," the doctor replied.

"Neil," Christy said as they whirled, "you have to tell James the truth, you know."

As suddenly as he'd swept her into his arms, the doctor let go of Christy. He went to the porch railing, staring out at the deep green woods.

"Tell James the truth? Tell him that I have to beg for medical supplies from old classmates? Tell him that I perform surgery in the most primitive conditions imaginable? Tell him that I spend my days sewing up the wounds caused by ignorance and hate and feuding?"

Gently Christy touched his shoulder. "Neil, what's wrong? Why all this self-doubt all of a sudden?"

"I don't know. Maybe it started when I sold that parcel of land to the Washingtons. They're good people, and I was happy to give them the chance to make a home here. But when I signed over that deed, I started wondering what's kept me attached to this particular place so long."

"You were born here. You have roots here."

"You were born in North Carolina. And here you are, far from home, because you wanted to help change people's lives."

"You've changed people's lives right here, too."

"I wonder sometimes . . ." He sighed heavily. "I just wonder if my life has come to anything. If what I've done here matters."

"Of course it—" Christy stopped short. She pointed toward the woods.

Two small figures were approaching fast. "That's Creed Allen," Christy said, waving, "and Della May."

Creed, who was nine, was holding his pet raccoon Scalawag in his arms, wrapped in an old shirt. His eight-year-old sister followed close behind.

"What a surprise," Christy said. "What brings the two of you here?"

"Hey, Miz Christy," Creed said softly.

"Hey, Teacher," Della May said.

"Is Scalawag all right?" Christy asked.

"He's feelin' a mite poorly is all," Creed said. He glanced over his shoulder nervously.

"Well, I generally tend to humans, but if you bring Scalawag on in, I'll have a look at him," Doctor MacNeill said cheerfully.

There was a noise in the woods. Della May gulped. "We'd best be headin' inside," she whispered to Creed.

"Creed," Christy said, "is there something worrying you?"

But before the boy could respond, Christy realized the answer.

A man burst from the thick trees. He was dressed in a worn black coat and was wearing a battered hat. In his right hand was a shotgun. The man was Bob Allen, the children's father. He was the keeper of the mill by Blackberry Creek.

"What do you young'uns mean, comin' here?" Bob cried. "I done told you not to go near this place no more!"

Christy had never seen Bob Allen so out of control.

"But Scalawag's sick, Pa," Creed said. "I had to do something."

"Bob?" Doctor MacNeill asked. "What's wrong?"

Bob strode up to the porch steps. A scowl was fixed on his grizzled face. He looked Doctor MacNeill in the eye and spat on the ground.

"I'll tell you what's wrong. What's wrong is you sold your land to them what don't belong here. Cutter Gap's a place for white folks, and white folks only. Now, I was goin' huntin' for squirrel, but these bullets will work just as well on a low-down skunk like you."

Slowly, his hand trembling, Bob raised his shotgun and aimed it straight at Doctor MacNeill.

"Bob," Christy whispered in horror, "please don't—"

"What the doc done was plain wrong, Miz Christy," Bob muttered.

He cocked the gun. Christy jumped at the awful sound.

"And now," Bob said, "he's a-goin' to pay for it."

⚛ Three ⚛

N̶o, Pa, no!" Creed cried.

Della May yanked on her father's arm, but Bob brushed her aside. He jerked his gun at the doctor. "You got no right mixin' up the races thataway."

"The Washingtons paid me for that land, fair and square, Bob," the doctor said. "They have as much right to be here as you and I do."

"My family and yours, we've been neighbors long as memory serves. My granny and yours were friends, Doc. Now you've done gone and put them people in amongst us. It ain't fair and it ain't right, and it's a-goin' to cause more trouble than you ever saw in all your born days."

"It was my land to sell," the doctor said firmly. "The Washingtons came to me and made a fair offer, and I accepted it."

Again Bob spat on the ground. The hate in his eyes made Christy shiver. She glanced at Creed and Della May. They seemed frozen in place, as frightened by their father's wrath as she was.

"My kin ain't never had nothin' to do with their kind. Never have. Never will."

"What kind is that?" Christy asked pointedly.

"You blind, woman? Take a look at the color o' their skin!"

"If they're good neighbors, Bob," Christy said, "does it really matter if they're black or brown or blue or purple?"

"It matters. It matters something awful. You oughta see Granny Allen. She's got herself all into a tizzy about this. Can't eat, can't sleep a wink for fear o' what could happen. I'm here today to stand up for her rights. And for all my kin."

"Bob, I understand you're upset," Doctor MacNeill said. "Why don't you put down that gun and come on inside? If we talk about this—"

"Too late for talkin'." Bob paused, closing his eyes for a split second. When he opened them, he seemed confused. Then his gaze seemed to clear.

"Pa?" Creed whispered. "You all right?"

"I'll be right as rain when the doc here tells me he's a-goin' to kick them squatters off'n his land."

"They aren't squatters, Bob," Doctor MacNeill said. "They bought that land. It's theirs."

Slowly, Bob climbed the porch steps. He jabbed the end of his shotgun hard against the doctor's chest. "I can't let this happen," Bob said, almost pleading. "Your kin go back as far as mine, Doc. You got blood in this soil, same as me." He looked into the doctor's eyes, his face full of pain. "Don't make me do this. I don't want to shoot you."

Doctor MacNeill stood perfectly still, the picture of calm. Christy couldn't believe his composure. She was trembling like a leaf.

"You do what you have to do, Bob," the doctor said. "But the Washingtons are staying."

Bob took a deep breath. Again he closed his eyes, swaying slightly. Della May sobbed softly.

Christy watched Bob's finger on the trigger begin to move, slowly, slowly—

"No!" she cried. She locked her hand on the cold steel muzzle. "Doctor MacNeill saved your life, Bob. I was there that day he operated on you in the Spencers' cabin. You would have died without him, Bob. How can you do this?"

Bob's mouth moved, but he didn't speak. He slowly released the trigger. His eyelids dropped. His face went slack. Suddenly the shotgun slipped from his grasp. A moment later, Bob slumped to the porch.

"Pa!" Della May cried, rushing up the steps.

Doctor MacNeill knelt down. "He's passed out. Give me a hand, Christy. We'll take him into the cabin."

With his arms around Bob's chest, the doctor lifted him off the porch. Christy took Bob's feet. They carried him to the doctor's bedroom and placed him on the bed. Creed and Della May stood at the end of the bed, watching solemnly.

"He's been havin' these spells some lately," Creed said. "Ever since that tree done hit him on the head and you operated on him."

"Why didn't he come see me?" the doctor asked irritably as he reached for his medical bag.

"He was afeared he couldn't pay—" Della May began, but Creed sent her a warning look.

"Hush, Della May," he snapped.

Della May shot him a defiant look. "Teacher," she asked, "is Pa going to be okay?"

"If anyone can help your father, Doctor MacNeill can," Christy said.

She stroked the little girl's hair. Della May was a dainty, fairylike child, with shimmering red-blond hair. Like her brother, she had a sprinkling of freckles across the bridge of her nose. Creed, who had a mischievous streak, had always reminded Christy of Tom Sawyer. Della May was much quieter, but she had more than a little of her brother's stubbornness.

"He's coming to," the doctor said.

Bob's lids fluttered. He sat up on his elbows, frowning. "What in tarnation am I doin' here?"

"You passed out," Doctor MacNeill said, "and I gather this isn't the first time, either."

Bob shrugged. "I get my spells now and again. 'Tain't nothin'."

"It may be a result of your accident. Some lingering brain damage. If that's the case, I'm not sure there's much I can do for you, Bob. In a bigger city, with better facilities . . ."

Pushing the doctor aside, Bob climbed to his feet. "One thing and one thing only you can do for me. Get rid o' them Washingtons. If you don't do it, someone else will."

Doctor MacNeill locked his hand on Bob's shoulder. "Let me make one thing clear. Leave the Washingtons alone, or you'll have me to contend with. Understand?"

"Ain't just me who wants 'em gone. Everyone in Cutter Gap feels the same as I do."

"Not everyone," Christy said.

Bob looked at her with contempt. "You'll be sorry for this, the both of you. Come on, Creed, Della May."

Christy and the doctor followed the Allens onto the porch, where Bob retrieved his gun.

"Did you want me to take a look at Scalawag, Creed?" Doctor MacNeill asked.

"Creed!" Bob snapped. "Come on, boy!"

Creed stroked the raccoon's head. "He'll be

147

all right, I reckon, Doctor MacNeill. He's just goin' through a bad spell. It'll pass."

Christy watched Creed and Della May race after their father. "Just a bad spell," she repeated. "I wish we could say the same for Creed's father."

❧ Four ❧

You really don't have to come with me,"
Christy said as she and the doctor made their
way along the path toward the Washingtons'
property a short time later. "I'm sure Bob
went straight home."

"Maybe," the doctor said darkly, "but you
can be equally sure that's not the end of
things. He's going to make trouble. And if he
doesn't, someone else will."

"The look on his face . . ." Christy shuddered. "Where do people learn that kind of
hate? These mountains are so beautiful, it's
hard to understand that kind of hate here."

Doctor MacNeill held back a low-hanging
oak branch so Christy could pass. "You've
been in these mountains long enough to
know the answer to that, Christy. They learn
it from their families and their friends. Look

at the feuds still burning in these hills. It's the same with prejudice like Bob's. It festers, like an old wound. Hate can grow in anyone's heart."

"Unless God is allowed to remove it," Christy added.

Up ahead, a sunny clearing came into view. In the center was a small, rundown cabin. The musical voices of children floated on the breeze. Two spotted hound dogs ran to greet Christy and the doctor, yelping happily.

"Pa!" a young girl in blue overalls cried. "Someone's comin'!"

A tall, thin man ran out from behind the house. In his hands was a shotgun.

"It's Neil MacNeill, Curtis!" the doctor called.

Instantly the man lowered his gun and broke into a smile. "Doctor! Thank goodness it's you. Good to see you again." He ran down the path and shook the doctor's hand.

"This is Miss Christy Huddleston, Curtis," Doctor MacNeill said. "She's the teacher over at the mission school."

"Please, you must excuse my manners, Miz Huddleston," Curtis apologized. "The gun, I mean. We're feelin' a little, well . . . nervous today."

"Problems?" the doctor asked.

"You tell me. Come on, I'll show you."

Curtis led them toward the house. "Children!" he called. "Come meet your new teacher. Margaret, we got ourselves some company!"

A pretty woman wearing a white apron emerged from the cabin. She smiled shyly.

"This is my wife, Margaret," Curtis said. "Margaret, you remember Doctor MacNeill. And this here's Miz Christy Huddleston, the mission teacher."

"It's an honor to have you visitin'," Margaret said. "I'm afraid we're just gettin' settled in. I wish I'd known you were comin'. I could have fixed up some o' my cornbread for you and the doctor."

"Don't be silly," Christy said. "We just wanted to say hello and meet the children."

Three barefoot children gathered in front of Christy with nervous smiles. "This here's Louise," Curtis said. "She's fifteen. John is ten. And Hannah just turned eight last week."

"Etta's in the cradle inside," Margaret added.

"And this here's Violet," Hannah said, pulling a small brown field mouse from her pocket. "I rescued her from an owl. She lost one foot, but I fixed her up good as new."

"Hannah's got a way with animals," Margaret said.

"All the children's been to school some," Curtis added proudly. "Louise could practically read better 'n her own teacher."

151

"Wonderful!" Christy exclaimed. "Most of the children at the mission school haven't had much schooling. There are so many of them that I often ask the better students to help out. It'll be wonderful to have you there, Louise."

"Do you have a library?" Louise asked hopefully.

"Unfortunately, no. Our school just manages to scrape by on donations. But we do the best we can." Christy smiled. "And if you want more practice reading, we have a Bible reading every week at the mission. Maybe you and your mother would like to come."

"We'd be right honored," Margaret said.

Just then, a branch snapped in the woods. Curtis spun around, gun raised, searching the trees.

"It's nothin', Curtis," Margaret said gently. She sighed. "He'll put himself in an early grave, fussin' and worryin' himself this way."

"Curtis," the doctor asked, "what was it you were going to show me?"

"I was fixin' to bury it when you all showed up," Curtis replied. "Follow me."

He led them to the back of the house and pointed. On the ground near a half-dug hole lay a dead skunk. Its stomach had been slit open. White maggots squirmed over the gaping wound. The stench was horrendous.

"That," Curtis said, "was waitin' for us on our

porch this mornin'. Nice welcomin' present, don't you think?'"

"Poor ol' skunk," muttered Hannah.

"Poor ol' us, you mean," said John. "That skunk's a warnin'. It's sayin' 'get lost.'" He crossed his arms over his chest. "Told you we shoulda stayed put. At least back home we knowed who our enemies was."

Margaret patted John's head. "Your pa wanted to get 'way from the city, John. Try his hand at farmin'."

"There's better farm land all over the place. It's too hilly here."

"Come on, everyone." Curtis gestured toward the front yard. "I'll take care of this later."

"Where did you move here from, Curtis?" Christy asked as they settled on the front porch of the cabin.

"Virginia. Fredericksburg, to be exact. Nice enough place, but it had its share of skunks, too, if'n you know what I mean."

"And what brought you to Cutter Gap, if you don't mind my asking?"

"Long story," Curtis said, smiling.

"My great-grandpa's why," Hannah volunteered. "Tell her, Pa."

"My grandpa, William, passed through these parts a long, long time ago," Curtis said. "Five years before the Civil War, in fact. He was a slave who escaped from a plantation in Alabama. Made it all the way

153

to Philadelphia, safe and sound, with some help. He always had a kind word to say about some folks in Cutter Gap, Tennessee—how they took him in and did right by him. How the mountains made you feel like the Lord was your next-door neighbor." He paused, staring off at the green peaks capped by golden sunlight. "So when we was lookin' to move on, this place came into my head. It was like my grandpa was tellin' me where to go."

"And once Curtis gets an idea in his head, you watch out!" Margaret said, laughing.

"I wanted to get away from the city, find me some land. And I liked the idea of bein' so plumb high that heaven's just that much closer, if'n I needed to do some talkin'." He laughed. "Anyways, a friend of mine knew a man who traveled to El Pano regular. And that man knew Ben Pentland, the mailman."

"And Ben knew I'd been thinking of selling part of my land to help buy some more medical supplies," the doctor finished.

"Well, we're awfully glad to have you here," Christy said.

John kicked at a rock angrily. "You be the only ones."

"John," Margaret said, "don't you be rude to your new teacher."

"I'm afraid John's right to be on guard," the doctor said. "I just talked to Bob Allen, your neighbor on the west side. He runs the little mill on Blackberry Creek." Doctor MacNeill gave a grim smile. "Let's just say this is going to take Bob some time to get used to."

"Should we be . . . worried, Doctor?" Margaret asked.

"I don't know, to be honest. Most of the people here are good, Margaret. But they take a long time to warm up to strangers, and they don't take kindly to new ideas. I'd be careful for a while. If you ever need anything, you know where to find me."

"And we'll always be there for you at the mission," Christy added.

"That's a start, anyway," Curtis said.

"Well, we should get going," Christy said. "I hope to see you children in school soon!"

"Thank you both for stoppin' by," Curtis said. "We'll have you over proper-like as soon as we get ourselves settled."

Christy and the doctor had just started down the path when they heard someone running after them.

"Miz Teacher?"

Christy turned to see Hannah rushing toward them. "What is it, Hannah?"

"I was wonderin' . . ." The little girl smiled shyly. She had huge, dark eyes fringed by long lashes. "I was wonderin' if'n you have any eight-year-olds at your school."

"Why, we have lots!" Christy exclaimed.

"Girls?"

"Plenty of girls."

"You s'pose . . ."

"Do I suppose what?"

"You s'pose you got any eight-year-old girls who'd be needin' a friend?" Hannah asked casually.

"I'm sure we'll find one for you," Christy said gently.

Hannah grinned. "I was hopin' so!"

Christy looked at Doctor MacNeill as Hannah ran off. "I just hope I'm right."

"So do I," the doctor said, shaking his head.

❧ Five ❧

That evening, Christy joined Alice Henderson in the mission house parlor for a cup of tea.

"You seem troubled, Christy," Miss Alice said.

"I can't seem to stop thinking about the Washingtons," Christy said. "I'm so worried the people here won't accept them."

She looked at Miss Alice hopefully. Alice Henderson was a Quaker mission worker who'd helped to found the school. She was a lovely, dignified woman, generous, thoughtful, and strong. Many times since coming here, Christy had turned to Miss Alice for help in understanding the people of Cutter Gap. She always seemed to have an answer, and her answers always carried a message of hope. She was known throughout the mountain communities and highly respected by all.

But tonight Miss Alice's deep gray eyes were troubled. "I wish I could tell you that these people will come to accept the Washingtons. I wish I could tell you that when they read in their Bibles 'Thou shalt love thy neighbor as thyself,' they will take those words into their hearts and act on them." She sipped at her tea. "But I don't know if that will happen, Christy. It may take years. It may even take lifetimes."

"I'm worried about the children at school. They can be so cruel sometimes. And some of the older boys, like Lundy . . . they can be downright dangerous."

Miss Alice nodded. "I've heard some talk about parents who plan to keep their children out of school if the Washingtons come."

"I suppose all we can do is try to help the children see that we're all really the same on the inside. In time, maybe they'll come to understand that."

"I hope we can say the same of their parents," said Miss Alice. "Sometimes it's easier for children to see the truth of things." She reached for the teapot. "More tea?"

"No, thanks. I should be getting to bed before long."

"You've had a long day. Thank you for picking up that medicine from Doctor MacNeill."

"I didn't mind."

"No," Miss Alice said with a knowing smile, "I don't suppose you did."

Christy went to the window. The stars glimmered over the dark trees like a thousand fireflies.

"Miss Alice?" Christy said. "What would you say if somebody wanted you to pretend to be something you're not?"

Miss Alice gazed at Christy thoughtfully. "Would that somebody be a certain physician who shall, for our purposes, remain nameless?"

Christy grinned. "Am I that transparent?"

"As glass."

"Neil told one of his old school chums that he and I are engaged. Now that friend is getting married, and Neil wants me to go to the wedding."

"As his fiancée?"

"As his rich fiancée who speaks four languages when she isn't busy winning waltz championships with him."

Miss Alice laughed. She had a glorious laugh, like bells ringing, that always made Christy feel better about life. Instantly, Christy found herself laughing, too, so hard it brought tears to her eyes.

"It is . . ." Christy gasped, "it is pretty ridiculous, when you think about it, isn't it?"

"Neil MacNeill!" Miss Alice said, chuckling. "The most down-to-earth, no-nonsense man I've ever met, caught up in a story that silly? Yes, I'd say it's quite ridiculous."

Christy wiped her eyes. "I told him I simply couldn't lie like that. What else *could* I have said?"

Still smiling, Miss Alice considered for a moment. "Don't worry, Christy. Neil is a reasonable man. If I know him as well as I think I do, he'll come to his senses and see the error of his ways."

"I think he was feeling a little jealous of his friend. James has all the things Neil has had to sacrifice—money, a thriving practice, a nice home."

"That's understandable. Jealousy is a perfectly human emotion. However, this little deception of Neil's is . . . well, it's going a bit too far."

"I'll tell him I'll go to the wedding, but only on the condition that he tell the truth," Christy said.

"It's certainly easier than learning three new languages overnight," Miss Alice said with a grin.

David appeared in the doorway. "What on earth are you two giggling about?"

"Men," Christy replied.

David raised his brows. "Oh? Anyone I know?"

"Actually," said Miss Alice, "he doesn't sound a bit like anyone we know. But we're hoping that will change."

Up in her bedroom, Christy climbed under her blanket with a sigh. She graded papers for a while. Then she pulled out her diary from her nightstand. She wanted to jot down the day's events before she drifted off to sleep:

I confronted two problems today. One, I think I can handle. Doctor MacNeill seems to be going through some doubts about his life here, but I'm sure he'll come to see how much he belongs in Cutter Gap. He has to. If he were to leave, the Cove would suffer terribly without a doctor. And I have to admit that I would suffer, too.

The other problem is very different. A new family has moved here, and it's already clear they aren't going to get a warm reception. Somehow, I have to find a way to help the Washingtons. Miss Alice says it will take time for them to be accepted, maybe years. But I'm determined to find a way to help them put down roots here. If I keep my eyes and my heart open, perhaps, God willing, I'll see the way.

❧ Six ❧

Della May settled into her desk at school the next morning, carefully sneaking a peek at her brother Creed. He winked at her, then put a finger to his lips. She knew he'd hidden Scalawag in his desk. She also knew that if Miz Christy found out, she'd be mad as a skinned snake.

On Miz Christy's very first day of teaching, Creed had brought Scalawag to school. She'd made Creed promise not to bring the raccoon again, and Creed had kept his promise until today. It wasn't like Creed had a choice. Scalawag had been acting plumb strange, moping and refusing to eat. He usually followed Creed around like a hound dog, but lately, he'd taken to slipping out of the Allens' cabin at night, heading off to who knows where.

This morning, when Scalawag wouldn't even eat the fresh possum meat Creed had saved for him, Creed had decided the only thing to do was take the raccoon along to school, hidden in a burlap sack.

There were six Allen children altogether, but Della May was the only one Creed had told about Scalawag. He knew he could trust her. They were almost like best friends, although Della May sometimes wished she had a *real* best friend. Brothers didn't really count. She always had Wanda Beck and Mary O'Teale, but neither of them liked to read the way Della May did, or just sit quietly in the woods and watch the animals and birds come and go.

Della May loved Creed, but sometimes he could be a bit of a troublemaker. She spent an awful lot of time pulling him out of one scrape or another. And she had a feeling today was going to be one of those days.

If Miz Christy found out about Scalawag, she'd be hopping mad. She might even tell their pa, and he'd been mad enough all on his own lately, fretting about the new folks down the road. Della May shuddered a little, just remembering how dark and mean his eyes had been yesterday.

Truth was, a lot of pas and mas were fretting lately. Many of Della May's schoolmates were missing today, on account of they heard the

Washingtons were coming to school. Her own pa had wanted to keep the children home, but Creed and Della May had begged and pleaded until he'd covered his ears and said "Be off with you, then," in a growly voice.

Suddenly a hush fell over the room. Creed nudged her with his elbow.

In the doorway stood Miz Christy, the preacher, and a woman Della May had never seen before. She was wearing a blue dress like Della May's ma wore sometimes, tattered at the edges, but clean. She had a smile like Della May's ma, too, the shy kind. But her skin was nothing like Della May had ever seen before. It was a warm brown acorn color.

"Her skin . . ." Della may whispered to Creed, "it's so purty."

Creed sent her a hush-your-mouth look, and Della May realized she must have said something very wrong.

The ma stepped aside and some children came into the room. There were three of them, a girl and a boy, both older than Della May, and another girl, who looked to be just about eight. The older children had a proud look in their eyes, but the youngest girl just looked scared and hoping all at once.

She met Della May's eyes. Della May started to smile, then stopped herself. She knew for a fact *that* would be wrong. Her pa had taught her that much.

"Pheww!" Lundy Taylor cried. "Somethin's stinkin' awful! Lordamercy, what *is* that smell?"

Some of the children giggled. Miz Christy's face turned hard as stone. The little girl moved closer to her ma. Della May wondered if the girl was going to cry.

"That will be enough, Lundy," the preacher scolded. Della May had never heard him sound so angry. "Quite enough."

"Children," Christy said, "I'm very pleased to introduce you to some new students who'll be joining us today. The Washingtons have just moved to a place between Doctor MacNeill's cabin and the Allens'. This is Louise, who's fifteen. John is ten. And Hannah is eight."

"They don't belong in this school," one of the older boys muttered. "They's too stupid. Their kind got the brains of a half-wit rabbit."

"Who said that?" Christy demanded.

Nobody spoke. Della May sneaked a glance at the girl named Hannah. No, she wasn't crying. But she looked right scared. Della May wondered how it would feel if Lundy and the older boys were saying those things about her. They'd made fun of her sometimes, the way did all the younger children. That was bad enough. But this talk had a meanness to it, sharp as a knife.

Della May knew that if she was Hannah, she'd probably be crying buckets by now. But maybe these people were different. Maybe

165

they didn't have the same kind of feelings as white folks.

"I want to make one thing clear from the start." Christy went to the front of the schoolroom. "That kind of thing will not be tolerated in this room under any circumstances. The next person who speaks that way will be sent home from school for a week. And if it happens again, that person will be expelled."

"Teacher?" Della May's brother, Little Burl, raised his hand. "What's ''spelled'?"

"*Expelled*. It means you can't ever come back to school again, Little Burl."

The preacher walked over to the big boys in the back of the room. He had a dark look on his face, worse even than when he was preachin' up a storm on Sunday mornings. He talked to the boys in a low voice. Della May couldn't hear the words. But she could sure tell he meant business.

Her pa had said it would be this way. The mission people siding with the Washingtons. Acting like they belonged here same as decent white folks. He'd said Miz Christy and Miz Alice and the preacher would be full of tales, just like Doctor MacNeill, but that the children shouldn't believe a word they said.

Christy searched the room. "We need to get you children settled," she said.

Della May sank lower in her seat. There was an empty desk right next to her.

"Louise and John, there's a bench on the left side available. And Hannah, why don't you take that desk next to Della May, right over there?"

Some of the children snickered. A few moved their desks.

Della May looked around helplessly. There was nowhere for her to move. She was trapped.

"You'll be all right," Creed advised. "Just pretend she ain't there."

While Christy said goodbye to the preacher and Mrs. Washington, the girl named Hannah slowly approached the empty desk beside Della May.

"You be Della May?" she asked in a soft voice.

Della May gave a nod, staring straight ahead.

"Then I guess this is where I'm supposed to be sittin'."

Della May tried to pretend she wasn't there, just like Creed had suggested. But it was awfully hard to pretend a living, breathing person was invisible.

"Maybe you and I could be friends," Hannah said. And then something deep inside told Della May it was going to be impossible to pretend that Hannah Washington wasn't there.

❧ Seven ❧

Hannah slipped into the desk. Della May sneaked a peek at her. Hannah had the same pretty brown skin as her ma. Her hair was caught up in two pigtails, tied with red ribbons. It was sparkly and dark and springy. Magical hair.

"Want to see my pet mouse?" Hannah asked in a soft whisper-voice.

Della May shook her head no. She could feel the eyes of the other students on her.

"Maybe later," Hannah said.

Della May ignored her. Behind her, she heard the sound of desks and benches scraping.

Della May looked at Creed. He shrugged. There was nowhere for him to shove his desk.

He opened the lid a crack. Scalawag's wet black nose poked out. Quickly Creed closed the desk, but not before Hannah noticed Scalawag.

"You got somethin' in there?" she asked Creed. "Can I see?"

Creed shook his head no.

Christy went to the blackboard. "We're going to start the day with a discussion of your arithmetic papers." A few students groaned. "Which, I am sorry to say, were not very impressive. Let's start with a review of addition."

She picked up a piece of chalk. It squeaked as she wrote numbers in a long column on the board.

"Creed Allen?" Christy called. "Why don't you come up here and help me with this problem?"

"I don't rightly like sums, factually speakin'," Creed said.

"That's exactly why I asked you," Christy said with a grin.

Creed looked over at Della May, worry in his bright blue eyes. He pointed to his desk. Della May nodded.

"The rest of you," Christy said, "work the problem at your desks."

Creed went to the board. He scratched his head, then took the chalk and went to work. Christy watched, her back to the class.

Della May reached for her little, cracked blackboard. The class fell quiet as the students worked, heads bowed, on the problem.

Suddenly, Della May felt a hand touch her shoulder. She jumped when she realized it was Hannah. How dare that girl touch her! She started to protest, but Hannah pointed her finger at Creed's desk.

The lid was opening! Scalawag poked out his head and blinked.

Della May tried to push him back, but he was in no mood to take orders. In a flash, he slipped out of the desk and leapt straight into her lap. Frantically, she held the struggling raccoon in her arms.

She had to get rid of him, and fast! But where was she going to put him? The lid on her own desk was broken.

She glanced around the room. Everyone was working. Miz Christy's back was still to the class.

"You're on the right track, Creed," Christy said. "Keep at it."

With one arm clutching Scalawag, Della May reached over to open the lid on Creed's desk. Scalawag squirmed out of her arms, straight into Hannah's lap.

Della May gasped. Now Miz Christy was sure to find out!

"Almost, Creed," Miz Christy was saying. "Can anyone tell me where he made his mistake?"

Scalawag was sitting quietly in Hannah's arms. She stroked him behind the ears, whispering something. Then she slipped him into her desk, easy as pie, just as Miz Christy turned around.

Hannah grinned at Della May, a big, I've-got-a-secret grin. She raised her hand.

She's going to tell, Della May thought, her heart galloping inside her like a frightened colt.

"I think Creed forgot to carry the one," Hannah said, calm and cool as could be. "So the seven should be an eight."

"Very good, Hannah," Christy said.

Della May stared at Hannah, her jaw dropped in disbelief. Hannah gave her a little wink.

"You can sneak him back later," Hannah whispered.

Della May didn't answer. For the life of her, she didn't know what to say.

～～～

When it came time for the noon dinner spell, Creed and Della May and Hannah waited until everyone else had left the schoolroom.

As soon as it was safe, Hannah opened her desk and lifted Scalawag into her arms. "He's a fine pet," she said, stroking the raccoon's head. Scalawag made a soft purring noise.

"Give him," Creed snapped. "He ain't yours."

"Creed," Della May said, "like I told you, she hid him for me. Miz Christy woulda seen him for sure if'n Hannah hadn't . . ." Her voice trailed off.

"Here you go," Hannah said, carefully placing Scalawag into Creed's arms. "Does it have a name?"

Creed shrugged. "Scalawag's his name. But don't you be tellin' anyone 'bout him, hear?"

"He's awful quiet," Hannah said.

"He's been feelin' poorly," Della May said, scratching the raccoon's ears. She realized with a start that she was talking to Hannah, just like she was a regular person.

Suddenly Scalawag struggled out of Creed's grasp. The little raccoon scampered over the desktops. He stopped by an open window, sniffed the air, then bounded outside.

"Scalawag!" Creed cried. "Come back!"

The three children dashed down the front steps of the school to the side yard. Scalawag was nowhere to be seen.

"He coulda gone anywheres," Creed moaned. "I'll never find him now."

"Raccoons are right smart about things. He'll come back, I'll bet you," Hannah said as she searched under some bushes.

"Ain't like him to run away," Creed said. "He just ain't been hisself lately."

Della May patted her brother's back. She could tell he was about to cry. "Don't fret yourself," she said. "Scalawag's your best friend. He'll come back. He probably just didn't like all that 'rithmetic, is all."

Creed frowned at Hannah. "Didn't like somethin', that's for sure and certain."

Della May watched her brother stomp off. It wasn't fair, exactly, blaming Hannah. She'd done her best to hide old Scalawag, after all. And Creed had been the one holding him when he'd run off.

She looked at Hannah uncertainly. "It weren't your fault," she said at last.

Hannah smiled a little. "I know. He was just bein' ornery. Got me a brother just like him. Feisty as a stepped-on bee sometimes."

Della May tried not to smile back, but she couldn't help it.

"Creed's all right. Most of the time."

"My brother John is all right most of the time, too. It's those *other* times that'll try your patience."

Quiet fell between them. Della May felt all twisted up and funny inside. She could almost hear her pa yellin' over her shoulder about how she shouldn't be talking to Hannah. But she sure seemed nice enough.

Maybe she'd just keep up her guard, to be on the safe side. See how things went. Granny Allen had a Bible quote she was always saying—"By their fruits ye shall know them."

Della May figured that meant she should give Hannah a chance. Judge her by the way she acted, not just by what others say, or the color of her skin.

In the meantime, she wouldn't say anything to her pa. No point in getting him angry and all riled up.

❧ Eight ❧

That afternoon, Christy rode over to Doctor MacNeill's cabin on Prince, the mission's black stallion.

The doctor was on his porch when Christy rode up. "So," he asked, "did the Washington children come to school today?"

Christy gave a terse nod.

"I'm almost afraid to ask how it went."

She climbed off Prince and tied him to a tree. "Let me put it this way. It was a long day. Longer still for those poor children."

"I'm sorry to say I'm not surprised."

"The older boys threatened them all day. Even when they didn't use their voices, I could see it in their eyes. And the younger children—well, they just acted as if Louise and John and Hannah were invisible."

"Give them time. They may come around."

"That's what Miss Alice said. But I'm starting to have my doubts."

"Come on in and sit awhile. You look worn out. What brings you here, anyway? Not that it matters. I'm always glad to see you."

Christy climbed the porch steps. "Well, Miss Alice asked me to pick up some more cough medicine. She's afraid two bottles won't be enough." She leaned against the door jamb, smiling. "That could have waited, I suppose. The other reason I'm here is to tell you I've decided to accept your kind offer to attend the wedding."

Doctor MacNeill brushed his hand through his hair. He gazed at her doubtfully. "Are you saying you'll go along with my little plan?"

"No. I'm saying I'll go if you'll agree to tell James the whole truth."

The doctor sighed. "You drive a hard bargain, Miss Huddleston."

"You'd have to tell him the truth eventually, Neil."

"I know. I know. You're right. I suppose this rivalry seems small-minded to you. Didn't you ever compete with a friend?"

"Mary Ellen Lanning." Christy settled into the doctor's old rocking chair. "She stole Gus Ricketts from me."

"Your first love?" the doctor asked.

"You might say so. I was all of twelve years old. But I was still heartbroken."

The doctor pulled up a chair beside her. "Imagine the jealousy you felt toward Mary Ellen Lanning, and multiply it by a thousand." He shook his head. "I know I shouldn't feel this way. I made my choice to live here. I ought to be happy with it. And I realize it's wrong to envy what James has. But still . . . don't you ever look at those seventy youngsters in your class and wonder if you'd be happier somewhere else? If you're really making a difference in their lives?"

Christy stared out the window. Two mockingbirds were making a ruckus as they chased each other through the sky. "Of course I feel frustrated, Neil. Especially on days like today, when I can't see any way to get through to those children. But there are good days, too—days when there is laughter and singing, instead of arguing and fighting. I try to concentrate on those."

"But the fighting doesn't ever really stop, that's the point. I patch up a man's wound so he can go right back to feuding. I sell land to some good people, hoping they'll be able to put down roots. And to what end? So they can be persecuted till they're forced to leave?" He rubbed his eyes.

Christy's heart ached at the pain in Neil's voice. She'd felt the same way many times, especially after she'd first come to Cutter Gap to teach. But it was harder to see someone she cared about suffer through the same despair and doubt.

She squeezed his hand. "Believe me, Neil. God brought you back to Cutter Gap for a reason."

"I wish I had your faith." He shrugged, forcing a smile. "But enough of this. We have some practicing to do."

"Practicing?"

"Even waltz champions need a little practice now and then."

"You know, I seem to remember that on our recent trip to Asheville, you weren't nearly so enthusiastic about dancing."

"That dance at the Barclays'?" The doctor groaned. "You were too busy dancing with your old beau, Lance, as I recall. The reverend and I stood in the corner all night like a couple of wallflowers. But I danced with you at the mission open house."

"That's true. I regained the use of my toes after a few weeks."

"Actually, you said I was a wonderful dancer. And remember that night we danced alone by the fire, after you rescued Ruby Mae Morrison?"

"Yes," Christy said softly. "That I will never forget."

"No broken toes?"

"None whatsoever."

The doctor stood and held out his hand. "I won't forget it, either," he said.

Christy gave a little curtsy. "I'll only dance if you promise to hum a *real* waltz."

"Strauss, then. Just for you."

Taking Christy's hand, the doctor led her out to the front yard. Slowly they spun around the grass in graceful circles while the doctor softly hummed.

It was so pleasant. Christy tried to forget about all the troubles that day. She tried to focus on the doctor's low, soft voice. The sun, warm on her shoulders. The wind, making the trees whisper secrets. The air, heavy with the smell of honeysuckle.

But every time she closed her eyes, she saw the frightened but determined faces of the Washington children. And the ugly faces of hatred on too many of her other students.

Suddenly the pleasant calm was interrupted by the sharp sound of gunshots.

One. Two. Three. Four.

Christy stopped cold. "It's coming from the direction of the Washingtons'!"

"Get Prince. I'll grab my gun."

Christy untied Prince's reins. The doctor bounded from his cabin. In one hand was his gun. In the other was his medical bag. He strapped the gun and his bag behind Prince's saddle, then leapt onto the stallion.

He took Christy's hand and lifted her up. "Hang on," he instructed as she settled behind him.

She wrapped her arms around his chest. They headed down the path toward the Washingtons' as fast as possible, dodging low tree limbs and bushes along the way.

They'd almost reached the cabin when they saw Hannah running toward them, waving her arms frantically.

"They shot John!" she cried. "They shot my brother!"

≈ Nine ≈

When Christy and the doctor reached the Washingtons' front porch, they found Margaret and Louise tending to John. His right arm was bleeding just above the elbow.

"Ain't nothin' but a scratch," John said. His voice was calm, but Christy could see the terror in his eyes.

"Scratch!" Margaret said furiously. "A few more inches the wrong way and it coulda killed you!"

Doctor MacNeill and Christy climbed off Prince. She retrieved the medical bag while the doctor examined John's arm.

"What happened, Hannah?" Christy asked.

"Ain't sure." Hannah's lower lip trembled. "Me and John was in the yard. All of a sudden we heard someone in the woods out yonder. They started firin', and we went runnin'. I fell in the dirt. Violet was in my pocket. Nearly crushed the poor ol' thing."

"You've just got a flesh wound, John," Doctor MacNeill said. "You're a lucky boy."

"Lucky," John repeated bitterly. "Yes, sir. I s'pose I'm lucky they didn't kill me outright."

"How could anyone do this?" Margaret demanded. "We haven't bothered anyone. This is our land, right and proper."

Hannah tugged on Christy's arm. "Why would somebody go shootin' at me and John, Teacher? I done tried to make friends at school today."

"I know you did, Hannah." Christy knelt beside the little girl. "Did you see who was shooting? Do you have any idea who did this?"

"Thought I seen a gray horse back in the woods," Hannah said. "But it's hard to say."

Christy exchanged a glance with the doctor. Bob Allen owned a dapple gray mare.

"Where's your father, Hannah?" the doctor asked as he cleaned John's wound.

"Ran up the path lookin' for the men."

"With his gun," Margaret added anxiously.

"That could mean trouble," the doctor said. "Christy, would you finish bandaging John's arm? I'm going to try to catch up with Curtis before there's any more shooting."

"I'm going with you," Christy said firmly.

"There's no point in you—"

"I'm going," Christy repeated.

Doctor MacNeill sighed. "Fine. I know better than to argue with you. Margaret, there are bandages in my bag. Apply one to John's wound with a little pressure. We'll be back as soon as we can."

"Be careful," Margaret said.

Christy and Doctor MacNeill climbed onto Prince. The doctor kept his shotgun at the ready, while Christy scanned the dense woods for any movement.

"You're thinking what I'm thinking, aren't you?" Christy said as they headed up the shady path.

"That you're the most incredibly stubborn woman in Tennessee and I shouldn't have let you ride along with me?"

"That Bob Allen's behind this."

Doctor MacNeill nodded. "Not that we'd ever be able to prove it. But yes. I'd bet my last dollar it was Bob. He could have been alone, but my guess is he brought along some help." They heard a noise in the bushes. Christy stiffened. By now she recognized all too well the metallic click of a shotgun being cocked.

"Hold it right there!" a low voice cried from somewhere in the underbrush.

"Curtis?" the doctor called. He brought Prince to a stop. "Is that you? It's me, Doctor MacNeill."

Slowly Curtis emerged from the woods, his gun at the ready. "They shot my boy, Doc," he said. "I gotta find the men who done it."

"Curtis, I understand how you feel," the doctor said. "But it's not going to help your family one bit if you walk into an ambush up the path."

"So you're sayin' just let it pass? Let the white folks shoot my boy and laugh about it?"

"No. I'm saying let Christy and me try to deal with these people. Calm them down, talk some sense into them."

"They shot my boy, Doctor—"

"John's fine. It was just a minor flesh wound."

"So that makes it all right?" Curtis demanded, his voice choked with rage. "Why should I listen to you? How can you talk that way? Whose side are you on, anyway?"

"Nobody's more upset about this than Doctor MacNeill, Curtis," Christy said gently. "And if anybody can talk some reason into these men, it's the doctor."

Curtis shook his head. "Ain't no reasonin' with hate."

"The doctor sold you that land because he thought you could make a home here. He thought the people of Cutter Gap were ready for a change," Christy said. "Give him a chance to make things right. You head on home and tend to John."

Curtis exhaled slowly. He stared off into the trees, considering. "All right, then. I'll do what you say, Miz Christy. But if anyone comes near my children again, they'll be answerin' to the barrel of a gun."

"I'll stop by later to check on John," the doctor promised.

They rode on in silence for a few minutes. "You may be stubborn," the doctor said, turning back to smile at Christy, "but you're also persuasive."

"That's not all," Christy said jokingly. "I speak four languages, too."

"Impressive," the doctor said as they approached the Allens' cabin. He reined Prince to a halt. "You may need all four to get through to Bob. Why don't you wait here till I check things out?"

"I know Bob and Mary Allen very well, Neil. And if Creed or Rob or Festus are mixed up in this, I'll have as good a chance as you of calming things down."

"All right, then. Stay a safe distance behind me, at least."

They dismounted and stepped into the clearing. The cabin was quiet, and so was the little mill beyond. The only sound was the babble of Blackberry Creek as it rushed past.

Bob's mare was in front of the cabin. There was foam on her mouth, as if she'd been running hard. Christy touched the mare's flank as she passed. It was damp with sweat.

Suddenly, the cabin door flew open. Bob appeared, his shotgun in the crook of his arm. "Howdy, Doc. Miz Christy. What brings you to our neck o' the woods?"

"John Washington's been shot," the doctor said. "But then, you already knew that, didn't you, Bob?"

❧ Ten ❧

Don't know what you're speakin' of, Doctor MacNeill."

"Put the gun down, Bob. We need to talk."

"If'n you come here about them no-accounts, I got nothin' to say to you. You come for socializin', then you're welcome."

Doctor MacNeill pointed his own gun right at Bob's chest. "I've come," he boomed, "to warn you that if you go near those people again, I'll—"

Christy put her hand on the doctor's arm to silence him. "Bob," she said sweetly, "I think I'll take you up on your kindly offer. I haven't seen Mary in such a long time. And how is Granny Allen doing?"

Without waiting, Christy marched up the front steps, walking right between the two guns each man had trained on the other. She brushed past a stunned Bob without even blinking.

At the door she spun around. "Coming, Doctor MacNeill?" she called.

"Might as well head on inside, Doc." Bob gestured with his gun toward the door. "Confounded women! Don't give no stock in argufyin' the way we men does."

Mary, Granny, and the Allen children were waiting in the cramped, dark cabin. "Come in, come in," Mary said, taking Christy's hand. She was a stooped, graying woman who looked much older than her years. "All this fussin' and carryin' on! Like to make a body plumb wore out."

Christy took a seat at the table, and Della May and Little Burl gathered close. The doctor stood in the doorway, his face set in a stony grimace. Bob leaned against the far wall, arms crossed over his chest. In the corner, Granny Allen sat in a wooden rocker. She was a tiny woman, well into her eighties, with a toothless smile and hands gnarled by rheumatism.

Silence fell in the crowded room. "Where's Creed?" Christy asked, to break the quiet.

"Mopin' out by the creek," Della May said.

"Moping?" Christy repeated. "Why?"

"Scalawag's done disappeared. Can't find him nowheres."

"When did he disappear?"

"Oh, that's hard to say," Della May replied a little evasively.

"He'll turn up," Granny said loudly. She was slightly deaf and tended to yell. "Mark my word."

Mary cleared her throat. "Could I fix y'all somethin' to eat?"

"This isn't a social call, Mary," the doctor said firmly, eyes locked on Bob. "This is about what just happened at the Washingtons' place. A young boy was shot."

"Shame, ain't it?" Bob said, with a hint of a sneer.

Della May and Little Burl looked at the floor, as if they were afraid to meet Christy's eyes.

"You did it, didn't you, Bob?" the doctor said.

"Prove it," Bob challenged.

"Your horse was seen there."

"That don't prove nothin'."

"Bob," Christy said, "Curtis Washington was on his way over here to even the score. The doctor and I stopped him. But next time, you might not be so lucky. We need to stop this madness before it turns into a war."

"That's a war I'd win," Bob grinned. "Purty much everybody's on my side, 'ceptin' you mission folks."

"Haven't you had enough fighting to last a lifetime?" Christy cried. "The Taylors and your clan have been feuding for generations.

189

Why do you need another enemy? Look what you're teaching your children."

"Teachin' 'em the way o' the world, is all," Mary said softly.

"But it doesn't have to be this way," Christy said. "The Washingtons are good people. Why can't you give them a chance? I invited Margaret and Louise to our next Bible study. You'll see then, Mary."

"She ain't goin' to no Bible readin', not if they be there!" Bob shouted.

"But I like goin' . . ." Mary said. "I get so lonely here. And Miss Alice makes us tea and reads Scripture to us—"

"You ain't goin', woman!" Bob screamed.

"Hush, Bob," Granny said. "You're a-hurtin' my ears, and I'm purt-near stone deaf. Let Mary go to the Bible study, if'n she wants."

"Didn't you hear? You want her near them two women that ain't our own kind? I won't have it, I'm a-tellin' you!" Bob pounded his fist on the wall. He beat it so hard that a needlepoint stitching in a crude frame—the only decoration in the cabin— fell to the floor. The frame splintered and broke apart.

"My stitchin'!" Granny moaned.

Christy picked up the faded fabric. The alphabet was carefully embroidered on it. The date "1841" had been sewn into the corner. Instead of a signature, like the other needlepoints

Christy had seen, Granny had stitched a tiny bluebird.

"This is beautiful, Granny," Christy said.

"Made it when I was just a wee thing," Granny said.

"I'm powerful sorry, Granny," Bob said, hanging his head like a guilty child. "I'm sure I can mend the frame."

Granny looked at him sharply through clouded blue eyes. "I'll tell you what you can mend. You can let that wife o' yours go to the Bible readin', just like always. I'd go myself, if'n I was a little more spry."

"But—"

"Hush! I've had mules with more sense than you, Bob Allen. Mary wants to go, she'll go."

Bob frowned. "Women!" he muttered.

"Bob, we haven't settled this," Doctor MacNeill said. "Next time I hear you've been near the Washingtons, I'll be using my gun. And I won't stop to socialize first. You understand me?"

"I understand you started this whole miserable mess," Bob shot back. "And I understand one other thing. You, Miz Christy, Miz Alice, the preacher, maybe two or three others are on the Washingtons' side. But I got me the whole o' Cutter Gap on my side. Who do you think is gonna win that war, Doc? We'll get you and those Washingtons. You started somethin' you ain't able to finish. You done

191

forgot your roots, Doc. You're as much a part of this place as the rest of us."

In two great steps, Doctor MacNeill placed himself squarely in front of Bob. He grabbed him by the shirt and shoved him hard against the wall.

Della May cried out. Mary gasped, her hand to her mouth.

"Don't you threaten me, Bob Allen," the doctor said between gritted teeth. "That's a fight you don't want. And don't you talk to me about my roots. Right about now, I'm embarrassed to be from this place."

Christy touched the doctor's shoulder. "Neil. Come on."

Doctor MacNeill released Bob, who slumped against the wall, rubbing his neck. "Traitor," Bob growled.

The doctor stomped out the door. Christy started to follow, then hesitated. "Come to the Bible study, Mary," she said. "Please."

When Mary didn't answer, Christy knew there was nothing more to say.

❧ Eleven ❧

On Monday during the noon break, Christy sat with David on the front steps of the mission school. The children were spread all over the lawn, lazing under the trees while they ate.

"So, any problems so far today?" asked David, who taught Bible study at the school and helped with arithmetic classes when he had time.

"Somebody put molasses on Louise Washington's chair while she was writing on the chalkboard. I tried, but I couldn't find the culprit. I'm pretty sure it was Lundy, though," Christy sighed. "I just can't seem to get through to these children, David."

"Join the club." David gave an understanding laugh. "How do you think I felt yesterday, during my sermon about brotherly love and tolerance?"

"It was a wonderful sermon, David."

"Too bad the church was only half full."

"I keep thinking if I could just get one or two of the children to make friends with the Washingtons, that would be a good start. I thought I saw Della May whispering to Hannah this morning, but I was probably imagining things. Given the way Bob Allen feels, it's difficult to imagine one of his own children defying him that way."

"It's hard for these children to take a stand like that," David pointed out. "It takes real bravery to go against your family and friends and do the right thing."

He pointed to Creed Allen, who was sitting under a tree, head in his hands. "Speaking of the Allens, what's wrong with Creed? He's been so quiet lately."

"Scalawag ran away," Christy explained.

"Oh, that explains it. Poor kid. Speaking of running away, I hear you're planning a trip with Doctor MacNeill."

"Word travels fast."

"You're going to a wedding?" David asked, brows raised.

"We'll see. If things don't settle down around here, I'm not sure I'll be comfortable leaving, even if it's only for a couple days. Miss Alice did say she wouldn't mind filling in at the school."

"I'll help out, too, if I can. Although I'd

prefer it," David added with a grin, "if you were going to a wedding with me."

Before Christy could reply, a sharp cry rang out. "Miz Christy, Preacher, come quick!" Ruby Mae called. "John and Lundy's a-fightin'!"

Christy and David ran to the other side of the school. A small group of students had circled around John and Lundy. John was on the ground. Lundy straddled his chest.

"Tell me, you slime-belly snake!" Lundy screamed. "Tell me what you did with it!"

"I don't know what you're a-talkin' about. I swear it!" John shouted.

Lundy raised his fist to strike. Just in the nick of time, David grabbed his arm. Together he and Christy yanked Lundy off John.

"Lundy Taylor!" Christy cried. "What do you think you're doing?"

"He stole my hat!" Lundy screamed. "Stole it right off my desk when I weren't lookin'."

"I didn't take his fool hat," John said as he climbed to his feet shakily. "What would I want with that dirty ol'—"

"I'm goin' to pummel you good for that!" Lundy started for John, but David held him back.

"Did anyone see John take Lundy's hat?" Christy asked.

Nobody answered.

"Who else woulda took it?" Lundy asked. "That's how they are, my pa says. Can't trust 'em as far as you can throw 'em. 'Sides, I ain't the only one what's had somethin' stole since they come to school."

"Someone took my bread last Friday," Wraight Holt said, glaring at John.

"And Mary O'Teale," Lundy added, "she done had her hair ribbon swiped."

Mary nodded. "It's true, Teacher."

"And that rag doll Vella Holt's always carryin' around with her like it's a real baby," Lundy said. "That's gone. All of it since *they*—" he jabbed a finger at John, "come to school."

Christy put her hands on her hips. "Has anyone seen these items taken? Does anyone have any proof that John or his sisters are responsible?"

"That's how thiefs is," Wraight said. "Sneak up on you when you ain't suspectin'."

"I didn't take your things," John said defiantly. "I ain't got no need of 'em."

"All right," Christy said firmly. "Here's what we're going to do. I want everyone to look high and low for these items for the rest of the noon break. Until we can prove what happened to them, there will be no more accusations. And Lundy, I want you to go home for the rest of the day. You know how I feel about fighting."

"But it weren't *my* fault!" Lundy screamed. "It was him—"

"That'll be quite enough, Lundy," David said. "You're lucky we aren't going to expel you."

Lundy sent a poisonous look at John. He spat on the ground. "You'll get yours," he growled. Then he spun on his heel and stomped off, muttering to himself.

~~~

When the fighting was over, Della May went over to her brother and sat beside him. "Bad fightin'," she reported.

"Lundy and John?" Creed asked.

"Yep."

"I figgered as much."

"You think they stole those things like Lundy said?"

"Don't rightly know." Creed leaned back against the tree trunk, sighed, and closed his eyes.

"Creed," Della May said, "Scalawag's bound to turn up. You heard Granny. She ain't hardly never wrong."

Creed didn't answer. That was a bad sign. Creed *always* had something to say.

"I ain't never heard Granny yell the way she did at Pa the other day," Della May said. She picked a piece of grass and chewed on it.

"Nope," was all Creed said.

Della May paused. "You think Pa was the one shot at John?" she asked softly.

"Most likely."

"If someone shot at you," Della May said, "I'd be powerful mad."

Creed opened one eye. "Thank you kindly, Della May." He smiled, but just a little.

"Creed?"

"Hmm?"

"You figger pas are ever wrong about things?"

"Hardly never. That's why they's pas and we's just children."

"Creed?"

"Lordamercy, Della May! Can't you see I'm restin'?"

"You figger Pa'd be right mad if'n I just talked to Hannah now and again?"

For that, Creed opened both eyes. He scratched his head, eyeing her like she'd gone plumb mad. "Talk to 'em to say mean things? Or talk to 'em to say friendly-like things?"

"Friendly-like."

Creed let out a low whistle. "Della May, you'd be a-walkin' on thin ice, girl."

"I've been givin' it some time. And I've come to figger out that Hannah's purty nice. Today she told me she's been lookin' for Scalawag for you every single day since he run off."

Creed gave that some thought. "Every day?"

"Every day. And I believe her, 'cause she likes animals same as you and me. Has a mouse in her pocket, name of Violet."

"Sounds to me like you already done your share o' talkin'."

"Some, maybe."

"Sounds to me like you already done made up your mind, Della May Allen."

"Maybe so."

"Then you don't need me a-tellin' you what to do, do you?"

"No. I s'pose not."

Creed closed his eyes again. Della May got up to leave. She'd only gone a few steps when she heard Creed call, "Della May?"

"Yep?"

"If'n you do decide to do more talkin', tell her thank you kindly about Scalawag."

❧ Twelve ❧

After school that afternoon, Christy hurriedly graded some papers and cleaned the chalkboard. When she was done, she headed straight to Miss Alice's cabin for the weekly Bible study.

Christy had always loved these meetings. Miss Alice would read in her soothing voice while the other women sewed or simply listened. It was a beautiful cabin inside, full of warmth and color. Polished brass candlesticks shone on the mantel. Cherry and pine furniture gleamed in the sunshine. Whenever Christy was there, she felt transported back to her old life in Asheville. It was a place of beauty, of sophistication, a place where the world was full of promise, not despair.

A world, she realized, like the one Doctor MacNeill seemed to be longing for.

Today, however, when Christy entered Miss Alice's cabin, the scene was not at all what she expected. In one corner sat some of the women who came regularly to the meetings. Granny O'Teale and her daughter-in-law, Swannie, were there. Aunt Polly Teague—at ninety-two, the oldest woman in the Cove—was in her favorite rocker. Fairlight Spencer, Christy's close friend, had come, and so had Lety Coburn. Christy was surprised and relieved to see that Mary Allen had come, too.

Still, many faces were missing. One look at the other corner, where Margaret and Louise Washington sat alone, explained why.

How did the word get out so quickly? Christy wondered. But of course she knew the answer. By now she understood that news had a way of traveling fast in Cutter gap—like "greased lightning," as her students liked to say.

"Christy!" Miss Alice exclaimed. "Come, sit down. We were just getting started. You see we have some new faces."

"Margaret, Louise." Christy sat down beside them. "I'm so glad you could come. You, too, Mary."

Mary gave a terse nod, but said nothing.

Christy gazed around her. Most of the women sat on one side. Christy and the Washingtons sat on the other. Miss Alice in the middle, trying to make peace. They were divided into warring camps, separated by hate and misunderstanding. Just like her classroom.

Miss Alice seemed to be reading Christy's mind. "I'll strain my voice, having to read to the east and west side of the cabin. Suppose we all try to move our chairs a little closer?"

No one moved. Margaret studied her Bible. Louise looked as if she were about to cry.

Fairlight cleared her throat. She picked up her chair and moved it next to Louise. "There," Miss Alice said. "That's much better."

Christy looked at her gratefully. Fairlight was a good woman, as warm and gentle as her radiant smile. She would be one ally, at least.

"How was school today, Christy?" Miss Alice asked, clearly hoping to break the icy silence.

Before Christy could answer, Lety Coburn spoke up. "Any more stealin'?" she asked, shooting a look at Margaret. "I hear tell things are disappearin' from that school right and left."

"I don't think it's anything serious, Lety," Christy assured her. "A doll, a hat, some odds and ends. I suspect the children just misplaced them."

"You suspect what you suspect," Lety said, "but I have my own ideas."

Christy sighed. "Is there some reason we can't at least try to get along? On my way here, I passed one of my students playing with Margaret's daughter, Hannah. They were laughing and giggling and having a wonderful time. I think we could all take a lesson from—"

"Whose child was it?" Swannie O'Teale demanded.

"That doesn't matter," Christy said, suddenly realizing she was just making things worse. The last thing she wanted was to get Della May in trouble for having shown some kindness to Hannah. "The point is—"

"Weren't my Mountie or Mary, were it?" Swannie pressed. "I done told those girls to keep their distance."

"Then why are you here?" Margaret spoke up for the first time. "You must have heard we were coming to the Bible study. Everyone seems to know everything in this place."

"I'm here 'cause it's rightfully my place to be here," Swannie jutted her chin. "unlike some."

"If we ain't wanted here," Louise said, leaping from her chair, "then I think we should go, Ma!"

"Louise, please stay," Miss Alice said in a calm, reassuring voice. "Everyone is welcome here in this cabin. This is a place for fellowship and love." She gave Swannie a stern look. "Not intolerance. Christy's right. Let's think about how we can get along. In God's eyes, we are all family, all worthy of His love. I think the key to understanding is to look beyond the surface and see what we all have in common. Before I start today's reading, why don't you tell us a little more about your family, Margaret? Once we get to know one another better, we'll have a better chance at getting along."

Margaret shifted uncomfortably. She clutched her worn Bible to her chest. Christy sent her an encouraging smile.

"Well," Margaret said in a soft voice, "my husband, Curtis and I, we been married all o' sixteen years. Got ourselves four children. Louise here, she's the oldest. She's fifteen. She loves to read, and she's mighty good with the others."

"That's always nice," Fairlight said helpfully. "I don't know what I'd do without Clara and Zady to help out with my young'uns."

Margaret managed a brief smile. "I got two other girls—Hannah, she's eight, and Etta, she's just the baby. Teethin' somethin' fierce, she is."

"Letting her chew on a nice cold rag will help with that," Miss Alice offered.

There was a long pause. Christy thought back to the many other Bible studies she'd been to. They'd been full of lively give-and-take—shared gossip and recipes and tears and laughter. Today, she could almost see the tension in the room.

"And then," Margaret added, eyes trained on the women on the other side of the room, "there's my son, John. He's a good boy—just ten. Somebody shot him the other day. For no reason, 'ceptin' they didn't like the color of his skin."

Her words hung in the air. Louise wiped away a tear.

"He's a fine boy, I'm tellin' you. All my family is," Margaret continued. She opened her Bible and held it up for all to see.

"This here's our family tree. All the names and baptisms wrote down proper-like. These was good people. 'Course, we can't rightly know 'em all—some of our folks were sold off as slaves, never heard of again." Tenderly, she passed the Bible to Christy. "Looky here, Miz Christy. These was good people, all of 'em."

Christy traced her finger over the names on the yellowed page. "I'm sure they were, Margaret."

"See there? William? That be Louise's great-grandpa." Margaret pointed a trembling finger at the name. "He run away from a plantation in Alabama, years before Abraham Lincoln done freed the slaves. Runnin' in leg irons, bleedin' and hungry.

He got hisself to Tennessee, to the mountains. Found a little hidden-away mite of a place. 'No bigger'n a tick's toe,' he used to say. Name o' Cutter Gap. He was fevered and near to dyin'."

Margaret took a deep breath. She looked at Swannie and Mary and the rest of the women. "A good woman from these parts saved Grandpa William. She hid him in a cave, brought him food, and tended to his wounds. She got herself a saw and took them leg irons off her own self. Without her, Grandpa William would have died. And that good woman she also gave him that there Bible and sent him off to freedom, she did."

"Who was this woman, Margaret?" Miss Alice asked.

"She never did give her name. Lots of folks back then used nicknames to protect themselves. Helpin' slaves was a crime. It was right dangerous. And it was mighty brave."

Christy studied the top of the page. There was a simple inscription:

Godspeed, William.
Birdy

"That's why we come here to Cutter Gap," Margaret said, her voice choked. "We knew the stories Grandpa William used to tell. We knew this had to be a place full o' good people. But we was wrong."

She leapt from her chair, pulling the Bible out of Christy's hands.

"Margaret," Christy pleaded, "please stay—"

"No, Miz Christy. Louise and me, we know we ain't wanted here. We'll read our Bible at home. I figure the Lord'll hear us just as clear from there."

❧ Thirteen ❧

I'm sorry the Bible study went so badly," Doctor MacNeill said.

The doctor had stopped by just after the Bible study at Miss Alice's had ended. He was on his way home from delivering a baby.

"It was awful," Christy said as she pulled weeds out of the vegetable garden by the mission house. "Poor Margaret and Louise. The other women were so cold—except for Fairlight, of course."

"Did Mary Allen show up?"

"Yes. But I don't think she said three words the whole time." Christy yanked out a weed, grimacing. "Sometimes I just get so discouraged about this place."

"Sometimes I do, too." The doctor gave a sad smile. "Which is why, I suppose, I'm thinking about asking James for a position."

"Position?" Christy echoed softly.

"Working in his practice in Knoxville. It'd take some time to get my skills up to speed, but I'm sure he'd take me on."

Christy stared at him, dumbfounded. "You mean . . . leave Cutter Gap for good?"

The doctor knelt down. He pulled a weed out of a row of carrots. "I'm not doing much good here, Christy. I have to realize that. I'm fighting a war I can never win."

"How can you say that?" Christy cried. "You just brought a beautiful baby into the world!"

"Babies will keep being born, whether I'm here or not. Miss Alice is more than competent to do what mending or stitching has to be done."

"But—"

The doctor put his finger to Christy's lips. "I know all the arguments. Please. Just let it go, Christy." He stood. "Well, I should get going. I just wanted to remind you that we haven't yet finished a single one of our dance practices. Perhaps later this week—"

"You just expect me to let you off the hook?" Christy demanded. "You tell me you may leave for good, and I'm just supposed to accept it?"

The doctor gave a resigned shrug. "Who knows? Maybe I'll go to Knoxville and get a taste of James's life, and this will look better. I doubt it, but it could happen."

Christy stared at him in shock. He couldn't leave Cutter Gap! The people here needed him.

She needed him.

Just then, two bluejays fluttered into the vegetable patch, ignoring the scarecrow Miss Ida had constructed out of a broom. One nipped at the other, which led to a dreadful screaming match.

"See?" the doctor said. "Even the birds can't seem to get along here."

Suddenly, Christy remembered the signature she'd seen in the Washingtons' Bible. *Birdy.*

Why did that name mean something?

The doctor started for his horse. "Wait," Christy said. "Don't go."

"You can try to talk me out of this later," Doctor MacNeill said wearily. "I was up all night, and I'm too tired to argue with you." He chuckled. "As it is, you usually win."

"No." Christy leapt to her feet, brushing off her dress. "I . . . I just thought of something. Remember that framed needlepoint that Bob broke? The one Granny Allen said she'd made?"

"Yes. Why?"

"Well, there was a bird on the bottom of it. And today, in the Washingtons' Bible . . ."

Yes. That was the connection. That had to be it, Christy thought.

Doctor MacNeill frowned. "I don't follow you."

"That's all right. You will. How tired are you, anyway?"

"Exhausted."

"Then I'll take the reins. Come on."

The doctor crossed his arms over his chest. "And where are we going, exactly?"

"To the Allens'. To do a little detective work."

~ ~ ~

Hannah and Della May skirted the edge of Blackberry Creek. They'd been together all afternoon, ever since school had let out.

For the most part, Della May had been careful to stick to the woods. She liked Hannah just fine, but there was no point in letting Lundy or anybody else see them playing together. That would just make for a heap of trouble. She had a feeling Miz Christy had caught sight of them this afternoon, but that was different. Miz Christy she could trust.

Della May sat on the bank. It was mighty peaceful. You could almost pretend that she and Hannah were just two friends, nothing special. Of course, that wasn't how it really was at all.

"We're gettin' on toward my cabin," she told Hannah. "You'd best be headin' home. If'n my pa caught sight of us, there'd be trouble for sure and certain."

Hannah dipped her toes in the rushing creek. "How come you figure your pa's so dead set against me and my kin?"

"Don't rightly know," Della May said truthfully. "I s'pose 'cause his pa was, and his pa before him."

"Don't seem fair."

"I know. I'm powerful sorry."

Hannah pointed downstream. "I still think we oughta check the trees and such around these parts. Scalawag coulda been headin' for home and got hisself hurt. Messed up with a hound, maybe."

"It's awful nice of you to help me keep lookin' for him. Creed's so sad he's all but given up. Never seen him so down-hearted."

"I had a dog once, got stole. Some white folks took him, drowned him in a well. Tied a rock round his neck." Hannah took a deep breath. "So I know what it's like, losin' a pet and all. We'd have better luck if'n we could look for Scalawag at night. Raccoons is night creatures by nature."

"We'll just have to keep hopin', I guess."

"Della May?" Hannah said softly.

"Yep?"

Hannah's eyes were wet with tears. "I . . . I heard Lundy a-sayin' as how he figured me and John stole Scalawag and skinned him alive. He says we done stole all sorts of things."

"Lundy's a fool. Half the time his head don't know what his mouth is sayin'." Della May patted Hannah on the back. "You don't pay him no never mind. None o' us believes him much either. Creed and me know what's what."

"Thanks, Della May."

"I oughta be thankin' you, for searchin' so hard."

"Let's just look another piece," Hannah said, getting to her feet. "Scalawag could be right around the corner."

"Not too close to my kin, though."

"I promise."

They made their way toward the cabin. It was just visible through the thick stand of trees. Suddenly Hannah jerked to a stop.

"Is that your gray horse?"

"That's Soldier. Pa's horse."

Hannah looked at Della May. Something in her eyes burned like hot coals. "The person who shot John. He was ridin' a gray horse with spots. I saw it through the trees."

Della May didn't know what to say. But she knew she couldn't lie.

"I heard my pa and ma whisperin' about that. I can't tell you one way or t'other what the truth is." She hung her head. "But I'd be lyin' if'n I said I was sure my pa didn't shoot that gun. If'n he did, I 'spect it was just to stir things up. Not to hurt nobody."

213

"But he did hurt somebody! He hurt John!" Hannah cried.

She spun on her heel and started to run. After a few feet, she stumbled on a tree root.

Della May ran to help her, but Hannah pushed her away. "Go away," she sobbed. "I don't want—"

A horrible scream, coming from the direction of the mill, cut her off.

Della May gulped. "That's my pa! Somethin' awful's happened! I have to go, Hannah. Will you be all right?"

"Go on. Git."

Della May ran as fast her legs would carry her. The screams kept coming, louder, each one more awful than the last.

She was almost to the mill when she saw Creed. "Pa!" he cried. "He passed out again. His arm's caught in the wood gears! We tried and tried, me and Festus and ma and Rob, but we can't budge him. We gotta get help, Della May. He's bleedin' bad."

"You stay here. I'll take Soldier and go for Doctor MacNeill."

Sobbing as she ran, Della May returned to the front yard. She grabbed Soldier's mane and hefted herself onto his back. She was a good rider. Still, she knew it could be a long time before she reached the doctor.

She'd only gone a few feet when she

heard a small voice calling from behind. "Della May! Wait up!"

Della May reined Soldier in. "Hannah?"

"I heard Creed a-yellin' about your pa. Give me a lift up."

"What?"

"We're ridin' to my cabin. It's closer."

"But . . . even after what you said?"

"That's about my pa and yours. This is about you and me. 'Sides, I can't stand to see my best friend a-sobbin'."

Della May shook her head. "You're plumb amazin', Hannah Washington."

"One thing. When we get close, you let me go first. My family ain't goin' to be none too happy to see this horse show up again."

❧ Fourteen ❧

Let me just say this," Doctor MacNeill said as he wrapped a bandage around Bob's arm. "You're a very lucky man that Curtis and John and Margaret came to your aid."

Bob gave a terse nod. The Allen family was gathered by his bedside—all except Granny, who was sitting in her rocker, watching the proceedings. The Washingtons—John, Curtis, Margaret, and Hannah—stood by the door. Louise had stayed home with the baby.

Christy patted John's shoulder. "You saved his life, John, you and your family. I'm so proud of you."

"We come 'cause Hannah begged us to," John muttered. "That's the only reason."

"It must not have been easy, pulling his arm free," Doctor MacNeill said.

"Pa stuck a log in the gears to make 'em

stop," Hannah explained. "Then everybody just yanked and yanked. For a thin man, Mr. Allen, you shore do weigh a heap."

Her remark was met with tense laughter.

"You're going to have to think about getting some help at the mill, Bob." Doctor MacNeill cut another length of bandage. "You can't be losing consciousness that way."

"Boys'll help me. Rob, Festus, Creed. They's old enough."

"But their schooling—" Christy protested.

"Schoolin' ain't nothin', compared to the mill," Bob said.

"Well," Curtis said abruptly, "we'd best be goin'."

"I . . ." Mary hesitated, glancing at Bob. "I want to thank you kindly for helpin'. You bound up his wound right proper, Margaret."

"She certainly did," the doctor said. "Bob would have bled to death without her."

"Had some practice not long ago," Margaret said sharply.

All eyes turned to the bandage on John's arm. Nobody spoke.

"Bob," Granny said sharply, "ain't there somethin' you want to be sayin'?"

Bob winced as Doctor MacNeill tied his bandage into place. "I said all I want to say."

"Ain't surprised," Curtis said. "Wouldn't 'spect no more from the likes of you." He strode over to Bob's bedside. "That horse o' yours. It's just like the one Hannah saw when John was shot. Now, I ain't sayin' for sure you shot my boy, 'cause I don't know. But if I ever catch you near my place with a gun in your hand, you'll be dead before you know what hit you."

The Washingtons filed out the door. Della May ran to the doorway. Nervously, she glanced over her shoulder at her father. "Bye, Hannah," she called softly. "Thank you."

"What's got into you, gal?" Bob shouted as soon as Della May shut the door. "What did I tell you about goin' near them folks?"

"Bob," Christy said, "those people just saved your life."

"I've just about had my fill with your meddlin', Miz Christy," Bob said, falling back against his pillow.

"Bob!" Mary cried. "Miz Christy and the doc are just tryin' to help you."

The doctor closed his bag. "I think we're just about done here, anyway, Mary," he said with barely concealed disgust. "You remember to change that bandage like I showed you."

"I will, Doctor."

"Before we go," Christy said, "we were wondering if we could have a word with you, Granny. It's about the Washingtons."

Granny narrowed her eyes. "I'm afeared I didn't hear you."

Christy smiled. She knew Granny had a way of not hearing when it was convenient.

Christy picked up the needlepoint she'd seen the other day. "This is some fine needlework, Granny. I was wondering why you didn't sign your name to it."

Granny shrugged. "No room, I reckon."

"But you had room to stitch a pretty little bluebird."

Granny yanked the needlepoint out of Christy's hand. "That's from another time, gal. Don't you be a-pesterin' me about such things."

"It's interesting," Christy continued, "because when I was looking at the Washingtons' family Bible, I saw an unusual signature. The woman's name was 'Birdy.'"

Granny studied the needlepoint, head lowered, ignoring Christy.

"Did you have a nickname as a child, Granny?" Christy asked.

"Can't hear you, child."

"'Birdy,' wasn't it?" the doctor said loudly.

"Pshaw." Granny waved him away. "Talkin' nonsense, the both of you. Crazy as March hares."

"I know it was Birdy," the doctor continued, "because I can remember my own grandma saying it. When Christy mentioned it today, it all came back to me."

"You're not sayin' that Granny is the

woman . . ." Mary gasped. "The woman Mary Washington was speakin' of at Bible study?"

"What in tarnation are you fools cacklin' about?" Bob demanded from his bed.

"Tell him, Granny," Christy urged gently. "Tell him what that young woman nicknamed Birdy did."

Granny just stared at the needlepoint in her lap, running her gnarled fingers over the needlework.

"Would somebody please tell me what all this nonsense is about?" Bob cried.

"Miz Christy's sayin' that Granny helped save one of the Washingtons' kin, Bob," Mary said. She was staring at Granny with a bewildered look. "A . . . a slave. Before the war. A long time ago."

"Long time," Granny whispered.

"It's true, isn't it, Granny?" Christy said.

Granny looked up at Christy. Her eyes were damp. She shook her head slightly.

"You can't squeeze milk out of a rock, Miz Christy," Bob said defiantly. "And you can't make what ain't true a fact. Why, Granny's the one who was all in a tizzy when she heard the Washingtons were movin' in! You got your stories all backward. But then," he added bitterly, "you got a lot o' things backward lately."

Doctor MacNeill knelt beside Granny. He took her hand and held it gently. "Granny," he said softly, "my own granny often spoke of you with such respect. She used to say you were tough as a laurel burl and braver than any man. Now, at last, I think I understand what she meant. I know you were afraid to admit it before. But now's the time. Tell them, Granny. Tell them what you did. Maybe it will help heal the wounds in this place. Maybe it's not too late to change things."

Della May put her arm around her great-grandmother's frail back. "Is it true, Granny? Is it true what the doctor is sayin'?"

Granny gave a resigned, faraway smile. "I can't hear you, child," she whispered.

❧ Fifteen ❧

That evening, Christy wrote in her diary before going to bed, hoping to rid herself of the heavy feeling in her heart. But she wondered if anything could really ease the pain.

Where are the answers when I need them? So much seems to be going wrong, and nothing I do helps. Doctor MacNeill says he's thinking of leaving the Cove for good. Granny Allen refuses to acknowledge her courageous act of so long ago. And I can't seem to get through to anyone.

Every day at school the hatred toward the Washingtons simmers. The accusations of stealing get more intense, but when I try to soothe my students, they ask me for an explanation. Why have things been disappearing from school? Why did it start right around the time John and Louise and Hannah arrived?

I know there must be an explanation. They're such good children. But for the life of me, I can't figure out what it is.

Today, after we left the Allens' cabin, Neil told me that some people will never change. That there will always be feuding and racism and hatred in people—especially the people of Cutter Gap.

Never have I seen him so cynical. So dark. Or so unhappy.

I told him that there is goodness in people. I told him how Fairlight had moved her chair at the Bible study. I told him how I'd seen Della May and Hannah playing together, despite all the risks.

I told him we just had to wait and work and pray.

And all he did was laugh.

Christy put her diary away. There was nothing more to say or do. Except, perhaps, to cry. And pray.

—— ～ ——

Late that night, Christy awoke suddenly, feeling anxious. She sat up, letting her eyes adjust to the darkness. Something was wrong. Was that smoke she smelled?

She ran to the open window. The smell of burning wood was in the air. Far up on Kildeer Mountain, red flames flickered against the night sky.

Christy's heart leapt into her throat. That was where Doctor MacNeill lived! It could be his cabin burning, or the Allens', or . . .

No.

Please, God, Christy silently prayed, *don't let it be the Washingtons' cabin. Let it be a forest fire, a campfire out of control, a woodpile . . .*

She threw on a dress and her shoes and raced down the stairs, just as David burst through the front door. Miss Ida was already up, dressed in her nightgown and robe.

"Looks like Kildeer," David said breathlessly. "I'm taking Prince up."

"I'm coming, too," Christy said. "Let me ride with you."

"Could it be a forest fire?" Miss Ida asked.

"Woods are pretty damp. No lightning," David replied. "But I suppose it could be."

"Do you think it's the Washingtons' place?" Miss Ida asked.

"I fear it is," Christy replied, "but I'm praying it isn't."

～～～

David urged Prince on as fast as he dared, but in the dark, every tree root and hole in the mountain path was treacherous. The closer they got to the fire, the larger it seemed to grow.

Red-gold flames licked at the stars. The air

grew acrid with the smell of burning wood. In the stillness of the night woods, the sound of the crackling fire grew ominous. Before long, they could hear the sound of desperate shouts.

Soon it was clear that the fire was located at the Washingtons'. "The flames are going higher," David said grimly, "but they're not spreading, the way they would with a forest fire. It must be their cabin."

"We should have kept this from happening," Christy muttered. "Surely there was something we could have done."

David glanced over his shoulder. His face was barely visible in the moonlight. "We tried, Christy."

"Not hard enough. And that makes me feel almost as guilty as the people who did this."

For the rest of the ride, neither spoke. There was nothing more to say. It was too late for words.

Just let them be all right, Christy prayed. *They can build another cabin. Just let the family be all right.*

❧ Sixteen ❧

By the time they reached the clearing where the Washingtons' cabin was located, the fire had quieted. It was more smoke than flame, but the damage was already done.

Doctor MacNeill was there, tossing buckets of dirt on the dying embers. His face and hands were darkened by soot. Curtis and John were still fighting the fire, too. They'd saved a few things—a chair, an iron pot, a photograph. But the cabin itself was nothing but charred logs, glowing an eerie red in the night. Christy ran to the spot where Margaret and the girls stood huddled together. Margaret was clutching their worn Bible.

"Margaret, I'm so sorry," Christy said, hugging the trembling woman. "Are you all right? Was anyone hurt?"

"We're fine. Curtis, he got some burns on his

hands. Doc, too." She let out a soft sob. "The children's all right. That's all that matters."

Doctor MacNeill came over. His brow was damp with perspiration. "Neil," Christy asked, "are you hurt?"

"A few burns. Nothing much." He shook his head at the dying embers where the little cabin had stood. "Do you see now why I want to leave this place? Tell me this, Christy. Can you look at this and still tell me there's good in the people of Cutter Gap?"

"You can't blame everyone, Doctor," David said. "This isn't the work of the whole Cove."

"No," the doctor said bitterly. "It's the work of Bob Allen. But there's plenty more where he came from."

Hannah tugged on the doctor's shirt. "Truth to tell, Doctor MacNeill," she said in a teary voice, "it weren't Bob."

"Hannah?" Margaret asked. "Did you see who done this, child?"

"I heard a noise, Ma, right before it started. Saw three men outa the window. All of 'em on horses, dark ones. Not gray like Bob's."

"She's right. With Bob's arm in such sorry shape, he'd be in no condition to ride," the doctor said wearily. "I shouldn't have assumed as much. But it doesn't help to hear there are others like him out there. Not that it's exactly a surprise."

Curtis came over, wiping his face with the

back of his arm. "Well, I guess they're gettin' their way," he said grimly. "I can fight words, maybe even bullets. But I can't fight fire."

"Yes, you can, Bob," Christy said firmly. "You fight fire with fire. When someone burns down your house, you build it up again. That way you don't let them win."

"It's too late for that, Miz Christy. I gotta think o' my children."

"Pa?" Hannah said softly. "What if we move on and they just burn us down all over again?"

"What if we stay," Curtis said, "and they do it again right here?" He knelt beside Hannah and held her close. "Sweetie, ol' Grandpa William was wrong about Cutter Gap. He said he felt closer to God here. But the truth is, I ain't never felt Him further away."

～～～

"Granny?" Della May said after school the next day. "I got me a question for you." She sat next to her great-grandmother on the dusty wooden porch outside the Allens' cabin.

"What is it, girl?"

Della May checked over her shoulder to be sure her pa and ma weren't around. "Where's Pa?" she asked.

"Out to the mill, the old coot. He ain't got a lick o' sense. His arm bandaged up and his head a-swimmin'."

"Well, it's like this. You know how the Washingtons' cabin done got burned down last night?"

"Could see those flames for miles."

"Well, Hannah weren't in school today. Her brother and sister, neither."

Granny looked up from her knitting. Her old fingers always moved very slowly, but now they stopped.

"Teacher said they was stayin' at the mission house. Said they might be a-movin' on soon, and it were all our faults for not bein' more friendly."

"Miz Christy's full of notions," Granny said softly.

"Granny, I have a confession to make. It's a-burning up my soul somethin' fierce."

"Speak your mind, then."

Della May took a deep breath. "Hannah Washington . . . well, she's the best friend I ever had, 'sides Creed. I don't want her to go, Granny. Is that wrong?"

Very slowly, Granny set her knitting aside. She reached for Della May's hand and grasped it tightly. "You're a fine girl, Della May. And it's a fine thing to have a friend, no matter what color she is."

"Is it true, Granny?" Della May asked.

229

"What Miz Christy said about you savin' that slave way back when?"

Granny rocked back and forth. "What if it was? What would you think o' your ol' granny then?"

Della May thought for a while. "I know how hard it's been to be Hannah's friend. Us always dodgin' from people and sneakin' in the woods and all. So I guess if'n you really *was* Birdy, I'd have to say I'd be powerful proud. Considerin' how brave she musta been."

For a long time, Granny didn't reply. She had thinking spells like that a lot, and Della May knew better than to bother her. She sat quietly on the porch by her great-grandmother, waiting and wondering and feeling sad. She felt like someone had torn a hole right out of her middle. She felt empty and smaller and very lonely.

"Child," Granny said suddenly. "I want you to go fetch your pa."

"He don't like it when I trouble him at the mill, Granny. What if he asks how come?"

Granny took a long breath. "Just tell him Birdy wants to see him."

ஃ Seventeen ஃ

W e sure can't thank you enough for givin' us a roof over our heads," Curtis said in the mission house dining room the next morning. The Washingtons had just finished breakfast, along with Christy, Miss Ida, and Ruby Mae. Miss Alice, Doctor MacNeill, and David were there, too.

"We were glad to help," Christy replied. "I just wish you would stay a little longer. There's plenty of room. Why do you have to leave so soon?"

"I got to find me some work as soon as possible, Miz Christy," Curtis replied. "There'll be somethin' in Knoxville. It's a big city."

"So Doctor MacNeill tells me," Christy said, sending a meaningful look at the doctor.

"Maybe we'll run into each other, Doctor," Curtis said. "If'n you decide to move on, too."

"I certainly wish we could convince you and the doctor to stay put," said Miss Alice.

"So it's true, Doctor?" David asked. "You're really leaving Cutter Gap?"

"I'm seriously considering the possibility. It feels like it's time to make a change." The doctor gave a wry grin. "Was that a note of hope I heard in your voice, Reverend?"

David grinned. "Not at all. I'll certainly miss you . . . professionally, anyway. This Cove needs a good doctor. Miss Alice has too much to take care of as it is."

"We'll get by," Miss Alice said. She sipped at her tea, then gave the doctor a sad smile. "Neil needs to do what's best for him."

"We've got plenty of work to be done around the mission, Curtis," David said. "You could stay for a while, work off your room and board that way."

"That wouldn't really solve the problem, now, would it?" Curtis shoved back his chair. "Come on, children. We've got a long walk ahead of us, if'n we want to make El Pano today."

"We're hopin' to leave before school gets started," Margaret whispered to Christy. "It'll be easier on the children that way."

On the porch, Christy knelt down beside Hannah. "I want you to promise to write me, Hannah," she said, "and let me know how you and John and Louise are doing."

"Miz Christy," Hannah said, her eyes full of tears, "would you tell Della May I said good-bye?"

"Of course."

"And would you tell Creed I'm a-keepin' my fingers crossed that Scalawag turns up?"

"Of course I—" Christy paused, shading her eyes from the morning sun. Who was that, heading down the path to the mission house?

"I have a better idea, Hannah," Christy said. "Why don't you tell them yourself?"

"Why, I'll be," Hannah cried. "It's all them Allens!"

"Even Granny," the doctor said.

"Probably come here to gloat," John muttered. "See us run out, just the way they wanted."

"Let's get goin'," Curtis said gravely. "Ain't no need for us to put up with them no longer."

But Della May was already running up the steps of the mission house, ahead of the others. "Hannah!" she cried. "Are you a-leavin' already?"

Hannah nodded. "We're movin' on to the city."

"But you *can't* go, you just can't! Least-ways, not till Pa and Granny says their piece." She tugged on Curtis's sleeve. "Please, Mr. Washington. Please hear them out."

"We heard all we needed to hear from your pa and his shotgun," John snapped.

"But my granny come all this way, with her rheumatis' and all," Della May protested.

Christy put her hand on Curtis's arm. "Maybe you should hear what they have to say, Curtis."

"Please, Curtis," Margaret said softly. "We been through this much. A few more words can't hurt us."

Hobbling slowly, clutching at Mary's arm, Granny Allen made her way to the house. Bob hung behind, hands in his pockets. The other Allen children followed.

"We come to talk," Granny announced when they'd reached the porch.

"Say what you got to say," Curtis said sharply. "We need to be movin' on."

Granny motioned to Bob. "Go on, then. Be a man and speak your mind."

Bob cleared his throat. "I been doin' some thinkin'," he said, choosing each word with care. "Well, mostly, Granny's been doin' some talkin'." He looked up at Curtis. "Granny's the one what saved your grandpa, turns out."

Margaret gasped. *"You? You're* Birdy?"

"That was my growin'-up name," Granny said. "Used it with William to protect myself." She shook her head. "Did a lot o' protectin' after that. Worryin' if'n anyone found out about what I done, what might happen. Never told a soul, 'ceptin' one friend."

"But why?" Louise asked softly.

"People woulda turned agin me. Maybe even strung me up to die. Things are better some now . . . but not much. I was afraid, child." Her lower lip trembled. "But Della May made me think maybe what I done weren't so awful after all. Maybe it was even a good thing. How many of us get the chance to save a man's life?"

"My granny's a good woman," Bob said. "Stubborn as a mad mule, but good. So I've been startin' to think maybe I might be wrong about some things."

"What he means is, I told this ornery, cantankerous old cuss that he better think twice about the way he was treatin' William Washington's kinfolk." Granny winked. "'Cause William was a friend of mine, and I aim to do right by him."

"Granny and Ma done yelled at Pa from sunup to sundown," Della May confided in a loud whisper to Hannah.

Bob rolled his eyes. "That's enough outa you, young'un."

Curtis stepped down to Granny and took her hand. "It's an honor to meet you, Ma'am. On behalf of all my kin, I want to thank you for what you done. None of us would be here without you." He sighed. "But that's all in the past. We still got to be movin' on."

"Not so fast, young man!" Granny cried. "My Bob ain't done with his speechifyin'. *Are* you, Bob?"

Bob kicked at the ground with his toe. "The thing is . . ." he cleared his throat, "the thing of it is, seems I need some help at the mill. I get these spells, and . . . well, if'n you'd be willin' to work, my boys and I could maybe help you build yourself a new cabin." He shrugged. "If'n you wanted."

"We're already set on leavin'," Curtis said tersely. "Why stay in a place where people burn your cabin to the ground?"

"There's good people, too, Pa," Hannah said. "Della May and Creed, they's good as they come. And Miz Christy and the preacher and Doctor MacNeill. And Granny." She smiled shyly at Granny Allen. "You said yourself Grandpa William woulda liked us settlin' here."

Curtis shook his head. "I just don't think . . ."

"My, but you're the spittin' image of William!" Granny exclaimed. "Never could argue him outa anything. I was afeared he couldn't make it north, but oh, he was set in his ways somethin' fierce. 'Birdy,' he said, 'scares me awful to try. But it scares me worse not to.'"

Curtis smiled, just a little. "He was a brave man, that Grandpa William."

"So are you, Pa," Hannah whispered. "You ain't a-scared o' tryin'."

For a long time, Curtis stared off at the mountaintops, reaching up to the morning sky. At last, he walked over to Bob. They faced each other, eye to eye.

"We'll try it for a month," Curtis said. He held out his hand.

Bob stared at it, hesitating. "I ain't never shook hands with one of your kind," he admitted. He gave a resigned sigh. "But I s'pose I ain't a-scared o' tryin', either."

Slowly, reluctantly, the two men grasped hands.

~~~

Before the Allens left, Granny motioned Christy and the doctor aside. "I want to thank the two of you," she said. "I was afraid to admit what I done. But that's who I am, and I s'pose, all things considered, I'm glad of it."

"I wonder, Granny," the doctor said, "who was it you told about William? My grandmother always looked up to you so. I wondered if . . ."

"Factually speakin', I did confide in your granny, Doc. I needed someone to fetch me a saw so's I could remove William's leg irons. I was desperate, and I took Helen aside and told her the whole truth."

"And she helped you?" Christy asked.

"Well, not quite." Granny hesitated. "She said she was afraid to help me. But on the other hand, she never breathed a word of my secret to anyone else. And that was a kind of help, don't you see?"

"So she was afraid," the doctor said, sounding a little disappointed.

"Oh, we all get afraid from time to time, Doctor MacNeill." Granny patted his arm gently. "She was a fine woman, your granny. You know how it is. We do what we can."

The doctor smiled sadly. "Some of us do, anyway."

✎ Eighteen ✎

A week later, Christy was sitting with the children during the noon break when she saw Doctor MacNeill riding up.

He dismounted and joined her on the lawn.

"I haven't heard from you in several days," she said. "I was starting to worry."

"I'm sorry. I've been preoccupied. I've been thinking, mostly . . . working some. The Washingtons' cabin's coming along nicely."

"It's nice of you to help out."

"It's the least I can do." The doctor lay back on the lawn, staring up at the sky. "I have to compensate for my dear departed grandmother."

"Not everyone can be as brave as Granny Allen was," Christy said. "I'm not sure I'd have that kind of courage."

The doctor sat up and pulled an envelope out of his breast pocket. "Has Ben Pentland been by yet with the mail?"

"No. But he's due today. Would you like me to give that to him?"

"Thanks." The doctor passed her the envelope. Christy slipped it into a book.

"Aren't you at least going to read the address?"

"Of course not. That's your private concern."

"It's to James," the doctor said.

Christy felt her heart plummet. "Is it about the job?"

"Yes. I felt it was time."

"I understand." Christy looked away to hide the tears threatening to spill down her cheeks. "I'm awfully disappointed, Neil . . ."

"I'm sorry. I know you had your heart set on waltzing at the wedding. Not to mention showing off your Italian."

Christy blinked. She looked at the doctor, eyes narrowed. "I don't think I heard you right . . ."

"Well, if I'm not going to take the job in Knoxville, I figured there was no point in going all the way there just to show you off. After all, you're a beautiful woman, Christy. Who knows what might happen if I let all those eligible young doctors get a glimpse of you?"

"You're not . . . you're not leaving us?"

240

Christy threw her arms around the doctor's neck and kissed him.

The children broke into wild applause, laughing and pointing. Quickly Christy pulled away, her cheeks ablaze.

"My, my," the doctor said. "I had no idea I was in danger of being so sorely missed."

"I'm just glad for the Cove," Christy said demurely. "That's all."

"Well, I very much enjoyed kissing you on behalf of the Cove," the doctor replied.

"But why did you change your mind?" Christy asked, smiling in spite of herself.

"Oh, a lot of things, I suppose. Seeing the Washingtons decide to stay. Whatever hardships I have, it's nothing compared to what they're up against. And hearing about my grandmother, Helen. I felt she'd let Cutter Gap down, just a little, that day Granny Allen asked for her help. I sort of feel like I need to make it up to this place. It's crazy, I know."

"Not at all."

The doctor leapt to his feet. "And then there was you."

"Me?"

He nodded. "See, I'm aiming to enter next year's state waltzing championship. And I know just the girl I want as a partner."

Christy stood, smiling. "Really? Anyone I know?"

"She speaks only one language. Her father

241

isn't a rich industrialist. And she's not much of a dancer, either."

"What do you see in her, I wonder?"

The doctor swept Christy into his arms, and they began to waltz, spinning around and around. The children watched, mesmerized.

"It's hard to say why I'm so fond of her," he said. "Could be because she loves these mountains as much as I do."

~ ~ ~

When the break was over, Christy herded the last of the straggling children into the school. They'd been teasing her about her kiss and her dance with the doctor for an hour now. It was going to be a long afternoon. But at least that would make for a change from the tension still hovering in the air around the Washington children.

It wasn't enough, she knew, for Bob Allen to hire Curtis. It wasn't enough that the Washingtons' cabin was being rebuilt. The older boys still tormented John and Louise and Hannah whenever they could. Ugly words were still being whispered. Even Hannah and Della May still hid their friendship.

Christy paused on the steps. Was everyone inside? She caught sight of Della May and Hannah, far off at the edge of the woods. "Girls!" she called. "Hurry up! No more dawdling!"

"Teacher!" Della May cried. She pointed to an old oak tree. "Come see! Bring everyone and come see, now!"

Christy frowned. The girls were taking an awful risk being seen together this way.

"It's important, Miz Christy!" Della May called. "I promise!"

Christy shook her head. Well, she wasn't eager to face a spelling lesson, either. After the doctor's good news, she almost felt like playing hooky herself. "All right, then," she called back, "but this had better be good, girls."

She poked her head in the schoolroom door. "Children," she called, "follow me."

Christy lead the way toward the old oak, trailed by her eager students. "Where are we goin', Teacher?" Little Burl asked.

"Actually, I have no idea, Little Burl," Christy confessed.

Della May and Hannah were standing side-by-side next to the tree. There was a large hollow under the lowest branch, just about even with the girls' heads.

"Well," Christy announced, "we're all here."

"We got somethin' to show y'all," Della May announced. She put her arm around Hannah's shoulder.

"What are you doin' with the likes o' her?"

Lundy demanded of Della May. "Your hand'll wither up and fall off now, sure as anything."

"Hush, Lundy," Della May said firmly. "First off, Creed gets to look."

The girls stepped aside and motioned for Creed. He peered inside the dark hole and gasped, hand to his mouth.

"Shh," Hannah said, grinning. "Don't tell!"

"It was all Hannah's doin', Creed," Della May said. "She done found the hole."

"Now for Miz Christy," Della May said.

Christy peered inside the hole. There, to her amazement, were a mother raccoon and four tiny babies.

"Scalawag?" Christy whispered.

"Sure as shootin'," Creed said.

"But I thought he was a boy."

"Guess he had other ideas," Creed said.

"Did you see the nest?" Hannah asked.

Christy looked again. The raccoons were nestled inside an old felt hat. It was lined with a hair ribbon, a rag doll, a plaid shirt, and a piece of chalk, among other things.

"He always was a bit of a thief," Creed admitted. "Can't help hisself. Or herself, I guess I should say."

"Class," Christy said, "Hannah and Della May have something I think you'll be very interested in seeing. It seems we've found Scalawag. And in doing so, we've also located our classroom thief. I think we all owe the Washingtons a very big apology."

Instantly, the children crowded around the hole, jockeying for position.

"My hat!" Lundy cried. "Why, you furry little crook, you!"

"My dolly!" Vella exclaimed. "The babies are sleepin' with my dolly!"

John and Louise watched silently, standing far off to one side. No one apologized. No one even acknowledged that they were there.

Christy heard laughter and turned. Behind her, heading up the school steps, were Hannah and Della May. They were holding hands and giggling, as if they didn't have a care in the world.

It wasn't enough, Christy knew. Not at all.

But at least it was a start.

Mountain
Madness

The Characters

CHRISTY RUDD HUDDLESTON, a nineteen-year-old school teacher.

CHRISTY'S STUDENTS:
    CREED ALLEN, age nine.
    LITTLE BURL ALLEN, age six.
    WRAIGHT HOLT, age seventeen.
    ZACHARIAS HOLT, age nine.
    VELLA HOLT, age five.
    RUBY MAE MORRISON, age thirteen.
    JOHN SPENCER, age fifteen.
    CLARA SPENCER, age twelve.
    ZADY SPENCER, age ten.
    LULU SPENCER, age six.
    LUNDY TAYLOR, age seventeen.
    LOUISE WASHINGTON, age fifteen.

ALICE HENDERSON, a Quaker missionary who helped start the mission at Cutter Gap.

FAIRLIGHT SPENCER, Christy's closest friend in the Cove.
JEB SPENCER, her husband.
(Parents of Christy's students John, Clara, Zady, and Lulu.)

AUNT BIDDY, relative of the Holt children.

BEN PENTLAND, the mailman.

DAVID GRANTLAND, the young minister.
IDA GRANTLAND, David's sister and the
   mission housekeeper.

GRANNY O' TEALE, superstitious
   mountain woman.

DR. NEIL MACNEILL, the physician of the Cove

BIRD'S-EYE TAYLOR, father of Christy's
   student Lundy.

BOB ALLEN, keeper of the mill by
   Blackberry Creek.
   *(Father of Christy's students Creed and
   Little Burl.)*

EDWARD HINTON, soldier at the Battle of
   Little Big Horn in 1876.

MARY DAVIS, Edward Hinton's sister.

❧ One ❧

Teacher! Look out! There's somethin' dangerous lurkin' up in that big ol' tree!"

Christy Huddleston paused on the tree-lined path. "Zach Holt, I'm not falling for that old trick of yours again. That's the third time you've tried to scare me since we started on this nature walk."

"B—but teacher, I'm a-tellin' you for your own good!" Zach, a painfully thin nine-year-old, pointed toward the canopy of sun-dappled trees. "He's a ferocious man-eatin' monster. I'm afeared!"

With a tolerant sigh, Christy followed Zach's gaze.

"G-G-R-R-R-R!" A blood-curdling roar filled the air.

Christy leapt back as the growling creature dropped to the path on all fours.

"Howdy, Miz Christy," it said.

Christy grinned. She pulled a leaf out of Creed Allen's tousled hair. "Creed, Zach was right about one thing. You really *are* a monster sometimes."

"Was you afeared, Teacher?" Zach asked hopefully.

"Not a whit," Christy replied. "It takes more than that to scare me, Zach."

"She'll be scared soon enough," Creed whispered loudly, "if'n we get any closer to Boggin Mountain."

"Not that silly story again!" Christy exclaimed. "That's an old superstition, Creed. Boggin Mountain is not inhabited by some strange, dangerous creature. He's just a figment of everyone's imagination."

Creed did not look convinced, which came as no surprise to Christy. The people in this isolated mountain cove of Tennessee were full of superstitions. When she'd first started teaching, many of the residents of Cutter Gap had actually been convinced that Christy was cursed.

"Lots o' folks has caught sight o' the Boggin monster, Teacher," Creed said. "He's big and mean, with eyes like a bear's, only a far sight nastier. He has hair down to his knees, and teeth as sharp as huntin' knives."

"And he's a-covered with warts," Zach added. "Big 'uns. And he has a big scar on his head, and only one ear."

"Let's concentrate on things that really do live in these beautiful woods," Christy suggested. "Flowers and trees and all of God's creatures." She waved them off. "Now, run up ahead and tell the older students not to get too far ahead on the path. This is supposed to be a nature hike, not a race."

With a fond smile, Christy watched the two boys dash off down the thin path carpeted with pine needles. On her very first day of teaching, Creed and Zach had played a trick on her. Creed had tied a string to Zach's ear, jerking it whenever Zach told a lie. She could still hear Creed: "All them Holts, when they tell a whopper, their ears twitch. . . ."

Had that only been a few months ago? Yes, just last January. How frightened she'd been that first day! Sixty-seven students—she was up to seventy now—in a one-room school that also served as the church on Sundays. She'd had almost no supplies. And worse yet, no teaching experience.

Most of the children had never even seen a book before. And they'd all been so cold and hungry! Coaxing them to concentrate on arithmetic or spelling had been next to impossible.

Still, with the help of God, Christy had persevered. Trembling in front of the class that first day, she never would have believed that she'd have the courage to take seventy students on a walk deep into the Great Smoky Mountains. But here she was, surrounded by children like the Pied Piper.

Up ahead, she could hear the older children marching along, singing "Onward, Christian Soldiers" in measured tones. Behind her, a group of the smallest children was singing a silly mountain tune:

> *Call up your dog, O call up your dog!*
> *Let's a-go huntin' to ketch a groundhog.*
> *Rang tang a-whaddle linky day!*

Truth was, her students were teaching Christy far more about the woods than she was teaching them. This lush, green forest belonged to these children. It was in their blood. They delighted in sharing its secrets with their teacher, the "city-gal" from Asheville, North Carolina.

"Miz Christy!" called Clara Spencer, a bright twelve-year-old. She was kneeling by a fallen tree. "Here it is! This here's pyxie lichen." She pointed to an odd-looking moss covering the rotting balsam log. "And that over there's reindeer moss."

Christy bent down to examine the delicate moss. "There are so many different kinds! It's amazing, isn't it?"

Clara nodded. "It's like that Bible quote about the lilies Miz Alice likes so much."

Alice Henderson had helped to found the mission at Cutter Gap where Christy taught. Miss Alice had become a good friend and advisor to Christy, and the children adored her.

"'Consider the lilies of the field, how they grow; they toil not, neither do they spin,'" Christy said. "'And yet I say unto you, That even—'"

"Solomon in all his glory was not arrayed like one of these," Clara finished proudly.

"See that pretty little flower over there?" Christy said, pointing. "Isn't that trillium?"

"You get yourself an A-plus, Miz Christy!" Clara cried.

"Your mother's taught me a lot about flowers on our walks together." Over the last few months, Fairlight Spencer had become one of Christy's dearest friends.

"Ma knows purt-near everything about these woods," Clara said. "Why, she—" A frantic shout interrupted Clara.

"Miz Christy! Come quick!"

Christy groaned. Creed and Zach were jumping up and down as if the path were on fire.

"What is it now, boys?"

"We found ourselves some monster tracks up ahead!" Creed cried.

"Don't you think we've had enough of that for one day?"

"I swear, Miz Christy! This ain't no pullin' on your leg. This is plumb serious."

"Could it be a bear?" Christy asked.

Zach shook his head. "Ain't no bear like I've ever seen. As sure as the sun's in the sky, Miz Christy. These is the tracks of a real live monster!"

"Creed, this joke is getting very old—"

"He's not joking, Miz Christy." John Spencer, Clara's older brother, joined the boys. His face was grim. "You'd better come take a look."

❧ TWO ❧

Christy ran up the path to the spot where the children were gathered in a tight circle. She could tell from their discussion that these were no ordinary tracks:

"Ain't never seen nothin' like it!"

"It's the Boggin, for sure and certain!"

"We oughta hightail it outa here before he comes to eat us!"

Several of the younger children were crying. Christy took Little Burl Allen's tiny hand as he sniffled. "Teacher," he sobbed, "I'm frightful scared."

"Don't listen to them, Little Burl," Christy said as the children parted to let her through. "They're just making up—"

Suddenly she paused. There, pressed deep into the wet dirt and pine needles, was the biggest, strangest footprint Christy had ever seen.

"Told ya it ain't no bear," Creed whispered.

Christy knelt down to feel the imprint. It was as long as her arm and half as wide. The four toeprints were the size of apples. Extending from those were sharp, deep claw marks. More footprints traveled back into the woods.

"What on earth is this?" Christy whispered.

"It's fresh," John said darkly. "That much is for sure."

Christy met his gaze. John, age fifteen, was one of her best students. He was tall and slender, like all the Spencer children, and had curly blond hair. Christy could see real worry in his light brown eyes.

"What do you think it is, John?" Christy asked.

"Creed's right. That ain't no bear," John said, scratching his head. "That ain't like nothin' I ever saw before."

"Could it be human?"

"That's not any human I want to run into," John said with a slight smile. "A foot the size of Little Burl, more or less, with four toes, and claws as sharp as an axe? No sir. I don't want to meet this fellow on a dark night."

Vella Holt had eased up as close to Christy as she could get. "It's the Boggin, ain't it, Teacher?" she asked in a trembling voice.

Christy hugged the little girl. "The Boggin is just a story, Vella. Like the haunt tales you children like to tell each other about witches and ghosts and other such nonsense. He's just superstitious silliness."

"Beggin' your pardon, Miz Christy," said Ruby Mae Morrison, "but why would they call that mountain over yonder Boggin Mountain, less'n he was real?"

Christy smiled. "Didn't we just pass a stream called Cuckoo Jig Creek? Does that mean I can expect to find birds dancing the night away by the bank?"

Ruby Mae tossed her wild red hair. "Could be. Cuckoos is strange birds. Besides, this ain't like Asheville. When we visited there 'cause Betsy needed her operation, I read all them road signs. They're all borin'. First Street, Second Street, and on and on." Ruby Mae jutted her chin. "Here, names got meanin'. Pinch Gut's a squeezin' place between two rocky spots. Stretch Yer Neck Ridge is a place where you gotta stand on tippy-toes to see the view. And Boggin Mountain is Boggin Mountain 'cause that's where the Boggin lives. Plain and simple."

Christy stood, brushing pine needles off her long brown skirt. "Tell me this. Has anyone ever seen this Boggin man?"

"Lots of people have," Creed replied. The other students murmured their agreement. "My grannie saw him once, sneakin' out by our woodpile. Had eyes as orange as a harvest moon."

"Nope. His eyes are fiery red," Zach reported. "My Aunt Biddie says so. She knows for sure, 'cause her horse got terrible spooked one day by the Boggin."

"His eyes are yellow," Ruby Mae corrected. "And big as plates."

"So I take it you've seen him, Ruby Mae?" Christy asked with a doubtful smile.

"Well, not exactly. But I heard Ben Pentland talkin' one day, about how he took a shortcut past Boggin Mountain to deliver mail to some folks on the far side. He was a-comin' home—" Ruby Mae lowered her voice to a whisper, "and all of a sudden, he run smack dab into a nest the size of a cabin. Made outa sticks and mud and bloody bones. And what do you think he saw, pokin' his powerful ugly head outa that nest?"

The children gasped. Christy groaned. "Let me guess. A very, very large robin?"

Ruby Mae rolled her eyes heavenward. "Miz Christy, for a teacher, you sure don't listen up when I'm doin' the lecturin'! It was the Boggin, of course. He had teeth as big and sharp as a bear. And a huge scar on his head. And his eyes, I'm tellin' you, were *yellow.*"

"That's why no one goes near Boggin Mountain," Creed explained. "The Boggin can swallow you whole in one bite, faster than a snake can suck down an egg."

Christy took a deep breath. How many

times had she battled the children's strange superstitions before? She had a feeling this particular story was going to be difficult to put to rest.

"Do all of you believe in this . . . this story?" she asked.

"Not me," Clara said loudly.

"At last," Christy cried, "a sensible voice! Clara's right, children. The Boggin only exists in your minds. He's not real."

"I'm not sayin' *that* exactly," Clara added. She paused, looking a little uncomfortable. "I'm just sayin' if there is a Boggin on the mountain, he's probably just like any critter in the woods. Like a wildcat or a 'possum or an owl. You know. Just wantin' to keep to himself—"

"Clara," John said in a warning voice.

"I'm just sayin' that's what I think, is all," Clara said, glaring at her brother.

Christy sighed. "Sometimes we're just afraid of what we can't understand," she said. "Maybe next time we'll take a trip up Boggin Mountain and see for ourselves that there's nothing to be afraid of."

"I wouldn't do that, Miz Christy," John said quickly.

"Don't tell me you believe in the Boggin, too, John—"

"It's just . . . well, that mountain's mighty sticky climbin', 'specially in a long dress. That's all I meant."

"Please, Teacher, please don't make me go up Boggin Mountain," Vella pleaded.

"That ain't a good idea, Miz Christy," Creed said, his eyes wide with terror.

"All right, then," Christy said gently. "It doesn't sound like an easy climb, anyway. I promise I won't make you go."

"I got a question for you, Miz Christy," Ruby Mae said. "You say there's no Boggin. But how do you explain these tracks?"

Christy pursed her lips. It was a good question. "I can't explain them, Ruby Mae. Perhaps two large animals crossed paths and we're seeing a combination of tracks. Perhaps the imprint was much smaller, but the wet dirt allowed it to expand. It's been awfully rainy lately. One way or another, I'm sure there's a logical explanation."

Christy could tell from her students' expressions that they already thought they knew the explanation.

She started back up the path. "I think we've had enough excitement for one day. We should really head back toward school. Remember, stay on the path and keep an eye on your friends. No dawdling, and no getting too far ahead."

After a few yards, Christy glanced over her shoulder to check for stragglers. To her surprise, she noticed Clara heading deeper into the woods.

"Clara?" Christy called. "Come on. We're heading back to school."

"I'm just followin' the tracks to see where they go," she called back.

"You can do that another time," Christy said, this time in her firmest teacher-voice. "Come on back now."

Clara headed deeper into the underbrush. "Just another minute!"

"John," Christy said, "would you go retrieve your sister?"

Suddenly, Clara let out a horrifying scream.

Frantically, Christy and the others plowed their way through the steep underbrush toward the frightened girl.

Clara pointed a trembling finger at a small clearing in the woods. Impaled on a sharp, tall stick was a shocking sight.

The skinned head of an animal—probably a bear—was stuck on the stick.

Beyond the awful sight, the tracks disappeared.

"Explain that," Ruby Mae said in a hoarse whisper.

Christy had no answer. But little Vella did.

"The Boggin done it," she sobbed softly. "It's the Boggin for sure, and he's sendin' us a warnin."

❧ Three ❧

I'm tellin' you, Miz Christy, that was the Boggin's doin'," Ruby Mae said that afternoon.

School was over, and Ruby Mae and Christy were the last to leave the schoolhouse, which also served as the church on Sunday. The teacher and student were walking the short distance to the mission house. Ruby Mae was the only student who lived at the mission. She'd had some problems getting along with her stepfather, and Miss Alice had suggested she stay in one of the spare bedrooms at the mission house.

"I'm not sure who did it, Ruby Mae," Christy said. "But I refuse to believe in some mythical creature who's been haunting a mountain for years and years."

They paused in front of the house, a large, wooden building set in a big yard. David

Grantland, the mission's young minister, was perched on a ladder, painting the frame around a second-floor window. His dark hair was splattered with white flecks of paint.

"It looks great, David," Christy called.

David wiped his brow with his shirt sleeve. "Yes, I'm quite the artist. I don't suppose you two would like to help?"

"But Preacher," Ruby Mae protested, "you're doin' such a fine job all by your lonesome. Me and Miz Christy, we'd just mess up your fine art work!"

David rolled his eyes. "Somehow I had the feeling that's what you'd say. Toss up that rag, would you, Christy?"

Christy retrieved the rag, careful not to walk under the ladder, and threw it to David. "Ruby Mae was just kidding, David. Is there something we can do to help?"

"Actually, I'm just about done. Although there is one thing—"

"Just name it."

"Promise me you'll never, ever send out letters requesting donations to the mission again!" David cried.

Some time ago, Christy had written several companies about the mission's desperate need for supplies. She'd asked for mattresses, paint, soap, window shades, cleaning supplies, food—anything she thought might make the lives of the mountain people a little easier.

To her surprise, she'd gotten plenty of responses. Week after week, Mr. Pentland had arrived at the mission with huge boxes brimming with supplies. Several months ago the Lyon and Healy Company had actually sent a grand piano. And the Bell Telephone Company had come through with wires and equipment for a telephone. That had been an especially exciting gift, since no one in the area owned a telephone. Most people had never even seen one before.

"So far," David said, "I've had to learn how to tune a piano and paint a house on account of those donations. Pretty soon, I'm going to have to figure out how to string telephone wires across a mountain. When I came here to Cutter Gap, I *thought* I was going to be a minister."

"The Lord works in mysterious ways," Christy said, grinning.

As soon as she was inside the house, Ruby Mae ran straight to the kitchen and began jabbering at high speed about the strange sights the children had discovered that afternoon.

Miss Ida, David's sister, was stirring a pot of soup. She was wearing a calico apron and her usual stern expression. Miss Ida was tall, almost gaunt, with sharp features and thin, graying hair. Sometimes it was hard to believe she was related to David, with his warm, brown eyes and friendly smile.

Miss Alice was also there sitting at the table, looking over the budget ledger, where she recorded every penny the mission spent. She was dressed in a simple blue skirt and a crisp white linen blouse. As always, she looked beautiful, with her clear, regal features and lovely gray eyes. Her hair was swept up in an elegant bun. Christy pulled a twig out of her own hair self-consciously. She probably looked a mess, after her adventure in the woods today.

"What *are* you babbling about, Ruby Mae?" Miss Ida said, clucking her tongue. "What's this about a bobbin?"

Ruby Mae sneaked a piece of carrot off the cutting board. "*Boggin*, Miss Ida," she corrected.

"Not that again," Miss Alice said, sighing. "I'd really hoped we were done with him."

"He left a footprint the size of a house," Ruby Mae exclaimed. "And a big ol' skinned animal head."

"You're exaggerating just a bit, Ruby Mae," Christy said. "Besides, I'm sure it was just a prank."

The screen door swung open and David stepped in. Paint splatters covered him like huge snowflakes. On the tip of his nose was a big white splotch.

"Looks like you painted more than the house, Preacher," Ruby Mae teased.

"David!" Miss Ida scolded. "I just washed this floor. Look at those boots! They're covered with paint!"

"Do any of you remember the story about the Little Red Hen?" David asked.

Ruby Mae frowned. "Is that in the Bible, Preacher?"

David bent down to unlace his boots. "No, Ruby Mae. It's the story of a hen who asks for help while she's baking bread. Nobody's willing to help her." He grunted as he yanked off one boot. "But everybody's willing to eat the bread after it's made."

"So you're sayin' you're the hen?" Ruby Mae asked.

"Exactly."

"But that don't make a lick o' sense. If you had feathers, Preacher, like as not you'd be a rooster, I'm a-guessin'."

David sighed. "Never mind. I can see my story is going to be wasted on you chickens." With one boot still on, he started toward the table.

"Preacher, stop where you are!" Ruby Mae screeched. She plowed into him, nearly knocking him down.

"What's wrong now, Ruby Mae?" David asked.

"Your boot!" Ruby Mae cried. "Don't you

know nothin' about nothin'? It's bad luck to step around with one shoe off and one shoe on! Every step is a day o' bad luck for you, sure as can be."

"That's nonsense, Ruby Mae." David gently moved her aside and proceeded to the table.

Ruby Mae watched in disgust. "I declare, you sure can be ornery, Preacher."

David took a chair across from Miss Alice and yanked off his other boot. "Where on earth do you get these notions, Ruby Mae?"

"Same place she learned to leave her old, tattered socks in the yard," Miss Ida said. "I was all set to throw them into that pile of rubbish you were burning the other day. But Ruby Mae would have none of that."

"Everyone knows if'n you burn a piece o' clothing, your body'll burn where the clothing was coverin' it. You didn't want me runnin' around with blisters on my feet, now, did you, Miss Ida?"

"Who tells you these things, Ruby Mae?" Christy asked. "I mean, things like the shoes and the socks and the Boggin stories?"

"They're just there, plain as the nose on your face." Ruby Mae glanced at David and giggled. "Or I guess I should say plain as the nose on *most* people's faces."

"Stories like these are passed from one generation to another," Miss Alice said. "I've heard the legend of the Boggin from dozens of different people. Many actually claim to have seen him."

"Where did they get that name, I wonder? It's not as if they've ever met him," Christy said. She rolled her eyes. "Listen to me! I'm starting to talk like this creature really exists!"

"But he does exist. You saw the signs yourself, Miz Christy," Ruby Mae protested.

"The name comes from the mountain people's Scottish background," Miss Alice said. "It refers to a ghost or goblin—a scary creature of some kind."

"And is he ever scary!" Ruby Mae let out a low growl, like a hungry wildcat. "That's how he sounds. Granny O'Teale done told me."

Christy laughed. "I can see I'm not going to get this superstition out of your head any time soon."

"You shouldn't act so high and mighty, Miz Christy," Ruby Mae said. "You've got your own superstitious side, after all."

"Me?" Christy cried.

David winked at Ruby Mae. "She has a point, Christy. Didn't I see you go out of your way to avoid walking under my ladder?"

"That . . . that's different," Christy said to David. "For one thing, I was just trying to avoid the possibility of your spilling paint all over me." She winked at Ruby Mae, turned back to David, and added, "I didn't want to end up looking like you!"

"And what is that supposed to mean?" David demanded.

"Go look in the mirror, Preacher," Ruby Mae said. "You look almost as scary as the Boggin."

❧ Four ❧

The mountains are so peaceful at night," Christy said that evening.

Christy and David were sitting in old wooden rockers on the front porch of the mission house. Crickets chirped noisily, while off in the distance, frogs carried on busy conversations. The damp air was sweet with pine. The Great Smoky Mountains towered around them, black silhouettes against the deep blue twilight sky.

"I always feel so calm when I take in this view," Christy said. "It's like a wonderful painting that constantly changes."

"God's canvas," David said, nodding.

Christy turned her gaze in the direction of Boggin Mountain. "I hate to think of the children fearing that mountain," she said. "It's such a beautiful place, really."

"Someone had to put those tracks there,"

David said. "And the skinned animal head."

"Don't tell me you believe—"

"Of course not. I agree with you that it sounds like a prank. Still, you were right near the base of Boggin Mountain. And having these stories start up again is troublesome."

"What do you mean?" Christy asked.

"I'd hoped to get together some volunteers to help me string the telephone wires—now that I'm almost done with my painting project. We're having a meeting here at the mission house on Saturday."

"Will stringing the wire be difficult?"

"Difficult? That's an understatement. We'll have to cross Boggin Mountain, then go over Bent Creek." He shook his head. "If the men are worried about the Boggin, they may refuse to help me string that wire. And it's not exactly something I can do solo."

"I'm sorry," Christy apologized. "I guess when I asked for a telephone donation, I didn't really think about the complications."

David gave a rueful laugh. "How could you have foreseen that one of the complications would be a mythical creature with huge feet?"

"I'm sure this will pass," Christy said. "By tomorrow, the children will be telling some new ghost story."

"Maybe," David said doubtfully.

"If not, I'll try to distract them with a nice, exciting grammar lesson."

"You're a fine teacher, Christy Huddleston," David said with an affectionate smile. "But even you aren't *that* good."

~ ~ ~

As she got ready for bed, Christy mulled over her lesson plans for the next day. With so many students in one classroom, it was always a challenge to keep their interest.

She stared into her mirror as she unpinned her hair. She looked so different from the Christy who'd come here a few months ago. Her skin was bronzed, her hair streaked by the sun. She was stronger, too. Her arms and legs were hardened by the physical demands of work here at the mission.

Still, she loved Cutter Gap—even this tiny, simple room, so different from her lace-trimmed, lovely bedroom back in Asheville. Her room here was not luxurious, to say the least—a washstand with a white china pitcher and bowl, an old dresser topped by a cracked mirror, two straight chairs, the plainest white curtains, and two cotton rag rugs on the floor.

But the furnishings didn't matter. It was the view outside her window that made this room so special. Eleven mountain ranges, folding one into another, the summits reaching up as if to touch heaven.

Christy retrieved her diary and pen. She'd been keeping a journal about her adventures ever since coming here to Cutter Gap. By now her pen was almost worn flat. Soon she'd have to switch to a pencil—that is, if she could spare one. Even with the recent donations, supplies were hard to come by at the mission school.

She climbed into her bed and began to write.

I've got to find a way to get the children past this Boggin nonsense. I've seen the way rumors and superstitions can take hold among these people. It's no different, I suppose, from the rumors that old Mrs. Dottsweiler back in Asheville used to spread about the neighbors while she hung out her laundry to dry.

And as Ruby Mae pointed out, I'm not exactly perfect when it comes to superstitions. After all, everyone "knows" it's a bad idea to break a mirror— that means seven years' bad luck. Or how about going out of your way not to walk under a ladder? The truth is, I have my share of silly superstitions.

But this Boggin nonsense—that seems so much worse, if it gets in the way of something important, like the new telephone. I would hate for Cutter Gap to lose such an important connection to the outside world. Especially if it's because of some ignorant superstition.

When I think of little Vella's scared expression today, I just know I have to find a way to make the

275

children forget about their fears. But they've learned those fears from their parents and grandparents, and I'm not sure if they'll be willing to "unlearn" them.

Suddenly Christy had a brilliant idea. If the children could learn from their parents, maybe the parents could learn from the children. If she got her students excited about the new telephone David wanted to install, maybe the children could get their parents excited.

And if their parents were excited, maybe they'd be willing to help out installing the wires—even if it did mean going near Boggin Mountain.

Now, if she could just find a way to sneak that grammar lesson in, too. . . .

❧ Five ❧

I have a surprise for you," Christy announced the next morning at school. "I know how disappointed you'll be to hear that instead of our usual grammar lesson, I have something special planned."

From under her desk, Christy pulled out two constructions of wooden boxes, paper, and string. She'd made them early that morning.

"What in tarnation are those, Teacher?" Creed asked.

"These," Christy said proudly, "are telephones. Well, they're not *really* telephones. They're practice telephones, until we can get the real thing. The Reverend Grantland is going to be putting up telephone poles and wires soon—hopefully, with the help of your fathers. When the new telephone is installed at the mission house, I want us all to be prepared."

"Teacher?" Little Burl waved his hand frantically.

"Yes, Little Burl?" Christy asked as she placed one of the makeshift "telephones" on her desk.

"Can I call my granny on that newfangled contraption right now?"

"That's not quite the idea, Little Burl," Christy said. She carried the other telephone to the back of the room and set it on a desk. "These are just pretend. You see, the telephone works by carrying your voice over a long piece of wire."

"How?" John Spencer asked.

"To tell you the truth, I don't know much about how they operate myself," Christy confessed. "I could try to find out more, if you'd like, John."

"Teacher?" Little Burl asked. "I figgered teachers knew just about everything in the world there is to know."

"Wrong, Little Burl," Creed said. "*Preachers* know just about everything."

"You're both wrong," said Clara Spencer. "In my house, it's my ma who knows everything. Just ask my pa."

Christy laughed. "Back to the subject, please. This box represents the telephone machine itself. The string is a wire. This paper cone is where you talk—the mouthpiece. And this other paper cone connected to the string is the earpiece where you listen."

"It's pure magic, it is!" Ruby Mae exclaimed.

"Now, the phones are really going to be connected by miles and miles of wires," Christy continued. "But I don't have enough string to spare for that, so you'll have to use your imaginations."

"Where do the wires go, Teacher?" Creed asked.

"Well, all over, Creed. But because Cutter Gap is in such a hard-to-reach place, with lots of high mountains, it's taken us longer to get connected."

Christy didn't add the other reason—that this area had simply been too poor to afford the luxury of telephones.

"My pa says those new-fangled contraptions is a heap o' nonsense."

Christy looked up in surprise. The low voice belonged to Lundy Taylor, a seventeen-year-old bully with a nose for trouble. Christy had suffered through her share of run-ins with his father, Bird's-Eye. Bird's-Eye made and sold illegal liquor—"moonshine." And whenever a fight broke out in Cutter Gap, you could always count on Bird's-Eye Taylor to be involved.

"Why do you think your father feels that way, Lundy?" Christy asked.

Lundy shrugged. He was a big boy, with dark, messy hair and a constant sneer. "Pa

says we got along just fine and dandy without no telephones for as long as his pa and
his great-grandpa was around. Says it's just a
way for you mission folks to sneak in with
your wires and poles and poke around
where you don't belong."

"But Lundy, that's not the reason for the
telephones at all. Suppose we desperately
needed supplies or medical help? The telephone is a wonderful invention, truly it is."

Lundy rolled his eyes. "Can't trick my pa
any sooner 'n you can catch a weasel asleep."

"Maybe so. But tell him to give this a
chance," Christy said. "Now, who would like
to be the first to try out the telephone?"

The classroom went wild. "Ruby Mae and
Clara. How about you two?"

Each girl took her place at one of the
"telephones" while the others watched, mesmerized.

"Now, Ruby Mae, I want you to pick up
the receiver—that's the little cone-shaped
thing. Put it next to your ear."

Ruby Mae did as she was told. "Cain't hear
a thing, Miz Christy."

"Remember, these are just *imaginary* telephones, Ruby Mae."

"I know. I was just imaginin' I couldn't
hear a thing."

"Next, turn the crank on the right side of
the telephone."

"Ain't no crank."

"I know. You have to pretend."

Dutifully, Ruby Mae made a circular motion with her hand.

"Excellent," Christy said. "Now, in a moment, you'll hear the operator's voice through the receiver. That's me."

Christy went behind the blackboard and pinched her nose. "El Pano operator," she said in a nasal voice, sending the class into a fit of giggles. "To whom would you like to speak?"

Ruby Mae considered. "I'd be tickled pink to speak to President Taft."

"No, Ruby Mae!" Clara cried. "You got to talk to me, 'cause I'm the one with the phone!"

"I was *imaginin'*," Ruby Mae said. "After all, it's a purty sure thing President Taft's got himself a fine telephone. Probably one made o' gold. But if'n you're goin' to get all sore about it, I'll talk to you instead."

Ruby Mae peeked behind the chalkboard. "I don't rightly see as I need a telephone to speak to Clara, Miz Christy. Seein' as she's standin' right over yonder, clear as day."

"Imagine that Clara's in El Pano, miles away. You're here at the mission, and you want to tell her something very important. As the operator, it's my job to connect your phone to hers. I'll plug in the right wire to my switchboard, and, as if by magic . . ." Christy grinned. "R-I-N-G, R-I-N-G!!"

"Are you there?" Clara asked, holding the earpiece to her mouth.

"That's the receiver, Clara. And say 'hello' when you pick up the telephone. Try again."

"Hello? Is that you, Ruby Mae?" Clara said, this time speaking into the paper mouthpiece.

"It's me! Ruby Mae!" Ruby Mae cried, caught up in the fantasy. "And have I got news for you! The Boggin's a-hauntin' us. And . . . let's see. Last week in church, Granny O'Teale fell asleep and snored so loud the preacher said she coulda purt-near waked the dead. And Doctor MacNeill brought Miz Christy pink flowers the other day, for no reason. 'Ceptin' o' course he's sweet on her. . . ."

Christy laughed. "That's probably enough about my social life," she said. She should have known that Ruby Mae, Cutter Gap's biggest busybody, would instantly fall in love with the telephone.

Christy watched in satisfaction as the two girls prattled on. The grammar lesson could wait. For the rest of the day, the children took turns playing on the pretend telephones. Even Lundy gave it a try. Christy had rarely been as happy with one of her lessons. She might not have much in the way of supplies. But sometimes a little ingenuity was all it took to create excitement about learning.

❧ Six ❧

I know the telephone machine's a fine invention," Clara said that afternoon. "But I'm afeared it's causin' a heap o' trouble." She gave her brother a meaningful look. "If'n you know what I mean."

"Shh!" John put a finger to his lips. "The little 'uns will hear you."

The four Spencer children were heading home from school along the sun-dappled path that led to their cabin. Up ahead, six-year-old Lulu and ten-year-old Zady were picking wildflowers for their mother. Clara and John hung back a little so that they could talk in private.

"Trouble with you is, you think too much," John scolded.

Clara stopped walking. John could be such a know-it-all! She shook her head at her big brother. Like all the Spencer children, he had wide eyes fringed by long lashes. And like the others, he was dressed in worn but clean clothes, carefully mended again and again by their mother.

"All I'm sayin'," Clara said, "is it *could* be him doin' it, John. To scare people off." She chewed on a thumbnail, something she did whenever she was worried.

"Stop chewin' off your nails," John said. "Ma says you keep that up, one day you'll wake up without any fingers."

Clara rolled her eyes. John was only three years older than she was, but he liked to act like he was her pa. It drove her crazy.

Of course, the truth was, they were a lot alike. They were always thinking, always looking at things and asking, "How come?" They loved school, and they both thought Miz Christy was the finest thing to ever happen to Cutter Gap.

"You got to admit, it could be him," Clara said, sighing.

"I don't know," John said darkly. "Could be you're right. It's like you were sayin' yesterday, when we found those tracks. About how the Boggin just wanted to be left alone, like a wild critter." He gave her a playful punch in the arm. "'Course, you shoulda just kept your tongue from waggin'."

"It just plumb popped outa my mouth," Clara admitted.

"I understand," John said. He frowned, scratching his head.

"Stop scratchin' your head," Clara teased, "or someday you'll wake up and be bald as a turkey buzzard."

"Hurry up, you slowpokes!" Zady called.

"We're comin'!" John yelled.

Clara gazed upward. Through the dense layer of leaves, she could just make out the towering peak of Boggin Mountain. They passed it every day on the way to school. She used to think it was beautiful. Like a fancy blue-green party skirt, the kind she could only dream about owning.

Now, with all the latest scary signs, it was hard to walk past it without shivering, just a little.

"Clara, John! Come quick!" Zady cried.

Zady and Lulu were standing next to a tall tree, staring at something.

"It's proof, I'm a-tellin' you," Zady said when Clara and John reached the spot.

She pointed nervously. There on the tree were huge, long gashes. It was as if a giant bear had scratched his claws deep into the bark.

"The Boggin left it as another warnin' to us," Zady said.

Lulu clutched at Clara, hugging her close. "He's goin' to eat us all for supper!"

"Hush, Lulu. He ain't goin' to eat us, not for supper or breakfast, either," Clara said.

"How do you know?" Zady demanded.

"'Cause you're too bony for eatin'," Clara replied.

"It ain't like you've ever seen him. Besides, you heard Ruby Mae a-talkin'—"

"Ruby Mae ain't seen him, either. And you know she just likes to hear the sound of her own voice," Clara said. Ruby Mae was one of Clara's very best friends, but Clara knew her friend had a way of talking on and on without thinking things through.

"Look," John said.

Clara followed John's gaze. Hanging from a branch high overhead was a man's shirt—or what was left of a shirt. It was shredded into strips and stained with what looked like blood.

Clara shuddered. "It's just more tricks," she said, trying to sound calmer than she felt.

"I'm not never comin' this way again," Zady vowed in a trembling voice. "I don't care if I have to walk clear over to Wildcat Hollow and cross the creek. I don't care if it takes me four hours to get to school. I ain't never comin' past Boggin Mountain again."

Clara put her hands on her hips. "You can't take the long way around. Besides, even if this is the Boggin leavin' warnings, he ain't mad at us."

"Maybe he don't want us goin' near the mountain. He figgers it's his, and that's that," Zady replied.

"That's just plain stupid, Zady," Clara said, rolling her eyes.

"I'm a-tellin' Ma you called me stupid!" Zady cried.

"I wasn't callin' you stupid, I was callin' what you said stupid."

"Same thing."

"Is not."

"Is too."

John cleared his throat. "That's enough, you two. You sound like a couple o' hens cacklin'."

Lulu's eyes went wide. "Maybe . . ." she whispered, "maybe he don't want the telephones and all. Maybe he figgers this is his mountain to haunt, fair and square."

"That's silly, Lulu," Clara said. She met John's worried gaze. "Now, come on." She gave Lulu a gentle push. "Ma's goin' to be worryin' somethin' fierce if'n we don't get home soon."

As Zady and Lulu ran ahead, Clara turned to John. "How will we ever know for sure and certain what's behind all this?"

"If it's the Boggin," John whispered, "there's only one way to find out."

Clara gazed up at Boggin Mountain, looming above them. Today it certainly didn't look like the pretty party skirt she dreamed about. Today, it looked like a place where an evil creature lived, hovering in the darkness, waiting to pounce.

She tried to smile at John. "Come on," she said, swallowing past a lump in her throat. "I'll race you the rest of the way home."

✑ Seven ✑

I'd hoped to see a better turnout today," Christy said on Saturday morning.

"So had I," said Miss Alice.

"I'm sure the reverend did, too," said Doctor MacNeill with a shake of his head.

"Don't they know how important this telephone is?" Christy asked with a sigh. "I guess my telephone lesson with the children didn't have much effect on their parents. And this rain didn't help, either."

She peered out the living room window. Half a dozen men sat on the mission house porch, waiting for David to start the meeting. The day was gloomy. An early morning downpour had been replaced by gray drizzle.

Jeb Spencer, Fairlight's husband, poked his head in the doorway. "Howdy, Miz Christy, Miz Alice," he said, removing his damp, broad-brimmed hat. "Howdy, Doc. If it ain't

290

no trouble, I was wonderin' if I might have a glass of water. As wet a day as it is, you'd think water'd be the last thing on my mind!"

"Come on in," Christy said.

"I'm glad you were able to come, Jeb," Miss Alice said as they headed to the kitchen.

"Wish more coulda come," Jeb said. "Puttin' up them poles and wires is goin' to be a heap o' trouble, I'm afeared. Hope the preacher knows what he's gettin' hisself into."

"It's my fault," Christy said as she poured Jeb a mug of water out of a white enamel pitcher. "I'm the one who asked for the telephone equipment. I guess I didn't realize how much trouble it would cause. Of course, this Boggin nonsense isn't helping."

Jeb took a long sip of water. "My kids saw another warnin' yesterday on the way home. Nothin' much—just some marks on a tree and a shredded-up ol' shirt. Still, little Lulu and Zady were mighty upset. Swore they'd take the long way to school from now on. Matter of fact—" Jeb shook a finger at Christy. "Weren't you headin' on out to my place today to see Fairlight? Maybe you should wait till I can walk you there, Miz Christy."

Christy gave a wave of her hand. "Don't tell me you believe in this nonsense, Jeb."

"I believe someone's tryin' to get our attention," Jeb said. "But that's all I know for sure."

"Jeb's right," said Doctor MacNeill. "These Boggin rumors come up from time to time, but nothing as persistent as this."

"Have you ever seen him, Neil?" Christy asked with a grin. "Or should I say *it?*"

"No." The doctor smiled back. "But I'm keeping my options open. I've certainly run into plenty of people in Cutter Gap who claim to have seen him . . . or it."

They walked out onto the porch. David was dressed in his old work clothes. He'd just placed on the porch floor a rough map he'd drawn. "I guess we can get started," he said, looking a little disappointed.

"There's some more a-coming'," said Jeb, pointing across the clearing past the church.

"That's Bird's-Eye Taylor and Lundy," Christy said.

"You sound surprised," said Jeb.

"I am. Lundy said his father isn't exactly enthusiastic about the telephone."

"And let's face it," the doctor added. "Bird's-Eye is not the first person you'd expect to volunteer."

"Unless you need help drinking down a jug o' moonshine!" Jeb joked.

"We'll take any able-bodied man we can get," David said. "We've got our work cut out for us." He pointed to the map. "We have to connect up to the nearest existing phone line. That's way over in Centerport."

"Three miles from the mission as the crow flies," said Bob Allen.

"Now, we can't fasten insulators and pins to live trees," David continued. "That means we have to cut tall, straight trees. Then we have to skin them and smooth them, lug them into place, and plant them up and down the mountains along the route. We'll have to hack off branches of any living trees that might swing against the wires, too." He stroked his chin, staring doubtfully at the map. "It's going to be slow-going, unless we recruit more men."

"We'd have more help," Bob said, "if it weren't for goin' over Boggin Mountain. Ain't there another way, Preacher?"

"Not without going miles out of our way." David shook his head. "Not to mention having to cross Dead Man's Creek. No," he sighed, "crossing Boggin Mountain is the only way."

"Only a fool lookin' for an early grave'll take that way," Bird's-Eye said as he approached. He had a shotgun slung over his shoulder. A big felt hat shaded his eyes from view. Lundy hung behind him, arms crossed over his chest, his wet hair plastered to his forehead.

"It's the only way, Bird's-Eye," Jeb said.

"Can I assume you're here to volunteer, Mr. Taylor?" David asked.

Bird's-Eye answered by spitting on the ground. "Not on your life, Preacher. You're a-lookin' for more trouble 'n you seen in all your born days, if'n you build that telephone contraption."

"Why are you here, then?" David asked tersely.

"Come to tell you what my boy done saw this morning." Bird's-Eye poked at Lundy with the muzzle of his shotgun. "Tell 'em, boy."

Lundy shrugged. "I was a-walkin' along, payin' no never mind, when all of a sudden—"

"Tell 'em where you was, fool," Bird's-Eye interrupted.

"I was over yonder." Lundy pointed toward Boggin Mountain. "With ol' Killer, my coon dog. All o' a sudden, Killer starts yelpin' and carryin' on like he's treed the biggest coon in all o' Tennessee. I look up, and hidin' on a rocky ridge is the Boggin. Big as all get-out, with eyes on fire. He aimed a rock as wide as that piano in the mission house right at me. Tossed it like it was the size of a pea. I jumped out o' the way, just in the nick o' time. Then I run home fast as I could and told my pa."

"And here we is to warn you, proper-like," Bird's-Eye added.

"Lundy," Christy said, "couldn't it have

been your imagination? Maybe the fiery eyes belonged to an animal. Maybe the rock just broke loose. It's been raining a lot lately. Mr. Pentland said he's come across some rock slides between here and El Pano."

"Nope," Lundy said defiantly. "I saw him, clear as day."

"Take my advice, Preacher," said Bird's-Eye. "You'd best be thinkin' twice before you head up that mountain."

"Thank you for the warning," David said. "But the mission is going to have a phone, if it takes my whole life to get it done."

"You keep this up," Bob Allen said ominously as Bird's-Eye and Lundy marched off, "you may not have a life."

"You're not scared, are you, Bob?" David asked.

"I ain't scared o' nothin', Preacher," Bob said. He reached for his hat and started down the stairs. "But I ain't no fool, neither."

They watched him leave. For a moment, nobody spoke.

"Well," David said with a grim smile, "I guess that makes the rest of us fools."

"What's that saying?" said Doctor MacNeill. "'Fools rush in where angels fear to tread'?"

"There's nothing to be afraid of," Christy said firmly, but she didn't sound quite as convincing as she'd hoped.

❧ Eight ❧

John? Clara? Is that you?"

Christy paused on the forest path. She was halfway to the Spencers' cabin and hadn't seen a single person on the long walk until now.

The two children hesitated, whispering to each other. After a moment, they ran to greet her.

"I'm on my way to your cabin," Christy said. "Your mother was going to give me another lesson about mountain herbs and wildflowers today. But the weather's so miserable, I guess we'll have to postpone it. Where are you off to?"

John and Clara exchanged a glance.

"To look for mushrooms," John said.

"To visit Louise Washington," Clara said at the same moment.

"Um, first we're gathering mushrooms,

then we're going to the Washingtons'," John corrected, "if there's time."

"I saw your father at the meeting about the telephone this morning. He said you and your little sisters came across some more odd signs on your way home yesterday."

"Up ahead aways, on the right." Clara nodded. "You can't miss 'em."

"Still, here you are. I'm pleased to see you weren't frightened off by this Boggin superstition . . . unlike most of the men in Cutter Gap." Christy shook her head. "Only a few people volunteered to help Reverend Grantland."

"Are *you* at all scared, Miz Christy?" Clara asked.

"Of course not."

"Not even a teensy bit?"

"Lots of things scare me, Clara. But the Boggin isn't on the list."

Clara chewed on her thumbnail, her thin, pale face tight with worry. "What *are* you afeared of, Miz Christy? If'n it's all right to ask."

"Well, that's a good question." Christy considered for a moment. "I suppose I'm afraid of not being as good a teacher as you all deserve, for one thing."

"But that's plumb crazy!" Clara exclaimed. "You're the best teacher in the whole, wide world!"

Christy patted Clara's shoulder. "Thank you, Clara. It makes me feel so good to hear you say that. Still and all, it's something I worry about. I suppose in a bigger way, it's a question we all face—are we strong enough to do God's work? That's something Miss Alice and I talked about when I first came to Cutter Gap. She said, 'If we're going to work on God's side, we have to decide to open our hearts to the griefs and pain all around us.'"

"So you're sayin' you're afeared of stuff *inside* you?" Clara asked, frowning.

"I suppose that is what I'm saying. Does that make any sense to you?"

"A little bit." Clara shrugged. "It's sorta like when we're learnin' arithmetic. I can see the numbers on the blackboard fine and dandy. But I can't always see what they add up to."

"Clara," Christy said with a laugh, "sometimes I feel that way about life in general."

John cleared his throat. "We'd best be gettin' on to the Washingtons', Clara," he said, a little tersely.

"You *mean* to the mushrooms," Clara corrected.

"Oh. Yep, that's what I meant, all right." John started down the path at a brisk pace. "See you later, Miz Christy," he called over his shoulder. "Tell Ma we'll be home soon."

Christy waved. *That's odd, she thought as she resumed walking. Clara and John are*

*both acting a bit strangely. But then everyone
is lately, it seems.*

She came to the deep gashes in the tree
Jeb had told her about. Christy knew there
was nothing to be afraid of. But she shiv-
ered just a little in spite of herself.

Since the weather was so damp, Christy
and Fairlight spent the afternoon in the Spencers' tiny cabin, reading together from the
Bible. When Christy had first come to Cutter
Gap, she'd taught Fairlight how to read.
Fairlight had caught on quickly, and now she
read almost as well as Christy herself.

Fairlight was a beautiful woman, in a
plain, simple way. She had a sweet, musical
voice that reminded Christy of silver bells.

"Are you sure you can't stay a little
longer?" Fairlight asked.

"I really should be going," Christy said,
gently closing Fairlight's worn family Bible.
"Miss Ida's baking pies all afternoon, and I
promised I would help." She laughed. "Although my baking skills are so bad, she usually just shoos me away after a few minutes."

"It is getting late," Fairlight agreed. "Clara
and John should be home by now."

"When I ran into them, they said they were
going to gather mushrooms, then visit the

Washingtons. But now that I think of it, they didn't have anything to carry the mushrooms *in*."

Fairlight tapped her fingers on the worn table. She looked as if she were about to say something, then seemed to reconsider.

"Fairlight? Is anything wrong?"

"Nothin' much. I s'pose these Boggin stories have everybody a mite on edge, is all."

"Do you believe in the Boggin?"

"Nope. Them's just pranks, I figger." Fairlight gave a gentle smile. "And if there *is* a Boggin, I like to think he's just one o' God's wild critters, tryin' to get by, like everyone else." She shrugged. "Anyways, if you do run into Clara and John on the way back to the mission, tell them I need them to come home and chop me up some firewood and kindling. And I need it today, not tomorrow!"

Christy grinned. "Yes, Ma."

"I do sound a bit cantankerous sometimes, don't I?" Fairlight said with a laugh. "Just you wait till you have young 'uns of your own, Christy Huddleston! You'll see."

"But Fairlight, I already have seventy!" Christy joked.

Almost as soon as Christy set out for home, a light, cold rain began to fall. She hurried along the shadowed path, anxious to make it back to the mission before a real downpour began. The sun was hidden behind thick, gray clouds. Off in the distance, thunder rumbled, low and ominous.

On a day like today, the sweet peace of the forest seemed to vanish. It became a dark, frightening place, full of strange noises and leaf whispers. It was a place that made Christy long for the warm, cozy comfort of the mission house kitchen. She couldn't wait to get home, change out of her wet clothes, and warm herself in front of a crackling fire.

She passed the tree with the deep gashes cut into it. This time, she didn't let her gaze linger. Boggin Mountain loomed above her. Somewhere in the forest, a branch cracked. Trees rustled. Thunder grumbled, a little closer this time.

Christy forced a grim smile. It suddenly occurred to her that when Clara had asked what she was afraid of, maybe Christy had left something out. Perhaps she should have added hiking alone through a dark, rainy forest, full of unfamiliar, creepy noises.

Christy picked up her pace. The last thing she wanted was to get caught in a forest during a lightning storm.

Suddenly, her shoe caught on a tree root. Christy tripped, crying out in surprise. She landed on her knees in a puddle.

"Oh, no," she moaned. "My skirt!"

As she struggled to get up, she heard footsteps nearing. They were coming from the direction of Boggin Mountain.

"Who's there?" Christy called. Her voice was just a thin whisper in the vast forest.

No answer. Nothing.

Still, Christy was certain she could feel the presence of another living thing close at hand.

Her breath caught in her throat. She could hear someone else—or something—breathing low and steadily.

It was watching her, whatever it was that was hidden in the dark, endless forest.

Christy didn't move. She seemed to have forgotten how to move. She peered into the shadows. A branch cracked to her right.

She looked, and then she saw it.

It was hideous. Monstrous. Its eyes glowed like an animal of the night.

It was the Boggin.

❧ Nine ❧

Somebody screamed.

A moment later, Christy realized it was her own voice echoing through the trees.

Then, as quickly as he'd appeared, the awful creature vanished into the dense forest.

Christy rubbed her eyes. Had she imagined him? Was she going crazy?

The creature she'd seen had been camouflaged by leaves and mist and trees. Christy *thought* she'd seen a man's face, buried in a mane of long, white hair. She *thought* she'd seen eyes, shining like tiny white moons. She *thought* she'd glimpsed a figure taller than any man she'd ever met.

She *thought* she'd seen it. But had she, really?

She tried in vain to brush the mud off her skirt. She peered into the woods one more time.

Nothing.

Just as she'd convinced herself she was a victim of her own imagination, Christy heard more footsteps.

But this time, she knew she wasn't imagining things.

"Clara! John!" Christy cried. "What a surprise! Am I glad to see you!"

"Miz Christy!" John called. He rushed to her side, with Clara close on his heels. "We thought we heard someone screamin'. Was that you?"

"I saw . . . I mean, I thought I saw . . ."

Christy hesitated. After all her talk about the Boggin being a silly superstition, what could she say? *I saw the Boggin?*

"You look like you seen a ghost, Miz Christy," Clara said, taking her hand. "You sure you're all right?"

"I tripped and fell. Then something startled me," Christy said. She could feel her cheeks burning. "I suppose it was just an animal, watching me from the trees. But still, it did unnerve me for a moment."

"Was it the Boggin?" Clara whispered. She cast a nervous glance at John.

"I'm not sure what it was," Christy said.

"This thing, whatever it was . . . it didn't try to hurt you, did it?" John asked gravely.

"No. It just seemed to be watching me. When I screamed, it vanished." Christy tucked a damp strand of hair behind her ear. "Chances are it was just some poor, wild animal. I probably scared him a whole lot more than he scared me. I'm sure he didn't mean me any harm."

Clara stared off into the woods. "I hope so, Miz Christy," she said softly. "I truly do."

The next day after church, Christy retrieved her diary and pen and went outside. The day was overcast, but at least the rain had stopped for a time. All of the congregation had headed for home by now, and the mission yard was empty and still. David was in his bunkhouse, Miss Alice was in her cabin, and Ruby Mae and Miss Ida were in the main house. Christy had the yard to herself.

She went to the chair swing under an old oak by the school. David had installed it a few weeks ago. He'd looped two long ropes over a thick branch, then attached the comfortable wooden swing.

Swinging gently back and forth, Christy opened her diary. It was so peaceful here, so calm. Her panic in the woods yesterday seemed silly now. And yet the experience had disturbed her more than she liked to admit.

Christy paused to gaze at Boggin Mountain, a silent, looming presence on the horizon.

Slowly, she began to write:

> *I haven't told anyone here at the mission about my experience yesterday in the woods.*
>
> *I suppose I'm embarrassed to admit how afraid I was. Or maybe I'm embarrassed to admit how quickly I assumed that the Boggin—something I'd dismissed as a figment of Cutter Gap imaginations—was real.*
>
> *Today, during his sermon, David talked a little about fear—about how, with God's love, we can overcome it. One verse in particular has stayed with me since this morning: "Perfect love casteth out fear."*
>
> *I know that he was directing his words to the people of Cutter Gap. I know he was trying to convince them not to let their own fears and superstitions overpower them.*
>
> *But as I listened, I felt as if he were talking right to me. I, too, fear the unknown. I fear what I can't understand. I fear that I won't be as strong as I want to be—as strong as God needs me to be to do His work.*
>
> *And now, as ridiculous as it sounds, I have a new fear to add to my list.*
>
> *As much as I hate to admit it, I'm even afraid of a creature lurking in the mountains I've come to love so much. The creature everyone insists on calling "the Boggin."*
>
> *Ironic, isn't it?*

Christy closed her diary. She smiled at the mountain she'd begun to fear.

She was going to have to go back, of course, just to prove to herself that the Boggin was nothing more than a superstition. It was an illusion—a trick of the eyesight and nothing more.

❧ Ten ❧

Boggin or no Boggin, it looks like you're making some progress," Christy said to David.

A few days had passed. David and his small group of volunteers had begun making telephone poles, cutting down trees, then stripping and smoothing them down. It was dirty, difficult, sweaty work. But slowly and steadily, they were making strides.

Most of the work was taking place in a clearing, not far from the base of Boggin Mountain. Christy had come to the site after school to deliver sandwiches Miss Ida had prepared for the men. At the last minute, Ruby Mae had decided to come along.

The truth was, Christy was glad for the company. It was the first time she'd been back to the area since her scare last Saturday. But just as she had promised herself, she *had* returned. Surrounded by the sweet scent of wildflowers and the merry discussions of warblers and tanagers, it was hard to believe she'd ever been so afraid.

"We've got a lot of the poles done, at least," David said. He paused to wipe his brow. "Today we've got seven men. Yesterday, we had three."

"Of course," Christy pointed out, "this is the first day it hasn't rained in a while."

"True. If the weather holds, I guess there's some hope we'll get this telephone of yours working before I'm old and gray."

"What's this I see?" Doctor MacNeill strode up, an axe slung over his shoulder. "Refreshments?"

"Miss Ida made sandwiches," Christy said.

"I helped a little," Ruby Mae chimed in.

Christy grinned. "Eating one of them doesn't really count, Ruby Mae."

"Doctor, any sign of . . ." Ruby Mae lowered her voice, "you know who?"

"No you-know-whats, no you-know-whos, no nothing." The doctor winked at Christy. "Sorry to disappoint you, Ruby Mae."

"Oh, I ain't the least bit disappointed!" Ruby Mae exclaimed. She shook her finger at him. "And I'm bettin' you wouldn't be actin' so sassy if'n you'd seen the Boggin for your own self, like some have." She gazed around the little clearing. "You ain't seen Clara Spencer, have you? I coulda sworn I caught a glimpse o' her on our way over here."

"No Clara sightings, either," the doctor said.

"I'm goin' to take a look around. You keep a sharp eye out for you-know-who."

"Clara or the Boggin?" the doctor asked, but Ruby Mae was already halfway across the clearing.

"You shouldn't tease her so, Neil," Christy said. "She really is frightened. And who knows?" She paused. "Maybe there's more to this Boggin thing than we realize."

"Uh-oh. Sounds like Christy's been bitten by the Boggin bug," said the doctor. "It's turning into an epidemic."

Christy looked away. "I'm just saying we should respect people's fears."

"No," David said firmly. "We should help them fight their fears. After all, if Lundy Taylor can do it, anyone can."

"Lundy's here?" Christy exclaimed.

"Two of your students just got here." David pointed to two figures at the far edge of the clearing. Sure enough, Lundy Taylor and Wraight Holt were sawing away at a tall pine.

"Amazing," Christy said. "Especially after his run-in with the Boggin . . . or what he thought was the Boggin."

"He said he wanted to prove to himself that he wasn't afraid of anything," David explained.

Christy smiled sympathetically. It was the same reason, she realized, that she was here.

"Perhaps your lesson on telephone etiquette inspired him," Doctor MacNeill suggested.

"I doubt—" Christy stopped in mid sentence. Something was flying through the air at high speed toward the middle of the clearing.

"What on earth is that?" David cried.

"Well, it's not a bird, that much is for sure," said the doctor.

"It's a bag," Christy said. "A burlap sack!"

The sack landed with a soft plop. It was loosely tied at the top with an old rope, leaving a small opening.

"It came from over yonder," said Jeb. He pointed toward a stand of trees at the edge of the clearing.

"I'll bet the Boggin sent it," Wraight said. "I'd bet you my last dollar, if'n I had one."

"I hear somethin' powerful funny," Lundy said, taking several steps back. "Somethin' that sounds like—"

"Hornets!" somebody screeched.

First one, then two, then dozens of yellow and black hornets buzzed free of the burlap sack.

"Hornets!" Ruby Mae cried. "It's a nest o' hornets! And they is *mad!*"

In an instant, the air was alive with the angry insects, swooping in wild circles.

Everyone scattered in terror. The doctor

grabbed Christy's hand and pulled. "But the sandwiches—" Christy began.

"Come on, city-girl. When their nest is disturbed, hornets want revenge."

Christy and the doctor ran several hundred yards before coming to a stop. A few seconds later, a winded David and Ruby Mae caught up with them. A nasty red welt was already forming on David's right arm.

"Let me take a look at that," said Doctor MacNeill. "Anyone else get stung?"

"Not that I know of," David said, wincing.

"You know why this happened, don't you?" Ruby Mae said as she struggled to catch her breath.

"Because the Boggin's mad at us?" the doctor asked with a hint of sarcasm.

"Yep," Ruby Mae replied. "But the preacher went and made it worse by walkin' around in the kitchen with one boot on. I *told* you it'd bring you bad luck, Preacher."

"It's not me I'm worried about," David said gloomily, glancing back toward the clearing. "It's the telephone lines. No one's going to help me with this project now. Not after this."

～ ～ ～

"Anyone coulda done it," Clara said.

She was perched on a fallen log in the

312

woods, not far from the spot where David and the men had been working. John was pacing back and forth in front of her.

"Sure, anyone coulda done it," John agreed. "But who do you think really *did* toss that hornet's nest into the clearing?"

Clara crossed her arms over her chest. "How should I know?"

"You're thinkin' what I'm thinkin', aren't you?"

"Don't you go tellin' me what I'm thinkin', John Spencer. I got my own mind and you got yours, and that's that."

"You're thinkin'," John continued, "that *he* did it."

"I'm not thinkin' any such thing."

John kept pacing. "You're thinkin' he's mad about the phone lines comin' over his mountain, and people trespassin' and all. You're thinkin' he's so mad he just up and started doin' mean things to scare people off."

"You may be thinkin' that way, John. But I ain't!" Clara cried in exasperation.

John narrowed his eyes. "Then how come we came here today after school, sneakin' around like spies? We were lookin' for clues, Clara. Lookin' to see if he'd do anything suspicious. And sure enough, he did."

"I don't want to believe that," Clara said softly. Tears burned her eyes. "I *can't* believe it, John. It makes me afraid. And I don't want to be afraid of him."

"I know," John said. "Me neither. But facts is facts." He sighed. "Truth is, I think Ma's right, Clara. I don't think we should go back no more."

A tear slipped down Clara's cheek. "I reckon you two is right."

For a long time, John didn't speak. He sat down next to Clara on the log and draped his arm around her shoulder.

"Of course," he said at last, "we could ask Ma about goin' up the mountain once more. Just to be sure we're right about him. She could come, too. We got to know the truth."

"We could go tomorrow after school."

"Tomorrow it is."

Clara wiped her cheek and nodded. "All right, then. One last time," she said softly, "just so we know the truth."

❧ Eleven ❧

Well, that's over and done with," David said the next afternoon.

Christy looked up from the papers she was grading. David was standing in the open doorway of the school. She'd just dismissed school for the day, and all the children were gone.

"What are you talking about, David?"

David strode in, leaving muddy footprints in his wake. It had started raining again that morning and hadn't stopped all day. The mission yard was full of deep, muddy puddles.

David sat on one of the desks in the front row, a scowl on his face. "The telephone. I'm sorry to report you can forget about having one." He combed fingers through his wet hair. "Nobody showed up to work today. Not even Jeb Spencer. Nobody."

"It could be the bad weather. Besides, after the incident with the hornets, I'm not surprised, are you?"

"I guess I'd hoped the men would find a way to see past it."

"It was all Lundy and Wraight could talk about today," Christy said. "Give it some time, David. Things will calm down in a few weeks."

"Maybe. But I doubt it."

"Who knows? Maybe it's for the best. I know the phone is important, but these incidents have been awfully frightening for these people." She gave a rueful smile. "Even for me, I have to admit."

"Don't tell me *you've* fallen for these Boggin stories, too?" David cried.

"Well, you have to admit there *have* been some strange goings-on."

David waved his hand dismissively. "Pranks. Probably one of our own students, just out to make mischief. Remember when you first started teaching? This same sort of thing happened."

"I don't know, David." Christy stared out the rain-spattered window. "The truth is, when I passed Boggin Mountain on my way to Fairlight's last week, I saw something . . . or some*one*. Whatever it was, it frightened me."

David leapt to his feet. He looked at Christy with a mixture of frustration and amazement.

"I cannot believe you, an intelligent woman—a teacher, no less—are buying into this, Christy!"

"I know it sounds crazy, David. And it was probably just a wild animal. All I'm saying is that if I can be scared, as skeptical as I was about the Boggin, can you blame the men who were helping you? They grew up hearing horrible stories about him."

"I guess I'd hoped my sermon last Sunday and your talk with the children about the telephone would have some effect." David gave a resigned shrug. "Sometimes I overestimate the influence I have."

"It was a wonderful sermon, David," Christy assured him. "It gave me a lot to think about. It affected me."

David smiled wearily as he started for the door. "Not enough, I guess."

"David—" Christy began, but he was already gone.

She looked at the stack of spelling tests. She'd only graded half of them. Besides that, she still needed to work on her lesson plans for tomorrow.

Again she gazed out the window. She could just make out the dark expanse of Boggin Mountain. She'd always loved this view. On days when she'd feared she couldn't handle the challenge of teaching these needy mountain children, one glance at that mountain had always steadied her. It had been her source of courage.

And now she was afraid of it. She'd stay afraid of it, too, unless she confronted her fear.

In her heart, she knew the Boggin was a myth, a silly story, a figment of her imagination. But there was only one way to prove it to herself.

She wanted her calming view returned to her. She wanted her mountain back.

It would be hard, climbing on a day like today, but no matter.

She could do the lesson plans tonight. First, there was something else she needed to work on.

— — —

"Slow down, John!" Clara complained. "I can't keep up. I keep slippin' and slidin'."

They'd climbed this route up Boggin Mountain many times, but today, the constant rain made every step hard.

John held out his hand. "Just a little farther."

"You're both too fast for me," said their mother, pausing to catch her breath. "Look at us, all a-covered with mud! What'll we tell your pa?"

"We'll tell him we got into a fearsome mud fight," John said with a grin. "And I won."

"I want to win," Clara said.

"We'll tell him it was a draw," said Fairlight. She sighed. "I hate keepin' a secret from folks this way. It just don't feel right. But I s'pose a promise is a promise."

"Ma?" Clara asked. "Are you afeared?"

"Don't worry. I'm here with you." She squeezed Clara's hand. "Come on. We're almost to the top."

They climbed on in silence. The rain made little tapping sounds as it hit the umbrella of trees over their heads. The ground was slippery as butter. Wet branches slapped at Clara's arms, stinging her. With the sun blocked by clouds, it was nearly as dark as twilight.

Clara wondered if they should have taken the other path up. It was much rockier, but it wasn't as steep. Because there weren't as many trees, John had been afraid someone would notice them heading up, so they'd come this way instead.

At last the trees began to thin. Rocks replaced the underbrush. Up ahead, nearly at the summit, was the place they'd climbed so far to reach.

It was a small, homely hut, even plainer than any of the cabins in Cutter Gap. On one side was a stack of logs. A small iron kettle hung outside the door.

It was a sad, run-down place. Seeing it

always made Clara glad for her own cabin, brightened by her parents' love.

But if the little hut made her sad, the space around it always made Clara smile. Hanging from tree after tree were the most amazing birdhouses Clara had ever seen. In fact, they were the *only* birdhouses she'd ever seen.

The first time she'd seen them, Clara hadn't quite believed her eyes. What a crazy notion, houses for birds! They had chimneys and windows and mailboxes and all manner of silly things a bird would never want.

Soon she saw that the wonderful carved birdhouses were like palaces to the birds who were lucky enough to nest in them. And she had to admit that the carving was something to behold. Finer than anything even her own pa could do—and he was the best whittler in Cutter Gap.

"Hello?" John called. He cupped his hands around his mouth and called again. No one answered.

"He ain't here," Clara said.

Cautiously, John poked his head into the little hut. When he looked at Clara, his expression sent shivers through her.

"He's gone, all right," John said in a whisper, "and so is his gun."

❧ Twelve ❧

Step, slide. Step, slide. Step, slide.

It seemed that for every step Christy took up Boggin Mountain, she slipped back just as far.

She paused, arm crooked around a thin pine, and tried to catch her breath.

John Spencer had been right. This *was* a tough climb. Especially on rain-slick rocks. Even on a sunny, dry day, this steep incline would have been hard. But today, in the rain, it was well-nigh impossible. She'd taken the longer, rockier route, hoping it would be easier. But nothing about this climb was easy.

Not for the first time, Christy considered giving up. She'd made it about two-thirds of the way to the top, after all.

And she'd proved her point. That was the important thing. She'd faced her fear.

Amazingly, she'd been more afraid back at

the school, just looking at this mountain. Now, as she struggled to climb it, all her energy was focused on taking the next step, and then the next. The notion that she'd run into some wild-eyed creature called the Boggin seemed almost silly . . . almost.

"Well," Christy said to herself, "I've come this far. I might as well go to the top."

She started her slow ascent again. She aimed toward a spot near a ledge of huge rocks. That would put her fairly close to the summit. When she got there, she promised herself, she could rest again.

Step, slide. Step, slide. This was crazy, all right. Brave, perhaps, but crazy.

The rain quickened. It was cold on her neck. The wind swayed the great trees around her. She was glad she'd borrowed Miss Ida's raincoat. Christy had told her she was "going for a little walk." What would Miss Ida say when she saw the mud streaks on her coat?

Step, slide. Step, slide. Suddenly Christy heard a strange grinding noise.

She looked up to see a great boulder tumbling down the mountain. It hit a tree, then another, then continued on its way.

There'd been rock slides recently because of all the rain, Christy recalled with a jolt. She stood rigidly, her heart pounding, her fists clenched.

Was that all? Just one boulder and nothing more? Was it safe to go on?

She took another tentative step, and then it happened.

With a thunderous crash, the rocky ledge crumbled like a tower of children's blocks. Tiny pebbles and giant, sharp rocks began to roll down the mountain. Boulders bounced as if they were rubber balls.

Christy spun around. She cut to her left, running down the mountain as fast as she could, hoping the slide would pass right by her.

Out of the corner of her eye, she saw a huge boulder hit a pine tree dead-on. The tree splintered with a horrible cracking sound, then began to fall.

She slipped, righted herself, and kept running. Her lungs burned. Just a little farther, she told herself, and she'd be safe.

The boulders rolled and crashed and thudded. Most were to her right, but some seemed to be directly behind her.

She wanted to turn to look. But there wasn't time. She had to run. She had to keep running.

Her skirt caught on a prickly shrub. She yanked it free. She stumbled. She ran another step.

And then she knew it was coming for her.

She heard the terrifying crash as the giant boulder hit a tree trunk directly behind her.

The tree snapped like a toothpick. Christy felt its shadow over her as it fell.

She looked up. She tripped. As the tree toppled, so did she.

She tried to crawl, but the tree was coming down too fast.

There was nothing else to do. Christy closed her eyes and covered her head. As she waited to die, she prayed.

✿ Thirteen ✿

Slowly, Christy opened her eyes.

She wasn't dead.

In fact, she was very much alive.

She tried to move but couldn't. Sweet-smelling needles tickled her nose. She was trapped in the great arms of a massive pine tree.

Christy lifted her head. She could just make out the huge boulder that had tumbled the tree. It was wedged against what was left of the trunk.

She wondered how badly she was hurt. She had some scrapes on her face and hands, and her right ankle throbbed, but she doubted any bones had been broken.

With all her might, Christy struggled to break free of the big tree's grasp. The massive trunk lay just inches to her left. Another foot and it would have landed directly on top of her.

It was a miracle that she hadn't been crushed.

"Thank you, God," Christy whispered.

Again she tried to free herself from the piney trap, but it was no use. The tree was huge, and she was not.

Suddenly, to her surprise, Christy found herself laughing. Now that she was out of danger, her predicament almost seemed ridiculous.

She could just see the surprise on the faces of her rescuers when they found her! Christy Huddleston, trapped by a man-eating pine tree. She'd gotten into plenty of hair-raising scrapes since coming to Cutter Gap. But Doctor MacNeill would tease her for weeks over this one.

Unless . . .

Christy gulped. Unless no one found her. Unless no one would even think to look for her here on Boggin Mountain.

After all, she hadn't told anyone where she was going. All she'd said to Miss Ida was that she was going for a walk. But nobody would expect Christy to have headed for the summit of Boggin Mountain. Nobody.

How long could she last out here without food, exposed to the elements? The awful possibilities marched through her head like an army. What if it stormed? How cold would it get at night? What if a hungry animal found her?

She could scream for help, but what would be the point?

No one came near this place. Everyone in Cutter Gap feared it.

She could scream till her voice gave out, and the only ones to hear it would be the wild creatures hidden in the trees.

And, of course, the Boggin.

"No!" Christy said out loud, trying to calm her frantic heart. "I am going to be fine! And there is no Boggin! The Boggin does not exist!"

Hearing the words made her feel better. She'd come here to conquer her fear, after all. She wasn't going to give in to it all over again. Especially not now, when she needed to keep her wits about her.

"Well, if no one's going to show up to rescue me," Christy said aloud, "I guess I'm going to have to rescue myself."

She felt a little silly, talking to herself. But the sound of a human voice—even it was just her own—was somehow reassuring.

Lifting her head a couple inches, Christy surveyed her situation. She was pinned down by layer upon layer of branches—some thick, some not-so-thick. Her only hope seemed to be to try to crawl her way out, inch by precious inch.

But that was easier said than done.

As she struggled to move, Christy began to sing an old song she'd loved as a child. It had helped her through many frightening moments. In fact, it was one of the first things she'd taught her students here in Cutter Gap:

> God will take care of you
> Through every day, o'er all the way,
> He will take care of you,
> He will take care of you.

She'd just started to sing it again when the loud snap of a twig silenced her. *She* hadn't broken it. Someone in the woods had.

"Is anybody there?" Christy called. "Please help me! I'm over here, trapped under this pine tree."

She paused. Nobody replied. Perhaps it had just been an animal passing by.

Still, Christy had the same eerie feeling she'd had that day on the path, when she'd been certain she'd spotted the Boggin. The sense that she was being watched. The feeling that there was another presence lurking nearby.

"Hello?" Christy called again.

She struggled to lift her head. She looked to the left. She looked to the right. And then she saw him.

He was only a few feet away from her. He towered over the fallen tree like some awful giant out of a fairy tale. He was clearly old.

His hair and beard were long and white, hanging in wisps down to his shoulders.

A horrible scar extended from his cheek to the spot where his right ear would have been. Even with his mane of hair, Christy could see that the ear was gone.

But it was his eyes that Christy focused on. They were the eyes of an old man, milky with disease, shining like white moons.

They were the eyes of the man she'd seen that day on the path.

"You're the Boggin," Christy whispered.

He came closer in two great strides. Only then did Christy see the gun and large hunting knife tucked into his belt.

Christy stared in horror at the hideous creature towering over her. "Please don't hurt me," she begged in a terrified whisper.

He didn't respond. For a moment, he didn't even move.

Suddenly, he lunged toward Christy. She let out a scream before realizing that he was reaching for a branch of the fallen tree.

To her amazement, Christy felt the weight of the tree easing. The old man could only lift the branches a few inches. But it was just enough to allow Christy the room she needed to crawl free.

When she was safe, the Boggin released the tree. Christy smiled at him. "Thank you so much," she said. "If you hadn't come along, I don't know what I would have done."

When he didn't answer, she wondered if he couldn't speak. He was staring at her with the same curiosity and fear he was probably seeing on her own face.

"You're the teacher," he finally said.

"Yes," she replied in surprise. "How did you know that?"

He didn't answer. "Can you walk?" he asked.

"I'm not sure. I think I may have hurt my ankle. Not to mention Miss Ida's coat."

Christy tried to stand, but her swollen ankle would not take any weight.

"I'll help you," said the Boggin.

"Really, I'm fine."

"You can come to my hut."

"No," Christy said, a little frantically. "I . . . I need to go home."

"I'll wrap up your ankle so you can walk on it," said the Boggin, as certainly as if he were Doctor MacNeill. "It's a long way down, Miz Huddleston."

Christy took a deep breath. This was the Boggin she was talking to. The creature of nightmares and superstitious stories. This was the Boggin, inviting her to his hut so he could tend to her ankle. And he knew her name.

"I . . . I don't even know your name, but you know mine," Christy said.

For the first time, the old man showed a hint of a smile.

"My real name don't matter no more," he said. "Boggin'll do just fine."

❧ Fourteen ❧

Christy and the Boggin made their way to the top of the mountain, step by slow step. She leaned on the tall old man for support, amazed at his strength. Twice Christy tried to start a conversation, but her questions were met with silence.

She had so many questions, too. Was he a hermit? How did he know her name? Was he the one who'd been frightening the people of Cutter Gap? And if so, why?

As they neared the summit, Christy thought she heard voices.

"Did you hear that?" she asked the Boggin.

He nodded. "My friends," was all he said.

The Boggin had friends? Christy thought in disbelief. As far as she knew, everyone in Cutter Gap feared him. How could he have any friends?

Up ahead, a tiny hut in a clearing came

into view. And then Christy saw who the Boggin's friends were.

"Edward! Christy!" Fairlight said. "Are you hurt?"

John and Clara ran to help Christy the rest of the way. "There was a rock slide," Christy explained. "A pine tree practically fell right on top of me. The Bog—" she stopped herself, "*Edward* saved me."

The old man shrugged. "I guess I might as well introduce myself formal-like, after all. My name's Edward Hinton."

"Edward Hinton," Christy repeated. "I like that much better than 'the Boggin.'"

"Me, too, I reckon."

"What on earth are you three doing here?" Christy asked.

Fairlight glanced at Edward. "That's a long story, I reckon. First things first. It sure looks to me like you need to set down and let me tend to that foot."

Clara retrieved a chair from the hut and Christy sat down gratefully. The hut, Christy noticed, was very small and crudely made. But surrounding it, dangling off of every tree limb, it seemed, were the most beautiful birdhouses Christy had ever seen.

Some looked like the elaborate Victorian homes back in Asheville. Some looked like the brick row houses in Boston Christy had seen pictures of in books. One even looked like the White House. And all of them seemed to be occupied by very happy birds.

"Those birdhouses," Christy said, shaking her head in wonder. "They're so beautiful!"

"Ain't they the purtiest things you ever did set eyes on, Miz Christy?" Clara exclaimed. "Edward made 'em all."

"They're amazing," Christy replied. "Just amazing."

"I whittle to while away the time," the old man said. "Tain't nothin' too special. I used to make 'em more fancy-like. But the eyes are goin' now. I have to go by feel more 'n sight when I'm whittlin' the little things."

Quiet fell for a moment, broken only by the happy chattering of the birds in their custom-made homes. Edward cleared his throat. "I guess I'll be gettin' you somethin' to wrap up that ankle with." He knocked his head with his hand. "Listen to me! I plumb forgot my manners, I ain't had company in so long—'ceptin' of course for Clara and John and their ma. Can I fetch you somethin' to drink? Or maybe to eat? I got some fresh fish I was goin' to fry up."

"No, thank you, Edward. But I do have some questions I'd like you to answer, if you'd be so kind."

Edward sighed. "Now I remember why I don't much like company," he said wryly, and with that, he disappeared into his tiny hut.

334

Christy looked at Fairlight and the children expectantly. "Well? Are you three going to explain to me why you just happen to be on the top of Boggin Mountain? What's this all about, anyway?"

Clara sighed. "Like Ma said, it's kind of a long story, Miz Christy."

"I have plenty of time."

"See, Edward's our friend," Clara said softly. "We met him one day pickin' flowers with Ma. Usually we never came up on Boggin Mountain, 'cause of all the stories and all."

"But that day, we kinda got carried away, lookin' for jack-in-the-pulpits," Fairlight said.

"Anyways, I found this baby wren on the ground, sickly as could be," Clara continued. "No ma, no nest in sight. And just as I knelt down to get her, I saw Edward. I like to nearly jumped outa my skin—" she lowered her voice, "'cause o' the way he looks and all. But he picked up that baby wren, gentle as could be, and took her back to his place, and fixed her up as good as new." She smiled. "And that's how we got to be friends with Edward."

"Why didn't you tell anyone?" Christy asked, leaning down to rub her tender ankle. "All those stories about the Boggin. They could have been put to rest for good."

"Ma and Clara and me promised we wouldn't tell anyone we'd met him. Edward just wants to be left alone, Miz Christy," John said quietly.

"But why?"

The old man appeared in the doorway of the hut. He was holding a strip of white cloth. "Because he doesn't much like people," he explained. His voice was bitter. "Because when you keep to yourself, no harm can come to you."

"But Clara and John and Fairlight are your friends," Christy pointed out.

"They're different," Edward said. "They're the exception that proves the rule."

Christy frowned. "Is that why you've been terrorizing everyone in Cutter Gap?" she demanded.

"I got nothin' to do with that," Edward said angrily. "The children told me about those goings-on last time they came to visit."

"But who else could be doing it, Edward?" Clara asked softly. "I mean, we've kinda plumb run out o' answers. That's why John and me and Ma come back today, to ask . . ."

"Ask what?" Edward crossed his arms over his chest.

"We were just thinkin' maybe with the telephone comin' and all . . ." John said gently. "I mean, it'd be natural as could be if you were mad about everybody pokin' their noses around. And we figgered maybe . . ." His voice faded away.

"You're my friends," Edward said sadly, "but you don't believe me when I tell you the plain truth. That's a sorry pickle, ain't it?"

"How come you went out today with your gun, then?" Clara challenged. "You told us you'd never ever use that gun again as long as you lived."

"Sometimes a man's gotta change his mind." Edward shook his head. "And I didn't count on Bird's-Eye Taylor."

"What do you mean, Edward?" Christy asked.

"Let's get that ankle o' yours wrapped up," Edward said.

"And on your way down the mountain, I'll show you just what I mean."

We're almost there now," Edward said.

They were halfway down the mountain. It had been slow going for Christy. But hobbling along with John and Edward for support, she felt certain she could make it all the way down.

After a few more minutes, Edward led them through thick underbrush to a spot by a tiny stream. "There," he said, pointing. "That's why I was packin' my ol' Colt forty-five."

"A still?" Christy cried.

"And there's plenty of moonshine to go with it," Edward added. "It's hidden under those bushes, mostly."

"How long has this been here?"

"Couldn't have been here long, I reckon. I know this mountain like the back o' my hand." Edward stroked his long beard. "First time I seen Bird's-Eye was a few days ago. Sneakin' 'round here like a low-bellied snake, he was."

"How can you know for certain it was Bird's-Eye?" Christy asked.

"Edward knows just about everybody," Clara explained. "On account o' we described 'em all."

Edward chuckled. "I'll bet I've heard more tales about the folks in Cutter Gap than they've heard about me."

"So you were out with your gun today lookin' for Bird's-Eye?" Fairlight asked.

"He comes just around nightfall mostly, near as I can tell. I was goin' to stake out a hidin' place, maybe shoot a couple rounds into the air to scare him off. I only want just to scare him," Edward said, his face suddenly grave. "You know how I feel about usin' my gun anymore."

"Edward was an Indian fighter, way back in the eighteen-seventies, Miz Christy," Clara said. "That's how he lost his ear and got all scarred up. He fought with—"

"That's enough, Clara," Edward interrupted sternly.

Clara bit her lip. "Sorry, Edward. I sorta forgot you don't like talkin' about it."

Christy considered pressing him for more information, but she could tell from Edward's icy tone that now was not the time.

"Well, I guess when I get home, I'll have to tell David and the others about this still," she said. "Then they can confront Bird's-Eye. There's no point in trying to scare Bird's-Eye off with some gunshots into the air, Edward. It would just start up a little war on this mountain. Bird's-Eye Taylor's spent his whole life feuding."

"Maybe you're right. Maybe the mission folks can fix things better than I can. But you won't go tellin' 'em about me," Edward said softly. It was more of a question than a demand.

"I suppose not, Edward. Not if you don't want me to. But I don't see—"

"Look, I just want my mountain back," Edward said. "I just want my peace. I've been here so many years . . ."

"How long *have* you been here?"

"So long, to tell you truthful, I can't remember."

"That must be how the rumors started so many years ago," Christy said. "People would catch a glimpse of you now and then, and one thing led to another. . . . Of course, that doesn't explain all the recent incidents."

"That still tells you all you need to know about the culprit."

"Bird's-Eye? Yes, that thought crossed my mind, too," Christy said. "But then I remembered that Bird's-Eye's son—"

"Lundy," Edward interrupted. "He's the

meanest bully in Tennessee." He winked at Clara and John. "Am I right?"

"You're right as rain," Clara said. "See, Miz Christy? He knows everybody."

Christy smiled. "Yes, he certainly does. Anyway, Lundy was helping the men work on telephone poles when somebody threw a hornet's nest at them. If Bird's-Eye were the one doing the pranks, I'm sure Lundy would have been in on it. So why would he have put himself in harm's way like that?"

"He was one o' the first to run, Miz Christy," Clara pointed out. "Maybe he was just tryin' to make him and his pa look innocent."

"I don't know," John said. "That's awfully smart for ol' Lundy."

"Wait a minute," Christy said. "How come you knew Lundy was the first to run away?"

"We was watchin'," Clara admitted. "Pokin' around, tryin' to figger out who was causin' all the Boggin trouble."

John met Edward's gaze. "Truth is, Edward, we was afeared it was you. But we was always a-hopin' we was wrong."

Edward nodded. "I s'pose that's all I could ask for from a friend. And then some." He gave a little smile. "I just want you to know I don't mind the telephone wires comin' over the mountain. Wires don't scare me. People do. I don't want no Bird's-Eye Taylors and their like disturbin' my peace. But the

341

preacher and his telephone-makin' . . . well, that don't matter to me, I s'pose. That'll come and go, soon enough."

As they neared the main path at the foot of the mountain, Edward hung back. "Can you all make it the rest o' the way?" he asked. "This is as far as I should go."

"We'll be fine," Christy said.

"You're welcome to come a-visitin' again. As long as you don't bring nobody with you but John and Clara and their ma."

"I just might take you up on that offer. And thank you, Edward, for all your help."

"I didn't mind so much," Edward said. "I ain't helped nobody but the birds in so long . . . it was kinda nice."

Christy and the others watched him weave back through the trees. Funny, Christy mused, the way Edward thought of Boggin Mountain as his own. Just the way she felt the soothing sight of it was somehow "hers." Peculiar as he was, he clearly loved this quiet place.

"I wonder if he's right about Bird's-Eye," Christy said.

"I figger Edward's a good man, Christy," Fairlight said thoughtfully. "He's a gentle soul. I don't think he'd ever try to scare anyone."

"No, that's the kind of behavior you'd expect to see from Bird's-Eye Taylor," Christy agreed.

"And Lundy," Clara added.

"You know," Christy said, "if it really has been Bird's-Eye behind these incidents, what he needs is a dose of his own medicine."

"I'd give anything to see him and ol' Lundy scared silly!" Clara exclaimed.

Suddenly, Christy had a very clever, very interesting, very amusing thought.

"John," she said, "run on back and get Edward. Tell him I have an idea that just might interest him."

✲ Sixteen ✲

Look at all of you!" Miss Ida scolded. "You look like something the cat dragged in!"

Christy, Fairlight, Clara, and John were gathered in the mission house parlor. Miss Ida had made them hot tea, and David was putting the finishing touches on a fire in the hearth. Miss Alice had found cozy quilts for each of the rain-drenched mountain climbers.

"I'm so sorry about your coat, Miss Ida," Christy said. "I feel just terrible—"

"Nonsense. A coat's a coat, a person's a person. The important thing is that you're all right," Miss Ida said, in a rare moment of sentiment. "Still," she added brusquely, returning to her old self, "I can't imagine why you chose today to go for a walk in the mountains!"

"It just felt like something I had to do," Christy explained.

She hadn't told anyone that the mountain she'd been climbing was Boggin Mountain, and fortunately, nobody had asked. Like Fairlight, she felt obligated to protect Edward's privacy. Still, in her heart, it made her sad to think of him all alone in that little, silent hut.

"Well, we should be heading on home," Fairlight said, getting to her feet. "Jeb's goin' to be wonderin' what's happened to us. You take care of that ankle now, Christy."

"I will. Don't forget we're getting together tomorrow evening for another walk in the woods."

"Christy!" Miss Alice exclaimed. "Don't you think you should stay off that foot for a few days?"

"I'll be fine, Miss Alice." Christy winked at Fairlight and the children. "Tomorrow, then?"

"Tomorrow," Fairlight said, waving. "We'll be there." John and Clara exchanged knowing looks and grinned from ear to ear as they followed their mother out the door.

"They're in a mighty fine mood," David said as he closed the door behind them. He sighed. "At least *some*body is."

"David," Miss Alice said kindly. "Please stop thinking about that telephone. Perhaps down the road in a few months, when things have calmed down, you can try again."

"Or even sooner," Christy said with a secret smile. "Who knows?"

"I feel like a real, live spy!" Clara whispered the next evening.

"Hush!" John chided. "Real, live spies know how to keep their mouths shut."

Christy, Fairlight, Edward, and the two oldest Spencer children were crouched behind bushes, near the little stream where Bird's-Eye had put his still. It was twilight, and the woods were shrouded in shadows.

"You did some scoutin' when you were in the Seventh Cavalry, Edward," Clara said. "I could be a spy, couldn't I?"

"You'd make a fine spy, Clara," Edward said, his eyes glued on the still.

Christy thought back to her history lessons for a moment. The Seventh Cavalry? Why did that ring a bell?

She started to ask, but just then, the sound of rustling nearby silenced her.

Crouching low, they all waited, holding their breath.

"False alarm," Edward announced after a moment. He pointed toward a blur of movement in the trees. "It's just a curious doe."

"Maybe we should go over our plan again," Fairlight said. "Does everybody know what they need to be doin'?"

"We done went over it a hundred times already, Ma," Clara complained.

Fairlight laughed. "All right. I'm sorry. Guess I'm not used to bein' so sneaky." She nudged Christy. "How's that ankle o' yours holdin' up?"

"The swelling's down. It's practically back to normal," Christy replied. "Edward, do you think it's about time to take your place?"

He nodded. "I got my kerosene lamp and my sheet."

"You be careful not to catch yourself on fire," Christy warned. "John, have you got your paper cone?"

"Just like the one you made for the telephones, Miz Christy. Only bigger."

"And Fairlight and Clara and I have plenty of Miss Ida's kitchen utensils. All right, then. I think we're all set. You sure you can make it up into the tree all right, Edward?"

"John'll give me a hand. 'Sides, I may be old, but I'm spry as they come." Edward stood. "Well, here we go. You really think this'll work?"

"Just remember," Christy said. "Tonight, you're not Edward Hinton. You're the Boggin."

Edward laughed. "I might as well be him. Everybody figgers I am, anyways!"

Edward climbed into position. John stationed himself nearby, behind a tree. Christy, Fairlight, and the children made certain they were well-hidden by bushes.

The sky was darkening fast. Already a few stray stars blinked through the trees. The leaves whispered softly.

Before long, the sound of footsteps and loud voices floated on the air.

"Here they come," John whispered. "Keep low—" he glared at Clara, "and no more talkin'!"

"What I needs," came a gravelly voice Christy recognized as Bird's-Eye's, "is to find myself a hundred o' them hornets' nests. Better 'n cannonballs, they is!"

The next voice was Lundy's. "Funniest thing I ever did see, all them folks a-runnin' like scared rabbits!"

Bird's-Eye and Lundy reached the still. "Think I'll have a swig or two o' brew before we get to work," Bird's-Eye said. He jerked an elbow at Lundy. "What're you lookin' for, boy? Ain't nobody comes to this mountain but us."

"Us and . . . and the Boggin," Lundy said nervously.

Bird's-Eye spat on the ground. "Fool! You and me *is* the Boggin!"

"Still and all, Pa, there's folks who say they've seen him, lurkin' around these parts."

Bird's-Eye gave a sharp laugh. "My uncle once swore he saw a three-headed mule. You think I believed him?"

Suddenly, an eerie light appeared, high up

in the branches of an oak tree. Above the white glow, a face scowled.

"Believe this, Bird's-Eye Taylor!" came a deep voice.

"There is only one Boggin! And here I am!"

❧ Seventeen ❧

P a?" Lundy whispered, grabbing Bird's-Eye's arm. "That there is the Boggin, for sure and certain! And he's every bit as ugly as they say!"

Christy and Fairlight smiled at each other. Edward had draped the white sheet around his neck. With the kerosene lamp glowing beneath the sheet, his body seemed to glow. The effect was terrifying.

"Let go o' my arm, boy! I'll shoot him right outa that tree!"

Christy looked at Fairlight in terror. She'd been so sure of her plan to scare Bird's-Eye. It hadn't occurred to her that he might actually try to shoot Edward.

"Shoot me if you will," John called through his paper cone. "But every shot you take, I'll spin that bullet clear around to take aim right at you!"

"Good job, John," Christy whispered.

Bird's-Eye hesitated. In the dim light, the fear on his face was obvious. He took a step back.

"He's talkin'," he said in a hoarse voice to Lundy, "but his lips ain't movin' none. How in tarnation can he do that?"

"He's the *Boggin*, Pa," Lundy squeaked. "He can do anything he wants!"

"Destroy your still now!" John boomed from his hiding place behind the tree. "And pour out your moonshine!"

"I . . . I can't do that," Bird's-Eye pleaded. "It's fine moonshine, the finest in Tennessee, uh . . . Mr. Boggin, sir. How about I just split it with you, nice and fair?"

"Destroy it now! Or I'll give you a taste o' my Boggin powers!"

Bird's-Eye shook his head. "How do you do that, if'n you don't mind my askin'? Talk without openin' your mouth, I mean?"

"Pour out the moonshine! Now!"

Christy nudged Fairlight and Clara. They began pounding pots and pans together, clanging and clattering like crazy. At the same time, they howled like wolves baying at the moon. It was such a horrible racket, Christy wished she'd brought ear plugs. But the effect was just what she'd hoped.

"All right! I—I'll do it!" Bird's-Eye cried in terror. Lundy clamped his hands to his ears. "J—just stop all that carryin'-on!"

Christy gave a nod and the commotion ceased instantly.

After that, the only noise was a steady glug-glug-glug, as Bird's-Eye and Lundy poured out bottle after bottle of their precious moonshine. Christy watched in delight as they dismantled the still, tossing pieces into the dark woods.

"There," Bird's-Eye said at last. "I hope you're satisfied, Mr. Boggin."

"I am satisfied," John said, "but there is one thing more."

"Confound it all," Bird's-Eye muttered. "You sure do know how to ruin a fella's evening."

"You must go to the people of Cutter Gap. You must tell them if they help with the telephone they will not be harmed. And you must confess that you're the one who's been scarin' 'em so."

"Aw, come on, Mr. Boggin. Ain't I done enough already?"

"Pa," Lundy pleaded. "Don't make him any madder 'n he already is!"

Bird's-Eye scowled. "All right, then. If'n you say so." With a sigh, he turned to go. "I never did like this mountain, anyways."

They were almost out of sight when John added, "By the way, Lundy—you really oughta stop pickin' on the little children at school."

"Nosy ol' Boggin," Lundy muttered. "Fella can't have a lick o' fun with him around."

✺ Eighteen ✺

The next week, when her ankle had fully healed, Christy returned to Boggin Mountain.

She found Edward near his hut, carving another birdhouse. Little curlicues of wood carpeted the ground, and the fresh smell of cut wood filled the air. He seemed surprised, and perhaps even a little pleased, to see her.

"I hope you don't mind my coming back, Edward," she said, taking a seat on a log.

"'Course not. You're welcome any time, like I said."

"That's a fine birdhouse."

Edward held it out at arm's length. "My birdhouses now are not as fine as they used to be. I'm gettin' on, I s'pose. My hands get tired and my eyes do, too."

"You know, there's a store back home in Asheville, where I come from. They sell handmade things, quilts and pottery and such. I'll bet you anything they'd be willing to sell your birdhouses, too."

Edward looked at her doubtfully, as if he thought she were making fun of him. "Naw."

"Seriously. I could send one to my mother, if you'd like. She could show it to the shop owner."

Edward shrugged. "Ain't got enough for sellin'."

"Suppose . . . suppose you taught some of the local people how to carve them? They could help you—"

"I done told you. I don't want nothin' to do with nobody."

"I'm sorry," Christy said. "I didn't mean to push you. Especially since the real reason I came was to say thanks."

Edward blew wood shavings off the birdhouse. They fluttered to his feet like bits of snow. "Thank me for what?"

"For helping us get Bird's-Eye to destroy his still and pour out his moonshine."

"He'll build another 'un, mark my words."

"Perhaps. But not on your mountain, at least. And he admitted he was behind the pranks, like we asked. You'd be amazed how fast word spread about that. He explained everything. How he'd put chicken blood on one of his own tattered shirts and hung it in the tree. How he'd made the big tracks using a piece of wood he'd carved and an old pitchfork. It's like I told the children—there's a logical explanation for everything." Christy laughed. "He told everyone he'd seen you, too, but I'm not sure anyone believed him. It was sort of like that old story about the boy who cried wolf one too many times."

Edward set the birdhouse aside. "Telephone line's a-comin', then?"

"Yes. They're making real progress on the poles already."

"I'd best be goin' into hidin' for a while, till they're done and gone."

Gently, Christy reached for the little birdhouse. It was only half-done, but she could already see the outlines forming. "It's the church!" she said.

"I reckon."

"You've seen it?"

"Once. 'Round midnight, right after the preacher was finishin' it up. Fine job he did."

"He'd be pleased to hear that. David doesn't fashion himself much of a carpenter. I think he'd rather stick to being a minister." She smiled. "You'd like him."

"Maybe."

"I wish you'd come visit us at the mission house sometime. Everyone would love to meet you."

Edward stared up at the pale blue sky. "Ain't likely."

With a sigh, Christy set the birdhouse

down. "I know this is none of my business, Edward. But the other night while we were waiting for Bird's-Eye, Clara mentioned the Seventh Cavalry. At the time, I couldn't remember its significance. But later, when I got home, I took out my history book, and all of a sudden it came back to me." She paused, almost afraid to say the words. "The Seventh Cavalry fought the Battle of Little Big Horn—Custer's Last Stand."

Edward gave a slight nod. He was looking at Christy, but his milky eyes were somewhere far, far away. "I ran from that bloody place in the Dakota Territory. And I never looked back. I been here on my mountain ever since."

"So many died that day," Christy said softly.

"I was ridin' with Major Reno. There was one hundred and twelve of us troops, green as new grass. We attacked the Sioux at one end of the Indian camp, and a fool thing it was, too. We was way outnumbered. The fightin' was . . ." he winced at the awful memory, "somethin' terrible. Lookin' back, I think those Sioux just wanted to be left alone on the land they loved, same as me. But I didn't know that then."

"It must have been horrible."

"Ain't no words to describe it. I saw men, troops and Indians alike, fight brave as you can imagine. In the end, Major Reno pulled us back, what was left of us. Some called him a coward." He sighed. "S'pose that's what they'd call me, too. Soon as I got the chance, I run off. I was just a boy, mind you. Bloody and tired and scared o' dyin'. Later, I heard about Custer and his men. Two hundred sixty-four troops, all dead. All those lives, wasted."

A lone tear fell down Edward's cheek. Christy reached out and touched his hand. "Edward," she said gently, "that was a long time ago. Haven't you suffered enough?"

"Maybe so. But it's been too long. I don't know how to be around people anymore."

"Sure you do."

"Even old men can be afraid, you know." He managed a half-smile. "Even the Boggin."

"I know a little about fear myself," Christy admitted. "Truth is, that day you found me pinned under the tree, I'd come up here to prove something to myself."

"Prove something?"

"I was afraid of *you*, Edward . . . or at least of the thing everyone called the Boggin. And it made me mad, and sad, too, because if I was afraid of you, that meant I had to be afraid of this beautiful mountain, too." She paused. "And I loved this place too much to let that happen."

Edward nodded. "I'm glad you were brave

enough to come. But I'm not like that. I'm somebody who learned how to run away a long, long time ago. And now it's too late."

"You ran away from the worst side of human nature, Edward. And believe me, it's never too late to change."

"Maybe so. Maybe not. You know what they say about teaching old dogs new tricks."

"I taught my poodle Pansy to roll over when she was twelve years old and fat as one of the hogs living under the schoolhouse."

Edward laughed. "You're comparin' me to a fat ol' poodle dog?"

"Hardly." Christy stood. "Edward, do you suppose you still have family living?"

"I had a younger sister in Raleigh. Could be she's still around. Mary Davis was her name, after she got hitched."

"Wouldn't you like to get in touch with her?"

Edward shook his head. "I'm afraid I just plain wouldn't know where to begin, if I did."

"I understand. Well, I should be going. But will you at least think about visiting the mission someday?"

"I'll think about it. That's all I'm promisin'."

"It wouldn't be like visiting strangers. After all, you already know about everyone in Cutter Gap. Don't you think they'd like to know about you?"

"I ain't so sure." Edward went over to the nearest pine tree. He pulled down a little birdhouse. "Here. This ain't got no residents yet. Send it on to your ma to show to the shopkeeper, if'n you want. I ain't promisin' anything, mind you. I'm old and stuck in my ways."

Christy grinned. "Funny—that's just what everyone said about Pansy."

❧ Nineteen ❧

Nine weeks later . . .

"I can hardly stand the waitin' another minute!" Clara cried.

"Settle down, Clara," Ruby Mae teased. "This ain't the first call we've got."

"Practically, though," Clara said. "'Sides, it's the first one that's come from out o' state. And it's the first one we've had such a big jollification over."

She gazed around the mission house happily. It seemed like all of Cutter Gap was here for the big occasion. The parlor was decorated with vases of wildflowers. Pies and cookies were waiting to be eaten. And all over the walls were pictures the children had drawn—pictures of the way they imagined the Boggin would look when they finally got to meet him today.

She adjusted the bow in her hair nervously. Miz Christy had given it to her in honor of the special day.

"Quit playin' with that bow or it'll fall right apart," John teased.

Clara punched him in the arm. "John, you think he'll really come? Miz Christy said he was powerful scared."

"He's come to the mission house twice now," John pointed out.

"'Course, there was only a few people to visit with then. Everybody in Cutter Gap is here today."

Suddenly, a hush fell over the room. Every head turned toward the door.

Edward stood in the doorway. He bit his lip, staring at the huge assembled group.

Clara could see the panic in his eyes. She rushed over and took his hand. "Everybody," she announced, nice and firm and proud as could be, "this is my friend, Edward Hinton." She pulled him inside. "You're late, Edward. I was afeared you weren't a-goin' to come, and Miz Christy and the preacher fixed up the finest surprise you ever did—"

Then it happened, right on schedule. The brand-new, fine-as-could-be telephone began to ring.

A hush fell over the crowd.

It rang again, a jangly, silvery noise like tiny bells coming alive.

"Confound it all, if that ain't the most beautiful sound I ever did hear!" someone cried.

"Ain't somebody goin' to answer it?" Granny O'Teale demanded.

"Edward, why don't you do the honors?" said Christy. She gave a sly little wink at Clara.

"I don't think . . . I don't know if I'm ready for . . ."

"Come, come, there's nothing to it." David led Edward toward the phone.

"Just pick up that earpiece and say 'hello,'" Clara explained. "Miz Christy done taught us all how."

Edward hesitated. Again the phone jangled.

"Hurry up!" someone hissed. "Or they'll give up on you!"

With a trembling hand, Edward lifted the earpiece and put it to his ear.

"Talk into that cone-shaped thing," Clara whispered.

Edward cleared his throat. "H—hello?"

He listened. His eyes went wide.

More long moments passed. Clara waited, breath held.

"Mary?" Edward whispered. "Mary, is that really you?"

Clara reached for Miz Christy's hand and squeezed it tightly. They both smiled.

"Finally, Miz Christy," Clara whispered, "he ain't the Boggin no more."

About the Author

Catherine Marshall

With *Christy*, Catherine Marshall LeSourd (1914–1983) created one of the world's most widely read and best-loved classics. Published in 1967, the book spent 39 weeks on the New York Times bestseller list. With an estimated 30 million Americans having read it, *Christy* is now approaching its 90th printing and has sold over eight million copies. Although a novel, *Christy* is in fact a thinly-veiled biography of Catherine's mother, Leonora Wood.

Catherine Marshall LeSourd also authored *A Man Called Peter*, which has sold over four million copies. It is an American bestseller, portraying the love between a dynamic man and his God, and the tender, romantic love between a man and the girl he married. *Julie* is a powerful, sweeping novel of love and adventure, courage and commitment, tragedy and triumph, in a Pennsylvania town during the Great Depression. Catherine also authored many other devotional books of encouragement.